www.jfclayton.com

J F Clayton

Moonday

www.jfclayton.com

Book cover original artwork by: C. Campbell
Book cover design by: Intentional Promotions
ISBN no: 978-0-9935521-5-1
Published in Great Britain by Intentional Promotions
www.intentionalpromotions.com

Thanks to Denise, Susanne, Rebecca, Hannah, Jamie, Caroline, Rob, Alison and to all the people who made it possible to go to the Moon.

Chapters

Alpha 12 - Moon Base
Date: Sunday 25th September 2157 - 14:23 CET

I never asked to be born, but if I would have, I would never have asked to be the first person born on the Moon. Apparently as Steve had told him that's what you get when you send Irish Catholics into space.

Patrick frowned as he kicked hard against the closed door of his room. He hated his mother. It was so unfair that she'd sent him to his room. He didn't deserve it. He knew he'd been clumsier than normal though. He gulped, and tears appeared in his eyes. It was just that he hadn't yet mastered the new dimensions of his body. He felt the corners of his mouth turning down and knew he looked just as sad and helpless as he felt. He tried, but failed, to comfort himself with the belief that it wasn't really his fault. He glanced down at his guilty arms dangling awkwardly by the side of his body, then he looked at his legs, which were shaking a little. A fresh wave of injustice swept over him, and the tears returned. He wiggled his legs to distract himself from the tears, then looked at them angrily, almost as if he was trying to give them the blame. He thought about how much they'd grown over the last six months, and his chest expanded with indignation at the unfairness of his life. He hadn't got used to his new height yet. He glanced at the bruises on the back of his hands as he raised them and turned them over. He thought about his constant stumbling and having to save himself from falling with his hands and arms. He shook his hands gently. It seemed to him as if the bruises had always been there.

Frustrated, Patrick shrugged his shoulders to try and get rid of the gloomy feeling. Then, as he leaned against the door and slowly and deeply breathed in and out a few times, he felt his facial muscles relaxing. He even managed a weak smile. He didn't know it, but he looked good with his short red-brown hair, his Irish complexion and his green eyes, especially when he smiled. His expression hardened back into a frown as he tried to remember what Paul had told him, how to calm down when he was annoyed.

Patrick liked Paul and automatically smiled when he thought of him. They were friends. Paul was the second youngest technician, after Patrick, on the Moon Base. Patrick was aware that he was still an apprentice, but he liked to pretend he had already qualified.

Patrick remembered that Paul had told him that he could understand Patrick's worries because he himself was very tall. At 188 centimetres Patrick was getting closer to Paul's height. Paul knew that Patrick was worried about how tall he was growing and had explained it was quite normal for teenagers to have a growth spurt. Paul had smiled and even laughed a little as he explained that the growth spurt would not last forever. He'd tried to reassure Patrick that this growing phase only lasted a few months at most. He could clearly remember his own adolescence and stressed that it would soon be over.

This recollection calmed him down a little. Patrick tried to convince himself that he wasn't really worried about his size, but he knew that this was a lie. He was worried because the Moon Base was built for people under 2 Metres tall. He felt his face becoming sad again. He didn't want to be too big for the Moon Base and he really did hope that his growing phase would soon be over.

Looking for something to distract him, Patrick glanced to his left and saw the small black marks on the door frame. He smiled as his eyes flicked from the lowest to the highest mark. They had recorded his height there ever since he was five years old. Paul had helped him to draw the lines. He smiled broader as he remembered the story. It had been such a great idea. There had been that little problem in the beginning, the Sauberbots had classified the marks as undesirable and had repaired them every night. That had gone on for a few months until Paul suggested that they reprogram the Sauberbots. Patrick didn't know back then what that meant, but he recognised Paul's enthusiasm and wanted to try anyway. He trusted Paul and had been sure it would be fun.

The task turned out to be more difficult than they had expected. At first, they tried to teach the Sauberbots that the markings were part of the interior decoration. Unfortunately, this hadn't worked. So, Paul had tried something else and it had taken Paul a while to teach the Sauberbots that the markings were modern art. Patrick remembered how Paul had laughed really hard when he saw that the markings had survived their first night. Patrick glanced at the markings again and smiled, it was now ten years later, and they were still there. Patrick didn't want to admit it, but he didn't know exactly what modern art was and he suspected that the Sauberbots didn't either. Patrick had asked Paul what it was a few years after the reprogramming, and Paul had told him that it wasn't easy to define, otherwise they wouldn't have been able to reprogram the machines so easily. Paul had laughed, and Patrick wasn't sure why.

He was proud that he had learnt to program a little and enjoyed when he had the opportunity to modify Paul's code.

He looked over at the pile of dirty laundry in the middle of his room and nodded appreciatively as he smiled to himself. He had come a long way with reprogramming the Sauberbots. He wanted to see how big his pile of clothes could get before the little robots started cleaning things up. Paul had told Patrick that the Sauberbots knew they were clothes because each piece of clothing was discreetly chipped on the Moon Base. Paul had smiled as he stressed that the clothing chips were only used to make sure they didn't get lost. Patrick stood up straighter as he looked at his pile of clothes and he smiled with pride, he was conducting his own experiment, just like his mother experimented in her laboratory.

He sniffed his armpit and wondered if he should throw another piece of clothing on it. He pulled a face. He was too lazy to change his clothes. Usually he relied on Beatriz and Paul's help to tell him when it was time to change. He shook his head gently as he decided against it. It wasn't necessary yet, and anyway, his clothes hadn't been soiled during the small incident in the lab.

He hadn't wanted to break anything, especially not the test tubes. He sighed. It bothered him that he couldn't remember all the different names of the scientific equipment. But he was sure that his mother was more bothered by it than he was. He did feel ashamed of his ignorance. He remembered that when he was younger, he'd desperately wanted to learn what his mother did at work, but after many hiccups in the lab, his enthusiasm had waned. Lately she had been dismissive towards him, and the last time he suggested that he could help her, she had made it clear to him that she didn't need his help while she was at work.

It was Paul's fault that they had tried to work together again. He had suggested that Patrick needed a little work experience before he could decide what he wanted to do with his life. The other eight people on the Moon Base had readily agreed with Paul's plan. They wanted to help Patrick. And because the others were willing to take part, his mother had been left with no choice. It had been his mother's turn today and he should have spent the day at work with her. Patrick remembered Paul had argued with his mother, Dervla, and that in the end she had reluctantly given in and agreed to them working together.

Patrick had already worked in his mother's laboratory and didn't want to do it again, but he also didn't want to offend his mother either, so he reluctantly went along with the plan. Tears came into his eyes as he remembered how mean and condescending she had sounded as she told him that under no circumstances did glass go in the Re-Do Recycle bin. He could clearly hear her words, "Surely you should know that. You aren't a toddler anymore."

Of course, Patrick knew that you only put plastic into Re-Do Recycle bins and not glass. He knew that glass would destroy the Re-Do Nanobots. He'd just wanted to clean up after he had broken the test tubes. He shivered slightly before kicking hard against the closed door. It hurt him, but he was so frustrated and angry that he didn't really notice the pain in his toes.

Someone saw his pain. A quiet voice sounded in his head or did it come over the intercom? "Use the punchbag."

Without thinking about it, Patrick lowered the punchbag with the Re-Do logo from the ceiling recess, took the Pulsera off his wrist and placed it on the small bedside table before starting his training. The effect was fast, and he felt it in his whole body. He felt himself getting happier and calmer as he fought his frustration with each blow. The dull, spasmodic pain in his arms disappeared a little with every movement.

After most of his frustration had disappeared, Patrick realised he was tired. He held the punchbag, and before stopping the swing, he put his sweaty face against it and let his body rock back and forth. It occurred to him that he would soon be sixteen. He grinned. She couldn't send him to his room anymore when he was sixteen.

He turned around and went over to his bed. Irritated and clumsy, he threw himself on the bed and bumped his head against the wall. He noticed the pain, but he didn't react. Instead, he sank onto the bed and made himself comfortable. He was bored and wasn't sure what to do next.

Peter, whose voice it had been, observed Patrick, wondering how far he was allowed to step over the boundary of the boy's privacy. He justified his surveillance by telling himself that it was his job to enforce the privacy policies, and he had to occasionally ignore the policies to ensure the general security of the Moon Base. He'd watched Patrick for a while before he decided to do something about it. He hadn't wanted to leave the boy alone. He tapped his console and called Paul and asked him succinctly to take Patrick to Beatriz as soon as possible. She needed to check his right foot. Then he transferred the permission to enter Dervla and Patrick's suite to Paul's Security-Pulsera.

Paul thanked the Moon Major and parked the two robots that he was using. As he turned around to go, he heard a soft rumbling from the small wheels on his toolbox. He turned around and said, "Stay there," as he walked off and left his work behind.

The clothing chips made it especially easy for Peter to locate everyone. As Peter watched Paul walk lankily towards Patrick's room, he rested his head in his hands and sighed. Didn't he have anything better to do than spy on people? From reading Paul's medical record, he knew that Paul had had a growth problem as a teenager. Paul was still a little clumsy, and Peter assumed that was the reason he and Patrick got along so well. Paul had an excuse for his clumsiness. He'd inherited damaged DNA from his father. His father had wanted to become a professional athlete and had taken a new growth drug when he was a teenager. The impact for Paul's father had been great, but the problems for his children only became clear later. When Paul was a teenager, he'd been forced to take a growth stopping medication, otherwise he would have grown much taller. Here on the Moon, DNA damage was a delicate matter. The shields were rarely used and the normal artificial deflecting field around the Moon Base was not effective enough to protect everyone from all cosmic rays. The decision had been made that a five year stay on the Moon would probably not cause significant DNA damage, but Paul wouldn't be able to renew his contract of employment after that. Peter chuckled to himself. Paul's contract had now been extended three times.

Peter called Beatriz and warned her that Patrick and Paul were coming to the infirmary and asked if she could also check if Paul was taking the right dose of medication. Beatriz seemed a little distracted, but she nodded. Peter hung up pleased with himself.

Paul looked at his Security-Pulsera. He had access to Patrick's room and could have gone straight in, but he didn't really want to intrude. For a few moments he smiled as he looked at the childish picture of the two moons that they'd painted on the door years ago, then he knocked on the door and announced loudly that he was there.

Patrick jumped up, it was Paul. Fantastic. He opened the door and smiled broadly. As he walked towards Paul, his forgotten Pulsera beeped. Patrick looked at his left wrist and was surprised that his Pulsera was missing. As he turned around to get it he smiled because he was the only Moon Base person who was important enough to always have to wear a modified Pulsera that was specially adapted by Dervla. The others wore an authorisation device, called a Security-Pulsera, but Patrick's Pulsera monitored his health, and he liked that. With a practised art he put it on and smiled as he felt the cold metal against his wrist.

They left the suite together and went down the stairs to Beatriz's infirmary. Patrick noticed the Sun shining through the window and the staircase lit with natural light. He looked out of the window and saw the slow flashing play of light, which meant that the solar panels were in motion. The light show was amusing, and it made Patrick smile. He liked the sunlight and seeing how the light was reflected, but he was only allowed to spend a small amount of time actually in the Sun. There was always a reason why it was too dangerous. He looked forward to when he would be able to enjoy the Sun without thinking about it, when he was finally on Earth.

It didn't take long before they arrived on the first floor and passed the large meeting room before they reached the infirmary. The gym was on the other side, and at the moment it was pretty quiet in there. Beatriz didn't hear them coming in and she continued with what she was doing. Patrick wasn't sure what she was up to, but she seemed to be treating herself or at least he could see that she was using a medication button. It looked similar to the medication button that Europa had used when she had had a bad cold. Patrick actually didn't know what a cold was, he'd never had one himself, but he had the impression that it wasn't good.

Paul asked gently and curiously why she didn't regulate it automatically. Beatriz looked at him surprised that he was there and replied that she was experimenting. Paul nodded and pointed his thumb at Patrick. Beatriz examined her necklace before she smiled and showed the richness of her wrinkles. She looked at Patrick with compassion. She felt sorry for him because he was the only child and the nine adults didn't have much time for him. She asked Patrick to sit on a comfy chair and as she looked at him she remembered that there were now only six adults who didn't have much time for him.

Beatriz glanced at Paul's silver Security-Pulsera that he was wearing on his right arm. He knew what to do and without taking it off, he put his Security-Pulsera on the electronic scale. It only took a few seconds for it to beep. Beatriz glanced at the screen and smiled at him. Everything was in the clear. Paul took his arm back, waved to Patrick, nodded goodbye and went back to his work.

Before Beatriz examined Patrick's toes, she asked him to blow into the Smellaid, hard enough to see the lights come on. She looked at the device and smiled. She took his foot in her hand and felt his toes. Everything was fine. She hadn't expected anything else. His bones were particularly strong. For a moment she was confused. She wanted to do a DNA test on Patrick, and she didn't know why she had forgotten.

Peter switched the surveillance system back to automatic and turned his thoughts to the annual meeting that was going to take place tomorrow morning. They needed to discuss the future of the Moon Base, and he didn't know what he was going to say. He pondered for a while, going over the same old thoughts and wasn't surprised when he found nothing new there. His eyes scanned the faces in the first team photo. The twelve young smiling faces looked at him with hope and enthusiasm. Pent-up anger rose up in his chest. He felt responsible for the situation and had no solution. Ashamed, he turned his eyes away from the photo, and it was then that it occurred to him, Patrick was about to turn sixteen.

Arrival

Date: Wednesday 7th October 2139 - 10:02 CET
Location: Alpha 12 - Moon Base

Peter took off his helmet and thought that he could feel a gentle breeze on his cheek. He turned his head towards where he thought the breeze was coming from and took a moment to enjoy breathing in the fresh air. He could feel himself relaxing and experienced the joy of the cool, clean air that slowly cleansed his lungs. He smiled, and his eyes shone as he looked around. He was relieved as he realised that they were finally here, and he was pleasantly surprised that space actually smelled a little like the sweet, agreeable aroma of barbecued meat. Hesitantly he looked closer at his surroundings and his eyes blinked involuntarily. He smiled broadly and almost laughed. They were finally here. He had waited a long time for this day. The journey, because of the advantageous position of the Earth and the Moon, had lasted just over three days. After twelve people, one less than normal, had spent three days in the Moon shuttle, the air quality wasn't the best. He wasn't aware of the gentle shaking of his head as he remembered the space authorities at Columbus claimed that the air was still good even after a journey that lasted several days, and they insisted that there was no reason to accelerate the Moon shuttle. Peter thought about their explanation that they were bringing supplies, and they were more important than the extra fuel needed to travel faster. He accepted the explanation, but they had also claimed that the journey time had no effect on air quality, because efficient air filters were in use throughout the journey. It didn't matter what they claimed, he still thought the air smelled musty.

Peter put his helmet carefully on the bench before gently twisting his upper body to try and relieve the stiffness in his back. He had been awake since the first braking manoeuvre and had not been able to stretch properly in the Moon shuttle. Only now in the Moon Base entrance area was there enough room for him to stretch his back. He felt the muscles struggling against his movements and enjoyed the relaxing small pains. It felt good. He felt alive. His body needed the exercise after two days of sleeping. It was a requirement that they sleep during the flight, at first he had been disappointed when he had found out that they had to sleep from the near-Earth floating space platform, which served as the terminus of the space lift and as the gateway to space, until the beginning of the braking manoeuvre, but now as he stretched his back, he was grateful. As he twisted his torso slowly and stiffly, he noticed a growing pressure on his bladder. Resigned to accepting Columbus' argument, he put his hand on his face and stoked his beard as he remembered the annoying inconvenience of emptying his bladder in space. Then he smiled as he realised that he was now on the Moon Base and the toilets were almost normal. Quietly he thanked Art Feldmann for her invention, the ability to control gravity. He frowned and metaphorically crossed his legs. He would still have to wait until the landing formalities were completed.

The rest of the team soon stood behind him. Paul, who had been the last to disembark, had just joined the others and was about to take off his helmet. Peter looked at his team briefly smiling to himself before his attention was drawn to the window wall, it was fascinating to see the commotion around the Moon shuttle. An engineer in a Moon Base outdoor uniform stood a little distance away from the action, overlooking the dance of the Art Feldmann Robots. He didn't seem to be doing anything. Peter watched the hypnotic movements of the hurrying machines and nodded gently, unconsciously along to the imaginary sounds of their rhythm. The work needed to be done quickly as the returning team wanted to take advantage of the Earth-Moon apogee when the distance between the Earth and Moon is at its minimum.

The other team members were stretching leisurely, in a similar way to how he had just been doing. They were also stiff and tired, and seemed to be relieved that they had finally arrived. He smiled when he saw them sniffing the fresh air. And he wondered if they also thought that space smelled of barbecued meat. He smiled again as it occurred to him that they would probably also appreciate the Moon Base toilets.

As soon as Peter noticed that the helmets were on the bench, he suggested that it was time to have the official Moon-arrival photo taken. The members of the eleven-strong team, who were still wearing their bulky orange spacesuits, came together smiling, laughing and full of anticipation. With calm, obedient movements, that showed both the extent of their training and their natural tranquil aptitudes, they moved into their predetermined positions and stood peacefully in an orderly line. The pilot took a step back and held her hands up to ward off the friendly and inviting gestures of the Moon crew. She was about to fly back, and she didn't belong in this photo.

Peter felt both proud and happy, he stood in the middle and looked around to make sure that everything was as planned. He breathed in sharply as he realised that he had almost forgotten someone. Luckily, Liam came in just then, and Peter waved to him to encourage him to take his place.

Liam nodded and smiled without enthusiasm as he joined the others. He wasn't happy, he'd had to leave the robots unsupervised to be in the photo.

Peter assumed that the robots probably didn't need monitoring if the work went well and there were no surprises. Then he noticed the mobile surveillance device in Liam's hand and nodded, satisfied. Liam was conscientious, and Peter felt pleased that Liam was the twelfth member of his team. Liam was going to bring continuity to the working practices because he had volunteered for a second shift on the Moon Base, even though he looked like an outsider for this photo. The others were still wearing their orange spacesuits while Liam was wearing the white Moon Base outdoor uniform, still holding his helmet in his hand.

On command they all smiled broadly, and that first photo was taken. The pilot, who was standing a little distance away, nodded encouragingly. They looked good.

Peter gave the order to have the photo displayed on the window wall. He nodded as he looked at it. They were going to get to see this photo on Earth. As he looked he felt both proud and sad. His wife was going to see him in this photo - her husband and his team standing in Alpha 12 Moon Base not far from the South Pole of the Moon. He smiled when he thought of his wife, then he remembered where he was, and for the first time he felt the emptiness of the deep chasm of distance.

He looked closer at the photo to distract himself from the sombre feeling. He was fascinated by how easy it was to recognise the smallest of details in the oversized photo. Filip and Damian's green eyes seemed almost uncannily green, and John's red hair stood in stark contrast to Peter's brown. Peter's eyes glided over the photo as he subconsciously checked the order of the team. They really were standing as they'd practised during training. Paul, the tallest, stood on the far right with his friend Filip, who the next tallest, next to him. Damian, who was smiling broadly was a smaller, older version of his son Filip, and was standing to Filip's right. It warmed Peter's heart and made him smile to see how much the two of them resembled each other. Next to Damian were the two scientists Dervla and John. Peter didn't quite understand what they did professionally, and he had the uncomfortable feeling that he might not want to know. He himself, the Moon Major, was stood proudly in the middle of the picture. On his right-hand side was his mentor, the Moon Base doctor Beatriz, with her elegant grey hair and her friendly smile. Steve was holding his shoulders straight and looked taller than normal. He seemed proud of his position next to Beatriz. Next in line was Europa with her ruffled short hair and a forced smile on her lips. Peter already knew that this was the best he could expect from her. He smiled amused. She really didn't like to have her photo taken.

Then came the beautiful Maria, she was standing next to Europa. Her stance was graceful and relaxed, and she smiled charmingly. Her disarming smile, which reached her eyes, seemed to absorb the nearby light allowing her to shine brighter than the others. Charlie stood, with a barely hidden grin, closer than the regulations allowed next to Maria. His left shoulder was behind and looked as if it was just touching Maria's right shoulder. The last person on the left of the photo, with maybe a little too much distance from the others, was Liam, who should have been standing where Steve was standing. Peter thought that Liam seemed a little distant, cut off from the rest of the team, but he was at least facing them, and it almost seemed as if he belonged. The others, who knew each well, had trained together on Earth. He hoped they would make Liam feel welcome in the team.

Smiling Peter looked at the others expressing his satisfaction with the photo. He asked the others if there were any objections. Everyone nodded contentedly, and they all agreed that the photo was okay. Peter had the impression that they were too excited to focus on the photo. He nodded and ordered it to be sent to the space authorities. He knew that they would make their own decision. He hoped that it would be appropriate to publish.

Peter glanced down at his bulky spacesuit. It was time to get changed. He grinned and thought he could try the toilets as well. After he was finished changing, Meichun, the returning Moon Major, approached Peter. She explained that her returning team was already waiting in the canteen and the pilot was sleeping in one of the guest rooms. She was taking the opportunity to rest for a few hours.

Peter understood immediately what Meichun meant and instructed his team to go to the canteen as soon as they were ready. They didn't need detailed instructions, they already knew that they had about three hours to discuss the handover before the Moon shuttle returned. Liam was ready first and was already waiting for the team. He needed to show them the way. Meichun pointed Peter in the direction of his new office. The route there took them past the Art Feldmann statue, which was in the communication area. As they arrived, Peter stopped and looked up in awe at the statue. She was as impressive as he had heard. In an attempt to preserve the mystery of the Art Feldmann statue, there were no photos on Earth. That was one of the reasons why it was particularly impressive when you first saw her.

With a small all-knowing smile, Meichun observed Peter as he looked the statue. She was remembering, with a pleasant easy feeling, how she had reacted in exactly the same way when she first saw this statue. And she knew intuitively that he needed a few moments to realise that he was really standing in front of this statue.

The full-coloured statue was magnificent. He'd heard that it represented Professor Art Feldmann at a younger age, but he had heard nothing about the wonderful colours and the almost lifelike hair. He'd never seen a complete picture of the statue. A few Moononauts had sketched the statue from memory after they had returned to Earth. Peter had seen these illicit rough sketches and hadn't been impressed by them. These Moononauts were obviously not artists, the pictures might have had a better quality if they had been. He found it ironic that contrary to all expectations of a flourishing Moon tourism, there had only been a few people who had ever made the journey to see the statue. Now the Moononauts were the only ones who made the long voyage, and before they could go to the Moon, they had to promise that they wouldn't make any reproductions of the Art Feldmann statue.

Peter shook his head. He could sense that his eyes were stretched wide open. He was really here. The statue was floating above him, almost touching the ceiling. It had been designed to prove that this woman was the one who had tamed gravity. Her body was almost horizontal, and she lay relaxed, as if she was on a chaise longue. He smiled more broadly, as he noticed that there was actually a glass of beer in her left hand. He had heard that it was beer, at least it looked like a beer glass, and the liquid in it was beer-coloured. It was this liquid that was most discussed on the Intellinet. There was no clear answer to the question of whether it was a liquid or only looked like one. He had heard that the statue had to be moved now and then. It was assumed that she was brought down for cleaning. And the tricky question was, if the statue within the local gravity of the environment was lowered too fast, would the liquid in the glass move downward at the same speed? If not, and the beer would fall slower than the statue, what would happen to the beer? Could it be possible for Art Feldmann to get beer in her face? People said that she had enjoyed beer a lot, but certainly not so much that she wanted beer on her face.

He thought it was strange that no one had tried the experiment on Earth, but it was claimed that it would cost too much to create an Art Feldmann's field on Earth. Up here, where the Feldmann field was permanently in use, it didn't cost much extra to let the statue float.

Peter looked at Meichun, remembering she was there. Embarrassed he opened his mouth to say something but lacked the words. He'd totally forgotten her. She smiled understandingly and suggested that they should move on. Peter nodded relieved. She led the way and as she walked past him, she whispered to him that she had been just the same when she first arrived. As they walked silently through the communication area, Peter looked around curiously. He noted that Damian and Liam would soon be working together in the communications area. The thought was pushed clean out of his mind when they entered his new office. He smiled unintentionally. It was exactly what he'd expected. They walked in the room together. Meichun automatically went towards her chair where she had been sitting for the last five years and put her hand on it. She managed to stop herself before she sat down in what was now Peter's chair. She turned to Peter and smiled at him apologetically. Old habits are difficult to change.

Peter suggested they hadn't finished the official handover yet. And that while she was here, it was still her chair.

They both sat down with a small, embarrassed laugh that released the confusion and tension. Meichun took her usual place and immediately began her official handover, "I know you've been getting weekly reports for the past few months.

Nevertheless, I think it makes sense for us to discuss the most important points." She radiated a relaxed self-confidence, especially when she smiled.

Peter was impressed by Meichun's quiet authority. He nodded and waited anxiously for what she would say next.

"The Moon Major is responsible for the entire Moon Base, but you mustn't forget that there is almost always back-up support on Earth." She looked thoughtful, "At first it's a bit strange with the communication delay, but you get used to it very quickly." She looked him straight in the eye, "On average it's about 1.3 seconds. I would advise you to contact Columbus as often as you can." She nodded gently, "The people at the Earth Base Columbus are very reasonable. And sometimes the returning Major joins the Columbus team," she smiled, and he wondered if she was going to do that.

But she shook her head as if to say, "Not me."

"The main tasks on the Moon Base are tourism, finding water and scientific research." As an afterthought, she said, "and of course there are the two storehouses for us and for the Mars Base."

She shrugged her shoulders and shook her head as she said, "There's not much to do with tourism, we haven't had any tourists in the last five years." A little pensive she added, "But before that during the previous Moon missions there was a tourist. She stayed longer than expected, if I'm not mistaken her name was Molly Brown."

She noticed Peter's worried expression and smiled, "But to be honest, don't worry about it. No one will come." She took a deep breath, "The third floor of the residential area in the main building, where we are now, is equipped with four VIP suites, and the robots know what to do if a tourist comes. The VIP suites are one floor up from the normal living area." She lowered her voice conspiratorially, "It's worth looking at them, they're pretty special." Then she continued in her normal voice, "We have fourteen normal apartments for the staff. The two extra ones are used by the pilots, and no one else. Have you thought about how to distribute the rooms?"

Peter nodded, "We planned that on Earth. Actually, we had no choice. The authorities told us which room we had been allocated."

Meichun nodded impartially and thought, "That's new."

"The second task is to find water. We are at the south pole of the Moon. Where the first water ice was found. The water-seeking robots search for new reserves of water and now and then they find something. Don't worry though," she smiled calmly, "we have enough water reserves for our requirements."

Peter nodded, "That's good to know."

"The third task is scientific research. There are two types of experiments that we do here, the long-term ones, which last more than five years, which my team will hand over to yours and the short-term ones, which are planned with each shift change. Who will do the research for the effect of Art Feldmann's field on dark matter?"

Peter replied, "Europa has already done the handover and is ready to begin." Peter didn't know much about the subject, but he trusted Europa. She was sometimes a little difficult, but she was an expert in her field. "She worked at CERN for a few years and was even involved in artificially creating the effect of Art Feldmann's field on dark matter."

Meichun nodded satisfied, but she looked at Peter seriously, "Always show respect for the statue. It's pretty risky and disrespectful to experiment with it."

Peter nodded seriously. He tried not to smile and said, "I didn't think about that at all." But he thought it might occur to someone after five years of being here. He thought Meichun was quite curious about his team, she wanted to know what everyone was going to do.

She cleared her throat and asked, "Who's going to take care of the biological experiments in the gardens?"

"Maria is our biologist. She's quite young but well qualified and if necessary, Charlie will help her."

Meichun seemed satisfied with his answer. Peter wondered if she had heard of Maria's professional reputation.

"To be honest, there's not much going on in the garden, but for everyday life it's extremely important that they work well," she paused briefly, "I prefer the small garden myself. It has dense plant cover and seems calmer." She smiled before she continued, "And the doctor is Beatriz. I am sure she's planned her own projects, and of course there is the extensive immune system research waiting for her. It is worthwhile to have everyone checked medically at the very beginning. Nothing happened to my team but in the previous team, there was a problem with someone's immune system." She looked serious again, "Not everyone can cope with cosmic radiation. He had to be sent home in the tourist escape pod, and they never replaced it." She lowered her eyes and looked at the table, "He died shortly after his return." She didn't want to reveal any more details and Peter didn't know if he really wanted to hear the story.

"We now have an immune boosting prototype to help with such problems, but we've not had a reason to use them yet."

He nodded, feeling a little reassured, "That's good to know."

"Finally, there are the other scientific projects, most of which are short-term and last up to five years, and the current ones have come to an end today." She gave a little smile, "You must have your own. Do you know what your team are planning on doing?"

Peter shook his head and shrugged his shoulders as he said, "I have no idea, should I?"

"There are two reasons why scientists want to experiment on the Moon, one is that they need the environment and the second is that the experiment is not allowed on Earth. On the Moon we are exempt from international law." She pointed at him, "Here, you are responsible for what is considered good and evil." She paused to let her words sink in.

He stayed calm and waited. He already knew all this. It had been explained to him shortly before his departure. He assumed Meichun had had it explained to her by the previous Moon Major and she wanted to return the favour.

"Before I go, I have a few tips." She smiled. "Always stay in contact with Earth, that helps to avoid going crazy. And over the years, every Moon Major has worked with an artificial intelligence, a so-called AI program, and has helped to develop it further. She can help with the decision-making process." She held her face in her hands as she said regretfully, "Don't forget, you'll need someone you can talk to openly. Keep your deputy, Beatriz in the loop and take care of the team's health."

He nodded. It seemed to him that Meichun really didn't want to let go, she had been here for five years and it was her home. This was the first time she had met Peter and he got the feeling that she wanted to be sure that he was going to take good care of the Moon Base.

"There's a father-son combination on your team, isn't there? Be careful, sometimes it can get really claustrophobic up here. Do you have any more questions?"

"Why does Liam want to stay for a second shift?" Peter couldn't understand Liam. Five years was a long time to be away from your family and he knew he was going to miss his wife a lot.

"All I can tell you is that Liam has his reasons, and I don't know what they are. If it was relevant or necessary, we'd have been notified." She shrugged.

"And one last tip before I go, watch the clothes. Up to a certain degree, they automatically adapt to the required size. There is a possibility to enter a maximum size. I can only recommend that you do that." She whispered, "Good luck" before she got up and left.

Peter watched the door as it closed. He chewed gently on his lower lip, uncertain what to do next. For the first time on the Moon, Peter was alone. A look of wonder crossed his face as he looked around his new office. He smiled bashfully and thought, "I work here. It's my workplace," but it was only a fleeting thought and was quickly replaced when he thought of the toilets. He wanted to try them again, and this time he wouldn't have to rush.

He smiled and nodded, impressed as he looked down at the toilet and thanked his heroine Art Feldmann for her genius, because of her the toilets could be flushed, and he could take a pee in relaxed luxury.

Peter stood in the entrance area a little way back from the returning team listening to their conversation. They were excited getting ready for the return flight. They were already wearing their orange spacesuits as they made the last adjustments He heard them laughing and talking about how pleased they were that their five-year shift was almost over, but he thought he could also hear an undertone of regret. They were joking that all they had to do was survive the commute home. He wondered if they were afraid something might go wrong.

He looked at the window wall and his eyes searched for the robots, which were now finished with their tasks and safety checks. He couldn't find them. It felt empty as he looked at the quiet scene. He looked towards the Moon shuttle, which was ready to launch, and then watched the Moononauts slowly approaching. Before she got in, Meichun turned around and waved. This image embedded itself in Peter's memory, and he knew that this would be how he was going to remember her.

He remained standing there and watched. It didn't take long until they were all onboard and the Moon shuttle was ready to go. He barely knew these people, yet he felt sad. He was aware of but didn't acknowledge when the members of his team, who had been there with him, left the entrance area. They were probably going to start work, or maybe they just wanted to orientate themselves better. Suddenly he felt empty. He forced himself to think positively. There was so much to discover in the Moon Base. He tried not to think about what they'd left behind on Earth. He stayed watching until the muted launch was over. Then he stepped closer to the window wall and watched the Moon shuttle slowly disappear into the distance. He knew that the escape velocity of the Moon was only a fifth of the Earth's. He smiled at his knowledge and knew that they needed less energy for the launch and that meant they could travel with less fuel. Then he thought about the journey ahead of them. The Moononauts, except for the pilot, would soon be asleep. As he watched the Moon shuttle, he thought that it seemed too small for twelve people, not to mention the thirteen it was supposed to be able to accommodate. He wished the crew a safe journey home. His wife was where they were going. Luckily, he could see the Earth through the window wall. He was glad he could see it, but it seemed so far away, so small and vulnerable. Had he made a mistake in coming?

He shook his head and reminded himself that he shouldn't think so negatively when he was facing such a great adventure. He turned his thoughts to work. The shift change was now complete, and he had a lot of work to do. He returned purposefully to his office and as he sat down on his chair, it occurred to him that he was now fully responsible for the Moon Base.

First Week

Date: Wednesday 14th October 2139 - 13:03 CET
Location: Alpha 12 - Moon Base

During the first week on the base everything was new and exciting. Peter smiled to himself because he felt like a toddler on its first adventure into the wilds of the back garden. He thought that there was a lot to discover despite the fact only the first building phase of the Moon Base had been completed. The second building phase had never been started since the tourists had stayed away.

As Peter tried out the features of the ingeniously built furniture in his office he marvelled at their design and construction. He found it difficult to understand why the tourists stayed away. He'd heard the pseudo claims from the Happynet that lots of people die during the strenuous flight to the Moon; that hardly anyone survives the physical stresses that they are exposed to during the Moon shuttle launch; and that during your stay they treat you like you are a lab rat because they turn the shields on and off to see how you will react which is why so many people go crazy and get Moon Madness. He shrugged his shoulders and shook his head gently as he thought about it. He couldn't believe that people actually took any of that seriously.

Everyone knew that the information in the Happynet was nonsense and not to be believed. He smiled and felt grateful that the Intellinet and Happynet were separate entities and that the project to keep them separate continued to find support. He tutted and shook his head again remembering more of the Happynet arguments, the high cost, and also that it made no sense to pay for the trip with your environmental credits, which had led to some truly unhinged conspiracy theories. A momentary look of sadness flashed across his face as he glanced down, but in reality, he believed that people were simply scared, and they used the spurious arguments from the Happynet to help them hide from the truth.

The completed domes were not just adequate for the crew, they were also big enough to serve as a storage facility for both the Moon Base and the Mars mission. Today was Peter's first weekly inspection of the Moon Base and he was looking forward to seeing the whole base. He put on his captain's hat respectfully and looked in the mirror. He smiled and tilted his head, then noticed that the peak wasn't straight, so while still smiling he adjusted it carefully.

He was going to pay everyone from the team a visit and wanted to look official while he checked if they were settling in as well as he had. He grinned. He felt the part, although he missed his wife a little. He had thought the distance would be harder to bear, but so far it seemed like a holiday and he could always send a video mail or watch one of his wife's again.

The communications area was right next to his office, so the first stop of his inspection was going to be Damian and Liam. Peter found it easy to chat to Damian. He enjoyed listening as he talked about his wife and how glad he was that his son was working with them. Damian found it easy to speak of his worries about his wife and that it must be a shock for her and his youngest son as it would be so much quieter at home. He'd already exchanged a few video mails with his wife and she seemed to be fine. Peter was pleased to see how

Damian smiled as he explained how much he liked the well-equipped gym.

Peter had already observed that Damian and Liam weren't very talkative with each other. They didn't say much, but they seemed to communicate well enough. It was clear that Damian liked the technology here and Liam was helping him get used to everything.

Peter tried to exchange a few words with Liam, but it was difficult. Liam wasn't very forthcoming. Peter had only managed to find out that he liked to walk in the main garden, where it was quiet, and he could be on his own.

Peter changed the subject and asked him about his work. He wanted to know more about the information exchange protocols with Earth Base Columbus. Liam smiled as he explained that the two-way communication worked well and always had priority over scientific reports. The reports arrived in a timely manner, and there was even enough bandwidth for receiving leisure communication. Peter watched him closely. It was obvious to see that Liam enjoyed controlling the flow of information and liked talking about it.

Peter turned to Damian, smiled friendly at him and asked what he thought of the Moon satellite. Damian nodded and grinned as he explained that they had just been talking about that. He was clearly impressed and reported that it was just like his training on Earth.

Peter wanted to know why they had been talking about the satellite, was there something wrong with it?

Suddenly unsure, Damian looked over to Liam, who nodded encouragingly. Damian didn't answer, so Liam took over and explained that they had been clarifying the process for the Annual Moon Base Closure. They were still checking with Europa to make sure if they needed to plan an early satellite manoeuvre to avoid any possible stray meteors. Damian smiled broadly as he spoke about the steering capability of the Moon satellite. He could hardly wait to bring the satellite home to safety and redeploy it after the danger was averted.

Peter could see the enthusiasm in his eyes as he explained the planned maintenance of the satellite and the tests for the replacement. Peter noticed Damian's relaxed smile and saw how Liam nodded in agreement and thought they are going to work well together.

Peter nodded his thanks as he left. He was thinking about the two-way communication with Earth. In many ways, Meichun was right. Initially, the conversations with Earth Base Columbus had been a bit weird, but he'd soon got used to the signal delay, and now he didn't think about it anymore, and it didn't bother him at all during his daily reports.

As he headed towards the second stop, he thought about how he had followed Meichun's advice and logged into the AI Program on the first day. He had been curious about what she had to offer. Her first question had taken him by surprise. He needed to choose a name for the AI program. He'd requested if he could continue using the existing name, and he was a little taken aback when his request was denied. He remembered looking at the window wall in his office, but there had been nothing to see as it was opaque, his unfocused eyes had concentrated on an image that wasn't there and even so he'd felt like he was looking right through it into the distance. He'd realised that he found it difficult to think while the AI Program was watching him, and he wasn't even sure how she could do this. He'd stood up, turned around and walked a few steps and with his back to the AI program robot he'd given his answer. He'd said the first name he'd thought of. He'd called the AI Program Meichun. She also had a talking face that looked and sounded like the real Meichun. A little embarrassed, he wondered whether Meichun had also used the name of her predecessor.

Still distracted and not concentrating on his surroundings, he continued on his way. When he noticed where he was and glanced up, he smiled broadly. He was standing beneath Art Feldmann's statue. He considered it an honour to look at. He was so lucky to be allowed to work here on the Moon. As he stood there, he started to get the niggling feeling of time passing. He should get back to work. Next on the list was the warehouse with Filip and Paul. He turned in the direction of the warehouse and began to walk with a light, easy step. The way there didn't take very long, and he enjoyed feeling the lightness in his legs and feet while walking. He had not yet become fully accustomed to the near-Earth gravity. The Moon's gravity was kept at approximately eighty percent of the strength of Earth's. After just one week, in which he had religiously done the muscle retention exercises, his muscles were almost as strong as they had been on Earth. With each light movement, he felt like he had the energy and strength of a small child and had to remind himself that as Moon Major it was not appropriate to run. With a thoughtful but serious expression and measured step he headed towards the main warehouse.

As Peter arrived at the main warehouse, Filip and Paul didn't notice him come in, they were otherwise occupied, and their work was apparently forgotten. Paul was trying to show Filip the secret of his amazing golf swing. Peter could hear a proud and confident voice as he approached, "I wouldn't be the first one to try it either."

Peter coughed softly.

They heard him and turned their heads in his direction abruptly.

Peter suppressed a smile as he noticed their wide-opened eyes and slightly open mouths. Paul still held the golf club in both hands above his head. As discretely as possible, he let it fall. The three of them stared at the golf club as it rattled loudly on the ground. Paul went very red and his arm movements betrayed his embarrassment as well. Peter couldn't hide his smile, but he managed to ask if Paul liked playing golf without laughing.

Paul's embarrassed gaze was keenly focused on the now silent golf club. He bent down and without saying anything picked it up with his left hand. Peter noticed that Paul was wearing his Pulsera on his right arm.

Filip, who was a few years older than Paul, took Paul's self-conscious silence as a signal to step in and help him. He spoke calmly, "He likes to play golf."

Peter nodded and asked curiously, "How did you get the golf club here?"

Paul steadied himself and managed to regain control of his voice as he blurted out, "I disguised the iron club head with some tools and put the shaft and handle together once I was here." He didn't dare look at Peter. "I wanted to experiment with my golf swing at different levels of gravity."

Peter laughed quietly, and his eyes twinkled in a friendly manner before he explained that he just wanted to see how everything was going in the warehouses. He knew that Filip and Paul were responsible for the warehouses and Peter would appreciate it if they would give him a quick tour of the facility.

Peter stood in front of one of the aisles of the warehouse and looked around. He was surprised as he said, "It's not as big as I thought it would be."

Paul had recovered from his embarrassment. He replied with a voice and face full of excitement, "There are loads of underground levels and we have forklift robots that move everything around. They are simply brilliant."

Peter nodded. Paul's enthusiasm for the highly automated systems made him smile.

Filip looked a little agitated as he spoke, "Everything is ready for the forthcoming Annual Closure." He breathed in deeply, and Peter waited, he sensed the but that was about to come.

"But what I don't like is the date of this year's closing. Why does it have to be in November? The Perseid meteors come in August and they can be more dangerous than the Leonid meteors. I think, it would make more sense if the closure took place in August."

Peter smiled, and thought Filip's birthday is in August, but he answered as if he didn't know, "I have no idea. We'll have to ask Europa. She knows everything about astronomy."

Filip nodded satisfied. He hadn't expected to change anything. He just wanted to have his say. And anyway, he thought, a November closure wasn't so bad. They would only have to wait a little over a month before the party. And they did need to practise working with the Moon Base robots. The robots reacted differently here, from their training on Earth. The lower gravity made a subtle difference to his expectations. They were going to have fun learning how their new toys reacted and worked.

Peter followed the robot and found his way through the main warehouse to the observatory without getting lost. It seemed strange how the observatory had been built on the side of the warehouses, but then he considered that they probably wanted to locate the telescope as far away from the lights of the residential area as possible. The dark shadows of the warehouses would probably shield the observatory from the light. He knew he was only guessing and wasn't really sure about it, but he had noticed that Europa was spending almost eighteen hours a day in the observatory. He was sure that she didn't sleep enough but he reminded himself to be respectful. The observatory was under her control, even though for six hours each day, the telescope could be controlled by Earth Base Columbus and used for their projects.

When he got there Europa didn't want to talk to him. She made it clear with her expression that she didn't want to be interrupted. She had waited a long time for this opportunity and was really enjoying working here. She was going to make the most of this research opportunity, and at this time of day the telescope was following her instructions, and she was in the process of going into her research in more depth.

Peter reassured her that he would only stay for a short while and that he only had two quick questions. He wanted to know if she was all right and did she know why the closure took place in November for the Leonid meteors and not in August for the Perseid meteors.

Europa turned her chair to Peter and looked at him puzzled. She didn't really understand what he was doing here but she knew the fastest way back to her work was to answer his questions. She considered what he would be able to understand before she answered, "It's true that both the Perseid Meteors in August and the Gemini Meteors in December usually have more meteors than the Leonid Meteors, but the Leonids occasionally come as a meteor storm and can be much more destructive than the other two." She looked directly into his eyes to see if he had understood.

He didn't react.

"Usually the Perseids and Geminides don't present any danger, and, of course, our automatic systems monitor these events and react accordingly if necessary." She looked at him quizzically. "The meteor storm doesn't come every year, but we humans need a regular break."

Peter nodded and remembered his decision to keep this visit as short as possible. She seemed to be doing fine. He slightly touched the brim of his captain's hat respectfully and nodded as he thanked Europa for her time and apologised for the interruption.

After he had left the observatory, he thought she was right, people do need a holiday, or they'll go stir-crazy cooped up here.

Peter took a relaxed stroll through the second warehouse on his way to the main garden. He was hoping to meet Maria there, but was in no hurry and enjoyed the alternating shades of light and the fragrances of the trees and plants. He knew there was a path at the edge of the garden, that people used for jogging, but he chose to wander through the middle. He'd been told that the many well-maintained paths that meandered through the garden resembled the one at the edge. He decided that he'd look at it another time, and one day maybe even go jogging.

Feeling relaxed, he lingered in the garden listening to the gentle sounds of unobtrusive music in the distance. He walked around a corner and was surprised to see Maria standing there. He'd almost forgotten why he was there. She smiled at him. She looked radiant when she smiled. It made him feel welcome and he returned her smile easily. They went for a stroll in the garden, falling easily into step with each other. He commented about the cover of the blossoming trees and plants. They looked greener, sharper than on Earth, and he wondered if that was because of the colouring of the protective glass?

Maria answered with a friendly smile. Her answer brief but polite, "There's no atmosphere outside the dome to filter the light. That's why it looks a little different than on Earth."

He nodded and felt comforted that there were so many experts working on the Moon Base. They meandered slowly and from time to time Maria knelt and inspected a plant.

Peter thought the plants looked like the ones on Earth. Although he had the feeling that this wasn't true, so he stayed quiet. He didn't want to show his ignorance, instead he asked, "Is there music playing?"

Maria stood up and smiled, "Yes, the plants like soft, gentle music." She pointed to a tree and said, "This one has been genetically modified to become a self-pollination variant and this particular variation likes it when they hear ABBA played quietly."

Peter was interested, "Are there many self-pollination variants?"

Maria nodded, "Yes, we have many, because some bees have a few problems flying and others don't adapt well to the lower gravity. We have as far as possible two varieties of each plant, one with and one without self-pollination." She smiled at him, "Dervla is working on the genetics to help produce more specimens. We are also experimenting with bee-like drones. Charlie's helping me." She smiled again and added, "We have more success with self-pollination."

Maria would have liked to have shown Peter both gardens. The biologist loved her work and thought that the opportunity to work on the Moon was simply awesome. She enthused about her own planned experiments and also about continuing the existing ones. Peter didn't understand every word she said but thought that she sounded like she knew what she was talking about. Their shift lasted five years after all, he could come back and find out more later. He let her keep talking without interrupting her.

Maria stopped suddenly and smiled broadly, "The gardens play a major role in our attempt to live as self-sufficiently as possible." Her eyes lit up, "Do you want to see the cultivated microalgae? There is a microalgae plant here in the main garden and another one in the second garden."

Peter saw how Maria's eyes sparkled. She loved to talk about her gardens and plants. He smiled at her and nodded.

She was beaming as she explained the details of the algae system to him as they walked there. When they got there, she pointed out the green water flowing under the plexiglass containers. Peter noticed small gas bubbles in the liquid and asked her why they were there.

"We cultivate two types of algae together. One is aerobic algae and the other anaerobic algae. It is a fantastic system. From the oxygen-dependent aerobic algae we get oxygen and from oxygen-independent anaerobic algae we get hydrogen. The products of this process can be used to produce energy and the by-product is water." She smiled, "And we also get an algae biomass, which is used in our food and serves as a basis for the food reconstruction machines."

Peter already knew that part of their food was made from algae, but he didn't really need to know or even to see it. He hoped his face wasn't as green as the water and was very pleased that he hadn't been part of the first Moon team, they had experimented with insects as a food source.

Maria noticed Peter's expression and she felt the need to explain to him how important algae are for their survival, "Algae belong to the system that keeps the carbon dioxide level under control, and they are also key in the water supply process." She looked thoughtful, "When I sit in the garden and listen, I can hear the artificial wind, especially when it blows from the north, rustling through the leaves and the sounds of small animals going about their business. It makes me think how important the algae are and how the whole ecosystem works together. Every part is important for our survival, without the gardens we wouldn't be able to keep the Moon Base running, not in the long term."

"There are small animals in the garden?"

"Yes, insects and animals as big as a snake."

Peter looked a little worried.

Maria changed the subject, "There's the soil creation experiment over there." She pointed to her right. Her voice sounded proud as she said, "We've been trying to create soil for the last thirty-five years, and it will take about another three hundred years to complete."

Peter looked at the seemingly unremarkable experiment. He would never have expected that it would take more than three hundred years until they could get something useful out of it, even with the accelerated soil creation process. He shook his head. Who would have thought that soil took so long to create?

"The experiment was a forerunner of the ones on the Mars Base. There is no soil on Mars. They have only loose rock. The soil biota is missing in the Mars regolith." She looked at him, "It is the absence of soil life that makes colonising Mars so difficult." She looked proud as she explained, "We started the experiments here first. They have similar experiments on the Mars Base, but they are not yet as far on in their experiments as we are."

Peter breathed in sharply, he wanted to ask something more, but Maria ignored him as she carried on talking, "The hydroponics, the water cultures, are in the second garden. It's pretty impressive how the mineral nutrient solutions flow through the system. There's no soil in the whole system. We are doing it in case the soil creation process fails."

Peter frowned, "The second garden, how big is it?"

Maria's shoulders fell, "Not really big. Let's do it next time." She'd already taken up a lot of Peter's time.

Peter asked, "Do you make moonshine in the garden?"

The question surprised Maria, and she frowned.

"I was just thinking of the Leonids and the upcoming Annual Closure. We'll need a little alcohol to celebrate." He smiled, and his eyes twinkled.

She laughed quietly and that calmed her, "The moonshine is delivered with the Moon shuttle, but I think we have the necessary equipment in stock if we really want to make it here. Filip should know."

To finish off the garden tour, Maria took Peter to the main attraction of the garden. The nocturnal moonflowers, which were already in flower, were closed at this time of day and didn't look as beautiful as they did in the artificial moonlight. Nevertheless, Peter could imagine what the climbing plants looked like, with their fifteen-centimetre diameter they looked like small moons. He bent over, took the name tag in his hand and read it, "Ipomoea alba, moonflower white, night bloomer, creeper."

Maria took her necklace in her hand, "We control day and night, but I don't want to confuse the plants by turning on night unnecessarily."

Peter understood Maria's concern and knew that there had been a lot of experiments over a very long time to find out the optimal times of day and night for the gardens and that even today the times of day in the two gardens were different.

Even though he seemed to understand she still wanted to justify her concern, "A normal Moon day lasts fourteen Earth days, and the Moon night also lasts fourteen days, I imagine that the plants and flowers would grow weary if we didn't control their environment." Maria corrected herself, "I know, in the base, that we are near the South Pole, and there would be ninety percent daylight if we didn't control it, but the idea is the same." She looked at him for agreement.

As Peter nodded, he realised how much the plants meant to Maria.

As they walked around the corner, they saw Charlie standing there working with a few of the robots. He was doing some gardening work for Maria. Charlie was already grinning as Peter looked at him. He'd noticed Maria and had pressed the red emergency park button on his BULcap helmet.

Peter liked Charlie because he was willing to help with every task, especially when Maria needed help. Officially he was a spacewalk specialist and technician, but today he was checking the flight pattern of the bee-like drones.

The drones landed and parked safely.

Peter looked at Charlie's BULcap. He'd tried to work with a Brain Uplink Cap, but he hadn't succeeded. He felt a little jealous that Charlie was able to control the drones with his thoughts.

Peter nodded respectfully to Charlie and smiled.

Charlie explained, "I'm checking possible flight patterns. The plants in the garden serve as obstacles for the flight training and I can simultaneously check and document the structures of the plants."

Peter was still looking at the drones, "You can park them very fast and accurately."

"New sensors have been installed in the drones, there are thermal images, X-rays, 3D geometric mapping and ultrasound crack detection. So, they are a little different and I need to practice before I can use the new sensors, but I can still park them."

There were so many new technologies, Peter was curious, "Could you show us what you've already learnt?"

Charlie blushed and stuttered, "I can't." He glanced briefly at Maria and then looked at the floor.

After a few uncomfortable seconds it dawned on Peter why Charlie couldn't do it. The brain-uplink connection is very sensitive to emotions, so much so that it had been necessary to install a red emergency parking button on the BULcap and given the fact that Charlie really liked Maria... Peter smiled as he thought, poor old Charlie, when he sees her, he can't clearly separate his thoughts from his feelings. He wants to be able to show Maria how good he is at controlling the drones, but he never can. Peter nodded at Charlie and said, "No problem. I'm going to see John and Steve. What's the best way to get there?"

Charlie and Maria pointed simultaneously towards the second lab on the northern edge of the main garden.

Peter smiled and left them without saying a word. He still felt a little sorry for Charlie, he'd really gone very red.

As soon as he was out of earshot, Peter laughed quietly to himself, life was sometimes very funny. He paid attention to which direction he was going and soon stood at the entrance to the second lab. John and Steve were Geologists, it wasn't a dangerous profession. Peter knew he could quite simply walk in there. After all he did have access to the whole Moon Base, but he found it politer and considered it less dangerous, especially when he was first entering a lab if he rang first. Peter looked at the Smellaid on the door frame and smirked as he thought he really could go anywhere, without hindrance. Each door on the base was controlled by a smart controller. They could be opened with breath or by permission loaded directly onto the Pulsera. Mostly he found it simpler to blow lightly into the sensors. The analysis took place almost immediately and access was either allowed or denied. The technology was similar to what he knew at home. The main difference was that they were much more sensitive here and he had the creepy feeling that the machine could actually smell him. He had already half-heartedly shared his concerns with Beatriz. She'd explained that the composition of his breath was checked for opportunistic pathogens every time he blew in one of the machines. It hadn't calmed him down. Just something else he needed to get used to.

Peter pressed the entrance buzzer and announced his name. The lock was released almost immediately, and he heard John's voice welcoming him. Peter walked in looking around as he went. It seemed well equipped or at least there was a lot of storage here.

As Peter turned the corner and saw John, he seemed pleased to see him and explained that he and his assistant were in the process of checking the status of the existing experiments. Steve was visibly annoyed. He didn't like John calling him his assistant. He was as well qualified a scientist as John.

John showed Peter the largest display screen that showed a map of the investigation sites and explained that the geologists mostly worked at the investigation sites. The information from the sources was relayed back to the Moon Base by radio waves. They used the Moon satellite and the automatic ground communication bases for this purpose.

Peter could hear the excitement in John's voice and could see him smiling broadly, John clearly liked the technology.

"The search for minerals and water uses drones with the new hyperspectral sensors. They were reworked and refitted during the last shift. That's why we're hoping," John glanced over to Steve, "for a significant discovery." They nodded and smiled together. "If we find something promising, we're planning an excursion and maybe we'll even set up a new site of investigation, or we could expand the range of an existing one." John continued, "The drones and robots bring any resources they find back to the Moon Base. This works well, as the robots return the samples cleanly including any ice cores. We get samples back in the lab without human contamination and then we analyse exactly what was found before-"

Steve interrupted John. He absolutely had to say something, "The finds could contain fossils. Ancient fossils, perhaps even the first evidence of life before the Moon and Earth broke apart!"

Nodding John agreed with Steve, "Yes, that's right. There is a very small chance that we might discover fossils from one of the ice cores taken from the permafrost in the shadow of one of the valleys near the South Pole. The core could originate from the beginning of the solar system. That's one reason why we're so close to the South Pole. The first scientists began their spectral analysis at the South Pole."

With widened, covetous eyes and a clipped voice Steve said, "By doing analysis of fossil and water samples we could even detect the original virus that spawned life."

"Do you really think so?" John seemed a little sceptical.

"And to make the connection to the Moon Madness," Steve added moodily.

John shook his head, "That is why we have our security measures. We want to make sure that no ancient germs have survived and escape into our environment."

Steve replied, "Not all scientists are as thorough as we are."

Peter distracted them by asking, "Analysing the whole Moon, wouldn't that be faster if we were using satellites?"

Steve explained, "A stable satellite orbit is difficult to find, and the drones and robots can do the job in more detail."

Peter thanked the scientists and left. He still needed to see Dervla and Beatriz today.

Peter decided to leave Dervla alone for the time being. He knew she would need some time to get her experiments going. He walked slowly from second laboratory through the main garden enjoying the soothing sounds. The green of the leaves seemed especially beautiful and he slowed even more as he wandered aimlessly around the garden.

Eventually he remembered that he wanted to talk to Beatriz. He looked up at the ceiling of the garden where there was a map of the Moon Base and chose the path towards Beatriz. It occurred to him, that the way back to his office led him past the infirmary anyway. He liked Beatriz. He thought she was very reasonable and liked to talk to her. The infirmary was located in the building directly next to the main garden. It was on the ground floor of the living area. It wasn't far away.

When he arrived, he looked around. Beatriz was sitting comfortably in an ergonomically correct position on her self-adjusting chair which she had configured to her favourite colour light blue. The colour matched perfectly to the scarf Beatriz was wearing. Which he noted wasn't strictly speaking part of her uniform.

She was happy to see him and was a little excited. She seemed in a hurry to show him all the medical equipment she had at her disposal before she drew his attention to one of the screens. The results of the first week's monitoring devices were displayed on the screen. There was a comparison with their original values and the display showed that all the measurements for everyone on the Moon Base were satisfactory. She tapped on her results and it instantly changed to show the results of the body chemistry analysis. Everything had been evaluated to look for potentially hazardous changes. Peter had signed the employment contract and knew that he had agreed to these conditions but seeing all the details on the screen, how every breath into a Smellaid, how every toilet flush was measured and recorded left him with the eerie feeling that he'd lost something.

Beatriz explained, "The machines don't only do an analysis of body chemistry, they can also do a DNA analysis and comparison in real time." She sounded impressed.

Peter looked at her smiling and thought she has settled in nicely. He could see that she was going to enjoy supervising the health of the team and that she would make the most of the opportunity to use these first-class machines for her own research. She was going to enjoy her five-year stay, and she was going to make the most of it.

Beatriz looked at Peter and smiled before saying, "I think it is great that you're visiting everyone today. They'll be glad that you're interested in their work."

Peter smiled and nodded in agreement to hide his guilt. He took a deep breath, as he thought, now he was going to have to pay Dervla a quick visit. He thanked Beatriz for her time and set off towards Dervla's laboratory.

The way to Dervla's lab was through the second garden. He liked the colours of the plant cover in the second garden better than in the main garden and it seemed calmer there, or maybe the light was different because it was later in the planned day.

Peter stood in front of the entrance to the main lab and looked around. The entrance door was the same size and looked the same as the second lab. He glanced at the Smellaid briefly, before he pressed the buzzer and announced himself. He wasn't sure what experiments Dervla was conducting and he suspected that her experiments were riskier than those of the geologists. It took a minute or so before Dervla answered. She came to the door and opened it without smiling.

Peter found it difficult to get close to Dervla. She was friendly enough but seemed distant. She willingly showed him the DNA plant experiments she was doing for Maria, but the other side of the laboratory was taboo, and he wasn't allowed to go there. Her own research projects were confidential.

Peter nodded as she explained. He already knew this was the case and confirmed his understanding with a little smile. He asked if she had settled in and if she needed anything. He could see that she wanted him to go so she could continue her research, so he thanked her for her time and set off back to his office. As he was walking back, he thought that Dervla seemed satisfied and obviously had her work under control.

Peter sat down in his black self-adjusting chair and smiled. He'd quickly got used to his new working environment and it already felt like home. He made himself comfortable and opened his captain's logbook and began writing. He chose every word carefully. His logbook belonged to the company and not him and he was very conscious that it could perhaps be used as evidence in a future lawsuit. This was why he also kept a second private diary, which only he knew about. In his secret diary he wrote his honest thoughts, but first he wrote the logbook. After only a few sentences he paused and tried to remember. This morning he had had the time to visit the VIP suites on the first floor of the main residential area and he had been impressed. The suites were luxuriously furnished and much roomier than his allotted accommodation. The Moononauts were only given the basics that were needed for their five-year stay. He wondered briefly if there were no tourists coming and they had at least four days warning before someone arrived, and the robots could clean the VIP suites really quickly, why he didn't take one of these luxury suites for himself. He sighed. He knew why he wouldn't. It was, of course, against the regulations and he was sure they'd certainly be supervised by Columbus. He laughed quietly. He certainly didn't want to get a tourist bill when he got home either.

He turned his thoughts back to work. So far, the team seemed to be getting along with each other very well. Peter was relieved. He definitely preferred working when everything was running smoothly. He thought about the relationships in the team. He smiled as he thought that Damian and Filip didn't seem to have any problems because of their close family relationship, and everyone else in the team seemed to have a professional respect for others.

Then he leaned back in his chair and stroked his chin with his hand, as it occurred to him that actually, so far there had only been Steve who had come to Peter to complain. He had turned up with an annoyed red face and had told him in no uncertain terms that he was more competent than Liam and it was difficult to understand why Liam was his supervisor. Peter was a little surprised by Steve's behaviour, but he managed not to let it show. Steve had been assigned two roles, his main role was as a geologist working with John, and his second was as an engineer supporting Damian and Liam. Steve's personality profile wasn't ideal for the Moon, but his qualifications were, and he had a lot of them.

Peter knew Steve well enough and had expected something from him, but not within the first week. Steve hadn't reacted positively as Peter had explained patiently that Liam had been working on the Moon for five years without any problems and he knew his job well. Peter remembered Steve's expression as he asked him, "Was there something special that was causing a problem?" Steve had remained calm, but you could see it in his face that the matter was not resolved. Peter didn't write about it officially, but he made some notes in his private diary.

There was a lot of different surveillance sensors available to Peter in his office. He'd tried a few of them before on Earth and he chose one he felt familiar with. It was the daylight camera with sound for the canteen and recreation room. Steve and Europa were there. He could see Steve standing there with his game helmet on. Peter didn't know which game he was playing, but he could hear Europa, who was standing next to him, laughing at him.

Peter heard Europa say, "You've given your opponent Avatar twenty percent brain damage. The option is meant for medical purposes and not just for people who can't play very well."

Peter watched Steve as he glared furiously at Europa who turned and returned to work laughing.

Peter turned off the device quickly. He felt like he had done something bad, intrusive. He had witnessed a private matter between the two of them.

Peter leaned back in his self-adjusting chair, closed his eyes and thought about life and working on the Moon Base. He imagined they would find a routine and live together for five years in a relaxed and professional way and work until it was time to fly home. Just a few more weeks until the Annual Closure for the Leonid meteors. He laughed to himself, then we'll see how people get along in party mode.

First Annual Opening

Date: Saturday 21st November 2139 - 12:00 CET
Location: Alpha 12 - Moon Base

There was a stillness in the communications area that masked the nervous anticipation. Peter leaned against the back of his safety chair trying to find comfort in its stability and security. It helped him feel less nervous. He looked up at the ceiling, he couldn't see them, but he could hear the soft scratching sound coming from the hydraulics of the moving shields as they slowly exposed the Moon Base to the outside world. It was his first Annual Opening, and it seemed to be taking forever. He glanced over to Liam and Damian. They looked busy and professional. He assumed they were familiar with the process and knew what needed to be done. He breathed deeply a few times and managed to calm himself. He smiled as he noticed the slight nausea deep in his stomach disappearing. He raised his hand uncertainly and touched his captain's hat briefly. He felt reassured. He hadn't forgotten it.

He heard Liam say, "Prepare for the gravity transition."

Peter relaxed further into his chair as he felt the force of the returning gravity. He closed his eyes and quietly thanked Art Feldmann for her discovery. He appreciated it now more than ever since they had just had four days of celebration with only the Moon's gravity. Now within a few minutes, the local gravity was being increased from sixteen to eighty percent of the Earth's gravity and he could feel the growing stresses and strains on his body.

He felt his head become heavier and he tensed his neck muscles to keep his head steady and upright. His felt his arms and legs pressing heavier against his body and the simple act of breathing became more difficult. He felt tired and heavy. He looked down at his body, had he gained weight during the holiday?

He knew he was going to need a few minutes to get used to it, but it didn't take long before he felt able to move normally again. He looked over to Damian and Liam and asked with a concerned voice, "Have you restored contact with Earth Base Columbus?"

They were sitting in front of their keyboards concentrating on the monitors. Peter thought they seem to be enjoying themselves. Liam pressed a couple of keys before answering. He knew that this was Peter's first time and could remember his own. The gravity transition took some getting used to. So, he took the concern in Peter's voice seriously, "We need to launch the Moon satellite before we can contact Earth Base Columbus." His voice was calm and didn't reveal any emotions.

"Luna is flying like an eagle." You could hear the smile in Damian's voice. He'd always wanted to say those words, to confirm that the uplink to the Moon satellite had succeeded and had successfully returned the communication handshake.

Liam watched the automatic confirmation messages scrolling up the monitor as the system prepared to go to the next step. The second step started, the uplink to a satellite in near-Earth orbit needed to be established before the connection to Earth Base Columbus could succeed. Damian was avidly watching and listening to the communication status. He heard it beep twice with a retry tone and smiled with relief as the longer successful tone sounded. The connection to Earth had succeeded. Almost immediately, he heard the rush of noise as the first messages from Earth Base began arriving. The expected, *"Welcome back to the real world"* message came first. It was followed by a short four-day summary of the events of the last few days.

Peter heard Damian sigh with relief and noticed how he visibly relaxed. He'd been worried about the many interfaces that could have caused problems. Damian thanked Liam for his help. The Moon Base was alive again.

Damian knew that it wasn't just his but also Peter's first Annual Opening, and they both had an important role to play. He had just finished his and Peter's was to come. So, he smiled and nodded encouragingly in Peter's direction, but didn't say anything. He didn't want to disturb Peter's thoughts.

Peter had prepared a short speech and was following the local custom, traditionally everything that happened during the closure stayed private, and he wasn't going to mention anything about it. He wouldn't even mention that they'd had four days of Moon Madness. He smiled as he thought about his joke. Then became serious as he stroked his chin with his right hand and felt his four-day old beard. He'd practiced his short speech many times. This was going to be the first message since the Leonid closure and he wanted to appear professional, an experienced and capable Moon Major. People were going to remember this moment, and his wife would be watching. He cleared his throat. He hoped that his voice would sound good.

As was expected of him, he hadn't shaved for four days. Peter thought it was a strange custom, but he did try to go along with the traditions, it seemed to make the people at home happy, and he thought he looked pretty good. He grinned as he remembered Meichun's first Opening, she'd worn a fake red beard.

The plan was to stand up and look straight at the camera and say, "We're overcoming the gravity of the situation" before giving his short report. It was surprising how many people on Earth still watched the speech, and Peter felt nervous as he performed his speech flawlessly.

After it was finished Peter sat back in the chair and relaxed. There were moments that you know you'll never forget. This was one of them and he was glad it was over.

An hour after the official Opening, the whole team were due to meet in the meeting room on the Moon floor. Peter was a few minutes early, but he was relaxed about punctuality today as he knew everyone was affected differently. It was going to take a little time for some of them to get used to the stronger gravity. Some of the team had adapted quickly, but others, he already knew, were having problems. It was different going to lower gravity, that had been easy. Although Peter thought that the alcohol had helped. He felt his leg muscles tense as he sat down, and he remembered that as part of their training they had been taught that gravitation sickness resembled seasickness, and you never know until you'd experienced it how you were going to react. Peter was thankful that he seemed to be coping well.

Peter was sitting in the meeting room chatting with Beatriz when the others started to come in. Charlie and Maria arrived together. Charlie was smiling broadly. Peter thought that the few days holiday had strengthened the team. Filip and Paul were both laughing as they arrived. Europa and Liam arrived very punctually but separately. The rest of the team showed up within the next minute or so. Peter was pleased that they were all there and no one was too late. He hoped it meant they weren't suffering.

Peter summarised the news from Columbus. Nothing particularly exciting had happened on Earth during the last few days. He smiled and looked at the team, as he explained that the outstanding requests for scientific reports and other work-related information would be processed today. Columbus had sent greetings and the family video mails were sent after the work requests.

"Well I just want to say, well done everybody for surviving the annual Leonid meteors." He laughed gently and looked at Maria. "If you get a chance, let me know what it's like in the gardens."

Maria nodded and smiled, "Sixteen percent gravity still keeps the plants under control. I will check, and Charlie will help me if there's anything that needs to be done."

Charlie looked at Maria and glowed.

Peter looked over to Filip and Paul. He sounded serious as he said, "Is there anything you'd like to report when it comes to damage?"

Paul looked at Filip, sniggered and looked guilty. Filip, who was the more reasonable of the two, answered, "Some of the drones had an accident. It has been discovered that mixing beer and sixteen percent gravity is a greater challenge to flying drones than we first thought." He put his hand over his mouth, his eyes opened wide, and a look of horror crossed his face as he burped long and loud.

Everybody in the room laughed.

Peter managed to stop laughing first and asked, "You can fix them, can't you?"

Both Filip and Paul nodded eagerly.

Peter smiled, and his eyes twinkled as he said, "And next time I would recommend you drink less carbonated drinks at sixteen percent gravity."

Peter ended the meeting with the words, "And remember what happens during the Annual Closure, stays secret."

After the meeting and before returning to his office Peter walked to Art Feldmann's statue. He wanted to see if she'd survived the closure. He looked up at her and saw her floating near the ceiling. Her system worked automatically. During the Closure her field was turned off and she was lowered safely to Moon level and after the Opening she floated back into her usual place near the ceiling.

Peter was pleased. He headed towards his office thinking how he was looking forward to the return of their routine and of course the party next year.

Lost Contact

Date: Sunday 20ᵗʰ November 2140 – 12:00 CET
Location: Alpha 12 – Moon Base

"Luna is flying like an eagle," Damian's voice sounded light and unconcerned.

Peter was sitting in the safety chair right behind Liam and Damian in the communication area, half listening to the proceedings. His thoughts were drifting. He could hardly believe a year had already passed. He was looking forward to the video mail from his wife. Last year she'd recreated the outfit from their first date and he wondered if she remembered what she was wearing on their first anniversary. He had absolutely no idea. She could tell him anything and he would be prepared to believe it.

He briefly touching his captain's hat, it reassured him that everything was as it was supposed to be. He thought back to last year's opening, restoring communication with Earth had taken longer than he'd thought. He hoped that they could connect faster this time.

Peter looked over to Liam and Damian, "Have we restored contact with Earth Base Columbus?" His voice sounded a little bored.

Liam turned to face Peter, he seemed relaxed as he muttered, "It sometimes takes a minute or two." Nonchalantly he turned his attention back to the monitors and rested his hands on the desk near the keyboard. He watched the messages scrolling on the monitor and then pressed a few keys before leaning back in his chair. The uplink to the Moon satellite succeeded and pinged back its confirmation. Both Liam and Damian were watching the system automatically go to the next step. The system was searching for a connection to a satellite in near-Earth orbit.

Peter speculated to himself that it might be taking a while because of the communication delay. He stared unseeing at the backrest of Liam's chair, with his right hand he played with his four-day beard and tried to remain patient. He practised his short speech in his head one more time and hoped that he wouldn't forget anything. He nodded to himself. The first message after the Leonid closure was a serious matter and he wanted to sound just as good as last year. He cleared his throat gently and wondered if his voice would hold for the speech as he started rubbing his nose.

Peter wasn't really paying attention, but Liam seemed to be doing the same thing repeatedly. He looked up as Liam moaned briefly. Peter watched him as he looked over at Damian. Damian continued looking at his monitor. Peter was puzzled, hadn't Damian heard him. Peter watched as Liam leaned over and pressed something on Damian's keyboard. Then he heard that double beep retry tone and asked, "How is it going?"

The tone of Liam's voice was a little higher than normal, and his words were slower and deliberate as he replied, "The system's been searching for a little longer than usual. It's trying to find a connection from the near-Earth satellite to Columbus."

Peter wished that he could just hear the longer successful tone and glanced around the room.

He heard Damian say, "Let's run the diagnostics again."

For a moment Liam looked at him like he was an idiot, then he nodded and started the diagnostics.

Peter started practising his speech again to distract himself and to relieve the boredom. He knew he couldn't help and didn't want to make the situation worse.

The diagnostics finished, both Damian and Liam looked closely at the result. Damian shook his head surprised, but still seemed quite relaxed as he said, "Everything seems to be working on our side, but we just don't have any feedback from Columbus." He looked over to Liam, and his expression changed as he realised that Liam was worried.

As soon as he finished practising his speech, Peter looked at the two of them, "Do we have a connection to Earth Base Columbus?"

Liam opened his mouth to say something as Europa came hurrying in, "Have you looked at the Earth? There aren't any lights."

Liam closed his mouth.

Damian pulled himself together first and brought a live feed picture of the Earth on to the window wall. As they looked at the picture, almost as if they had planned it, their jaws fell open simultaneously in surprise. The part of the Earth in daylight seemed normal but the part in darkness, where you could always see the street lights, was dark.

Peter was relieved as Europa cleared her throat to begin speaking. He was still shocked and hadn't quite pulled himself together. The three of them turned to Europa listening attentively.

Europa was standing almost in the middle of the communications area. She seemed more open, more vulnerable than normal. Her pain, which normally wasn't visible, was evident on her face, "The Columbus scientists have been playing a prank on and off for weeks. When they're done with the telescope, they point it towards Earth.

The first time I complained." She paused and swallowed, "I don't think the first time was intentional. But they obviously thought it was funny to annoy me because I had to reset the telescope regularly. When I saw the picture today, I thought they had done me a favour by bringing back the telescope where I'd left it."

Somewhat sceptical, Damian asked, "But I thought the telescope didn't work while the shields were closed."

A little surprised, Europa looked at Damian and replied, "Yes, of course, you're right. Last Thursday morning, I finished early and handed the telescope over to Columbus for a few hours before the closure."

Damian nodded, he accepted Europa's explanation.

Europa folded her arms, looked at him and said, "But it doesn't change anything, the Earth remains dark."

His speech preparations forgotten, Peter seemed to wake up, "Try to connect again." His voice sounded harsh. He couldn't believe it. He needed more information to be able to assess the situation. He looked at Europa, "The telescope stays set up pointing towards Earth."

"It's not a normal telescope. It's designed to take long, slow exposures observing very distant objects. The Earth is too close."

Peter looked at her sternly.

She capitulated, "Okay, it is possible, but in order to do that, I'll have to recalibrate the telescope and that disturbs my work." Europa didn't want to jeopardise her research. She looked at Damian and Liam, surely, they'd soon be able to make contact again.

"Just do it." Peter sounded angry. He didn't have any patience for excuses.

As Europa left the room, Peter said, "We'll meet in two hours in the meeting room." Then he turned to Liam and Damian, "Some of the satellites that are in near-Earth orbit for observational purposes are controlled directly from Columbus. I know we don't have direct access. But can you try to hack one of them?"

Damian was impressed that Peter knew that and replied, "It's not that simple, but we'll try." Damian looked at Liam, who shrugged, they both knew that hacking satellites was explicitly forbidden in their employment contracts, and neither of them wanted to lose their job. If they were successful, it could cost them their job. They decided to continue trying to re-establish the connection for now.

Peter left with the words, "See you in the meeting room in two hours."

Peter went back to his office. He needed a moment alone. He wasn't sure if they had an emergency procedure. He thought of Meichun and asked her if there was an emergency plan? There wasn't one.

Peter sat down and held his head in his hands. He let an overwhelming feeling of panic sweep over him. Everything had worked out fine last year. They must have done something wrong. Somehow made a mistake with the connection. The problem had to be on their side. Something was wrong on the Moon Base. He tried to think what it could be. He took off his captain's hat and put it on his desk before he stroked his beard. He snorted with frustration and said very quietly, "We're not coping with the gravity of the situation." He felt the beginnings of tears welling up in his eyes. For the first time since the incident, he thought of his wife. How was she doing? He was worried and felt helpless, but he knew he couldn't do anything. He put his captain's hat back on, sat up straight and he pulled himself together. He was responsible for the entire Moon Base. He couldn't let himself be distracted by his wife's situation. He could think about it later, but not now.

He felt the brim of his hat between his fingers and tried to be honest with himself. He knew the problem was probably on Earth, but what could be the cause of it. He tried to remember if there had been anything special on the news just before the Annual Closure. He couldn't think of anything. Nothing had struck him as unusual. Maybe Meichun could work through the news with her Big Data module. Maybe she could find something for him.

"Meichun, I need your help." When he heard his voice, he wondered, am I asking the program Meichun, or am I praying to the real Meichun?

He asked her to analyse the news for the few weeks before the Leonid closure, to see if there was anything unusual that could explain the situation.

Before she started, Meichun warned him that the information needed updating. It was missing the last four days.

He over exaggeratedly raised his eyebrows and shook his head gently. He stopped himself from exclaiming angrily, "Like I don't know that." He took a deep breath calmed himself and prayed that she would find something.

It took Meichun less than two minutes to get the results. There were two topics that had gotten the most attention and they had the hashtags #Redo and #WaterPolitics. Hashtag #Redo referred to improved Re-Do Recycle machines and hashtag #WaterPolitics was about a political summit on water sources. The second topic got the most lines in the Intellinet newspapers. Countries without a coastline were complaining about other countries polluting and endangering their water sources. They also complained about the costs of transporting water because they were getting higher and higher.

He thanked Meichun and thought of the saying, "Big Data - no information." Frustrated he took off his hat and placed it on his desk. He wondered if the Happynet could contribute something useful. He knew the information was unsourced and unreliable, and they only uploaded a fraction of it, but sometimes it was fun to look at the theories. He started watching a conspiracy video and didn't realise how fast time was passing. Soon it was time for the meeting.

With a nimble finger movement, he saved his notes. He would need them at the crisis meeting. From Thursday to Sunday was only four days. He shook his head and stood up. They'd been separated from the outside world for four days, and there was no indication in the news of what could have happened. As he walked through the door, he paused for a moment, he had the feeling in the pit of his stomach that he had forgotten something. He shook his head to shake off the feeling before continuing.

His captain's hat was still on his desk.

They met in the meeting room on the Moon floor next to the infirmary. When Peter arrived, everyone was already sitting in their seats waiting. They were whispering to each other frantically. As he stood at the end of the table, the noise level gradually dropped until the muttering became silent. Everyone was looking at him anxiously. He could see in their faces that they wanted an explanation.

The picture of Earth was being projected on to the window wall opposite Peter. He looked at it briefly. Still no lights on the dark part of the Earth. He hadn't been expecting any, but he'd still hoped anyway. He looked at Damian.

With a grave expression Damian shook his head, he mouthed, "No luck."

Liam, who was sitting next to Damian, looked for the umpteenth time at the mobile communication device lying on the table in front of him. The device remained quiet.

Peter sat down and glanced at his notes before he spoke, "You already know why we're having this meeting." Peter's voice sounded serious and appropriately sombre for bad news.

Everyone sitting around the table nodded. Some were staring at the table while others looked directly at Peter. It didn't matter where they were looking, they all looked sad and a little lost.

"We haven't been able to restore contact with the Earth Base Columbus - and we're not sure how long it will take to find a solution." He looked at Damian and Liam as he said, "Damian and Liam are working on a solution to the problem." He stopped and wondered how much he should say. They're adults. Surely, they can handle the truth.

"I'm sorry, but it seems the problem is with Earth Base Columbus." Why had he apologised? It wasn't his fault. "But I'm sure the problem is only temporary, and I'll let you all know as soon as we are back in touch with Columbus."

He faltered and cleared his throat and reached for the brim of his captain's hat. It was a habit that comforted him. He was surprised that the cap wasn't there, and it confused him for a second. The hat didn't make him Moon Major, he was the Moon Major and it didn't matter whether he was wearing the captain's hat or not. He was still the Moon Major. He straightened his back, held his head high and continued, "I know you're all waiting for video mails from your families. It's a special holiday season for the people at home too, and they're waiting for our messages too. We just need to be a little patient. I am sure we will have communications up and running soon and -"

Maria interrupted him, "Why did we have to close the shields anyway? We could have just left them open." There was a faint wobble in her voice.

Compassionately, Peter looked at Maria, but didn't say anything. He didn't know what to say to her.

Europa answered the question literally, "The Leonids sometimes come as meteor storms, which could overload our automatic defence systems. That's why we use the shields and a negative gravity field to support the defence system. It is unfortunate that the bulky shields block communication, so we lose contact." Europa looked smug.

In order to try and ease the depressed mood, Peter said, "Let's not forget that we were on vacation, and surely Columbus will get back in touch soon. Does anyone have anything to report?"

Paul and Filip looked at each other and laughed then Filip explained, "Paul drank his first whisky. We have a lot of bottles in the tourist stores, and most of the bottles are very old. Older than Paul, and some even older than me." At the ripe old age of twenty-five, Filip felt very experienced and looked upon Paul as a child at the young age of nineteen, "There are even older whiskies are in the elite tourist store, and also some in Mars stores as well." He smiled broadly and seemed proud of his knowledge.

A few of the others joined in the laughter it helped Peter to relax and he felt the mood in the room lighten.

Before the laughter had fully died down Beatriz asked, "Do we know what happened?" She looked surprised as if she hadn't meant to ask.

Peter remained calm and answered, "Meichun has analysed the news of the last few weeks looking for clues. She has come up with two suggestions. The most popular topics are improved Re-Do Recycle machines and a political summit on water resources." His voice sounded flat.

With a little more energy, he managed to say, "Of course, Meichun is missing the information from the last four days just like we are." Thoughtfully, he added, "I guess we'll have to ask her the right question if we want a sensible answer."

He looked around to see if anyone wanted to say anything. They avoided looking at him and no one said anything, so he carried on, "I don't know if it's worth it for all of us to go looking for a cause." He said it even though he knew that they would. They needed the Happynet to distract them, to take comfort from the tiny shots of dopamine induced by the stealth marketing techniques. He wanted to do that as well, to sink into the Happynet and forget everything for a while. The price was just a waste of time, not a hangover or long-term consequences when you didn't overdo it. But he was a little worried about the uncontrolled freedom of speech that existed in the Happynet, and he didn't want anyone believing any of those crazy conspiracy theories.

"The information in the Intellinet is out of date. We are missing the last four days. It is highly unlikely that we will find anything." Europa informed Peter factually.

Peter smiled at Europa and nodded in agreement, of course she was going to get her information from the Intellinet. Then trying to be more upbeat he asked, "Okay, any more questions?"

Maria cleared her throat, everyone looked at her as she whispered slowly, "Is everyone dead?"

Despite the low volume of her question, everyone heard clearly what she asked. All eyes turned immediately to Peter.

The first thought that popped into his head was, "my wife is dead." He leaned forward in his seat and covered his mouth with his hands. Unconsciously he held his breath. He felt his head shaking gently in his hands, his heart, his body were denying the statement. That wasn't possible. He breathed out loudly. He'd know, he was sure he'd know if his wife was dead. He managed to sound reasonable as he replied, "No, certainly not. I assume everyone is still alive, but we've just lost communications. Let's not jump to conclusions."

Paul, who wanted to help, suggested, "Maybe there was a war and they destroyed the whole world within four days."

With a sceptical expression, Liam looked at him and said condescendingly, "We would still be able to see the flames of destruction."

With morbid curiosity Steve asked, "Even with a nuclear war? If they were all bombed out and everything was complete evaporated?"

Liam replied a little disconcerted by Steve's vision, "Nevertheless, we would see them, with a nuclear war there would still be fire and flames."

Maria added in a small voice, "In an extreme weather event, there might not be any flames. Storms don't cause many fires, and we haven't yet been able to bring global warming under control."

Speculating on the topic was helping no one, Peter took control of the meeting again, "Back to the agenda. Do we have everything we need for the next few days?" Again, he was confronted with silence. Peter looked at them and thought, we need to keep busy. We need to try and not think about the situation. They need something to do, "The solar systems are due for their regular maintenance and could also do with a clean."

Peter looked at Charlie and smiled, "Maybe there's just not enough power, so the signal isn't strong enough, and after we clean them everything will be fine." Peter knew it didn't make any sense and that it was just a crazy idea, but he didn't regret saying it.

Against Peter's expectation, Liam reacted with understanding, "Good idea, brainstorming is a great method for finding new ideas. It's conceivable that the signal strength wouldn't be enough if the current flow from the solar panels is too low. But then if the solar panels get dirty, from a solar storm or something, and don't produce enough electricity, the nuclear fusion reactor kicks in automatically to keep the electricity flow constant." He looked at Peter, "We have enough fuel in stock to last for a few hundred years."

Charlie felt left out and added, "The solar systems have a ninety percent exposure to the Sun. Even when we are in a lunar night, they are still in the sunshine."

John turned to Peter and asked, "Is there anything we can do to restore contact?"

Peter looked at John and felt sorry for him. He guessed he was thinking of his family, "Damian and Liam are trying to re-establish contact, but Columbus has full control over their satellites. So, we don't have any access. This scenario wasn't foreseen, and we don't have a contingency plan. We're in the process of creating one." Peter smiled at his weak attempt at humour.

Damian sat bolt upright, looked at his son and said, "We want to go home." Filip nodded. He agreed with his father. Damian continued, "We want to terminate our employment contract and fly home."

Surprised, Peter replied, "Cancellation of a contract is only possible in special circumstances and they need to be agreed with Earth Base Columbus."

"What options do we have?" asked Damian, his voice sounded deep, controlled and hard.

Peter tried his best conciliatory tone and said, "Not everyone wants to go back, and we need three people per escape pod before we can launch, otherwise we wouldn't have enough escape pods for everyone." He pondered briefly, "And we'll have to wait for an optimal flight day."

Europa informed the others, "The next possible optimal flight day would be December 22nd, but it'd be better to go in June 2141 if you want to arrive alive."

Peter smiled at Europa. She knew her stuff.

"I'm sure the next time that we meet, there won't be a problem. For the time being, we'll continue with our daily tasks as if nothing has happened, and please prepare your reports as normal." He looked at Damian, "We'll wait until we have more facts." Then he looked directly at each one of them one after the other and his gaze demanded approval. They all nodded.

Peter got up he put his hands on the table and he looked around one last time. As he was looking at them wondering what they were thinking, his stomach growled. Peter looked down at his belly, he'd forgotten lunch. He lifted his head, and apologised for the disturbance, then smiled and said, "What we need is patience. We'll meet again in three days." His voice had sounded worried. He smiled again to indicate that the meeting was over. He'd chosen three days to give people time to calm down. And he knew that it was going take him a few days to assess the situation.

He looked at the picture of Earth and thought the first year had gone so smoothly. Why would it be so different now?

As the others started to get up Maria remained seated. She was looking at Peter and asked, "Could you perhaps say a few comforting words?"

Peter felt emotionally empty inside. He was still shocked by the facts. He didn't have anything left in him. He couldn't manage a few words of comfort. He knew he was overwhelmed and looked to Liam for help, "You were a lay preacher. Can you please say a few appropriate words for us?"

Liam nodded his agreement respectfully. Everyone sat back down as he closed his eyes and started speaking, "We had a huge shock this morning when we opened the shields and couldn't establish radio contact with Columbus. Now we are sitting here in ignorance and unable to send out good wishes to our friends and loved ones. We hope that everything on Earth is okay and that we will soon be able to contact our families again." He paused for a moment and looked at the others. They kept silent they were waiting for him to continue.

"The next few days will be difficult. Please remember that none of us are to blame for the disconnection. Courage and patience are the qualities that we need during the coming days. And I know, if I may speak for Moon Major Peter," he looked at Peter questioningly and Peter nodded, "that we know, we are a brave team and together, we will be able to overcome the gravity of the situation."

There was a quiet giggle.

Second Meeting

Date: Wednesday 23rd November 2140 – 11:00 CET
Location: Alpha 12 – Moon Base

Peter walked calmly and quietly into the meeting room and was now standing at the head of the table. He looked down trying to avoid eye contact. A heavy silence hung over the room, they were watching his every move, watching closely as he took off his captain's hat and placed it carefully on the table in front of him. Their eyes stayed focused on the hat for a few seconds and then slowly returned to look at Peter.

He smiled to break the silence, and because he would never have thought that his captain's hat could be so interesting. Everyone was sitting in their usual safe places. They remained silent and waited. They were expecting news from him. Information that he didn't have. His expression became more serious, his eyes saddened, and his smile disappeared, barely noticeably he shook his head. He hoped that they would, on an unconscious level, recognise the significance of the movement and perhaps be more realistic with their questions.

With a heavy heart he sat down and looked at the people waiting for him and he thought I promised them a meeting, knowing that I was hoping a solution would be found before we had to come together. He sighed, now they were here. He tapped on the table-screen and then looked down at his notes and thought, at least he'd organised the meeting as he'd promised even though he hadn't wanted to, he'd kept his promise. They were having their meeting, he hadn't called it a crisis meeting, even though it felt like a crisis. He didn't want to say it out loud or even write it down. He didn't want to admit it. He didn't want it to be real.

He looked up and looked at them. He could sense the mood in the room. It was complex but consistent. They were confused, insecure and some were already showing signs of being upset. He wanted to reassure them, to give them comfort and to make them feel better than he did. The problem was, he didn't know how. He steadied himself and called upon his good manners and training before he thanked them for coming and before smiling half-heartedly. As he was looking around he stopped at Damian and with a glimmer of hope in his eyes he looked at him questioningly. Damian sat rigid with a sad, hard expression and didn't react to Peter's look. Peter glanced to Liam who shook his head slightly. Peter knew exactly what it meant.

He glanced down at his notes. He didn't need to look at them, he'd knew what he was going to say. He explained that the contact with Earth Base Columbus had not yet been restored. He kept his voice as flat, as emotionless as possible and avoided using adjectives. There were enough feelings in the room, they didn't need his as well. He told them that Meichun hadn't found anything new. He looked at his notes to try and hide his sadness and his disappointment. He swiped his finger on the table-screen, looking through his notes. If they were watching they would have seen that his eyes weren't concentrating. He was thinking that there was no result from Meichun because he was not able to ask the right, or even a halfway decent, question. He looked up at the window wall. It was simply illuminated, there was no picture of Earth on it. He was grateful for that. He didn't want a reminder that they were alone.

He could see and feel their stares. He wanted to give them something. He told them the background information he had from Meichun about how expensive water becomes when it is extracted from the sea and how landlocked countries need very long pipes stretching over the neighbouring countries. He voiced his opinion, "Clean water should be self-evident. How can that not be the case these days?"

Damian wasn't interested. Bluntly, he interrupted Peter, "We want to go home." He looked at his son as he spoke. Filip nodded in agreement.

Peter said quietly and compassionately, "We are all thinking of our families and want to be with them." He had a picture of his wife in his mind's eye, she was smiling, as he spoke.

"We want to do something. Not just sit around and talk. We want to return as soon as possible." Damian's voice sounded harsh without any sign of patience.

Peter opened his mouth to reply, to ask for a little patience, but before he could get a word out, a strong voice sounded, claiming that this was foolish. Everyone turned to Europa.

She continued confidently, "The journey takes approximately thirty-six hours to fly on the perigee. The next perigee comes on December 22nd and after that one in June. June would be the better option the distance between Moon and Earth is optimal."

Damian frowned. He seemed to be calculating in his head, "There's a more favourable date tomorrow."

Europa smiled knowingly and said, "We are too close to the meteoroid shower. It is too big a risk."

Steve smiled snidely and said tauntingly, "And you can't go faster than thirty-six hours. If you use all your fuel accelerating, you won't have enough to brake. Or do you want to burn up from the friction when you hit the Earth's atmosphere?"

Steve looked at Europa and smiled. She replied with a scowl.

Damian looked at Steve angrily but kept quiet.

"It won't do your wife any good if you're dead." Steve taunted. He wasn't hiding that he was looking for a fight.

Beatriz sounded calm and peaceful as she explained, "The escape pods aren't very comfortable, and they're only intended for emergencies. They might not be able to take enough oxygen if the journey takes too long. Waiting for the perigee is highly recommended if you want to survive the journey."

Filip didn't want to give up. His voice sounded tense and pleading, "There's a safety margin for the oxygen."

The compassion was clear to see in Beatriz's eyes, "The oxygen safety margin is there in case something unexpected happens. In case the journey takes longer than expected." Beatriz looked at both Damian and Filip and shook her head gently, "It's not worth deliberately risking an oxygen deficiency."

Damian, who had listened to his son quietly, had an expression that was a mixture of stubbornness and anger. He wanted to return with his son as soon as possible. It didn't matter if there were problems with the escape pod or not. He wanted to risk it.

Peter was watching Damian closely. He believed he understood how Damian was feeling. He too was worried about his wife and wanted to go home to see her, to know that she was safe, but he was also responsible for the Moon Base and needed to find a solution before he could go home. Peter took a deep breath and explained, "We have twelve people and twelve seats in the escape pods. There are four escape pods with three seats each. There's no escape pod available for two people, and we aren't leaving anyone behind."

Peter waited for Damian's reaction, but Damian remained sullenly silent. Peter looked over to Filip before he added, "The tourists' escape pods were never built. They were started, but didn't get very far, after the Moon Madness stories started and the tourists didn't come as had been expected." Peter paused. That was a dangerous thing to say out loud. The disease was just a rumour, and no one had even proved it existed. He looked around warily, people got what they believed. He needed to destroy this idea before it took hold. He changed the subject, "We should wait. It could be that the connection problem is only temporary."

Charlie didn't seem to have heard Peter and added thoughtfully, "They did finish building the escape pods for the tourists. I mean, I read that one was used for a rescue operation. A few years ago, a Moononaut got sick and had to be sent home. They used one then, and Columbus said that if a tourist comes, they'll build a new escape pod and send it to us because we don't have the resources or the right equipment to build one ourselves."

Peter looked at Filip and Paul. "Do you know if we have the resources?"

Paul panicked and froze, his face turned pale. He didn't know what was in stock. He looked at Filip with his eyes wide-open and shook his head.

Filip smiled at Paul before answering Peter, "We don't know exactly what we have, but we can check it out." He turned to Paul and said quietly, "We don't need to know everything."

Liam interrupted, he seemed thoughtful when he asked the question, "How would we land?" He looked at Damian. "There'll be no one able to pick you up from the sea."

"We'd be wearing our orange spacesuits. They'll find us." Damian sounded stubborn and confident.

Steve, who appeared worried, said, "The pods are made so that they begin to break apart from the heat caused by the air friction braking. There is a parachute, but it was only designed for emergencies."

Liam nodded in agreement. Damian looked at them as he thought about it. He knew they were right, and a speedy return home had just been ruled out. With a level voice and slumped resignation, Damian said quietly, "We'll have to check the landing gear and probably adjust it. Especially if we don't have the safety net of a Columbus pickup."

Peter was relieved but tried not to let it show. He said encouragingly, "Liam, Damian and Steve, can you look for a solution."

Peter stood up, but before he could say anything, Beatriz lay a picture of her sisters on the table. She looked at the photo and said quietly but clearly, "I miss my sisters, and I'm waiting for a video mail from them."

Surprised, Peter looked briefly at Beatriz, until he regained his composure. He sat down and glancing at Beatriz's photo before saying quietly, "I miss my wife Jean."

Maria added spontaneously, "I miss my younger sister Vickie and my parents Theofilos and Catherine."

Charlie, who was sitting next to Maria, looked at her and smiled before saying, "I miss my brothers Albert and Bruce and my parents Zach and Yvonne." Charlie looked to Steve, who looked away shaking his head.

Europa noticed the silence and added, "I miss my sister Callisto."

John looked sad and looked the others in the eye and held his head high, as he said, "I miss my ex-wife Charlotte and my son Daniel."

Dervla, who was sitting next to John, looked at the table and shook her head almost imperceptibly.

Beatriz looked at Damian, who with sad eyes and a wobbly voice, said, "I miss my wife Justine." He looked at Filip, "and my younger son Hubert."

Liam shook his head without smiling. He didn't want to say anything.

Filip looked at the table, trying to hide his emotions, as he said quietly, "I miss my mother Justine and my brother Hubert."

Paul noticed some of them looking at him and he blurted out, "I miss my brother Andrew and my dog Astro. Andrew's looking after my dog."

A few people laughed. Peter was grateful for the laughter. It eased the tension a little. He looked at the group. They'd shared something and seemed closer now. He stroked his chin and felt his seven-day beard and wondered if it was too soon to shave. As Peter stood up he thought, would he still need a beard for the first message after opening? He wanted to keep to tradition.

He looked at the group and said, "We'll meet again on Monday." He hoped that somehow something would happen on Earth over the weekend. He just couldn't believe that Columbus couldn't find a solution. When contact was restored, he was going to shave.

Third Meeting

Date: Monday 28th November 2140 – 11:00 CET
Location: Alpha 12 – Moon Base

Peter looked at the calendar and couldn't quite believe that it was already Monday. He'd promised them a meeting, but there was still no news from Earth. He stood up determined to put on a good show. He knew they'd be waiting for him when he got to the meeting room. He walked calmly, but he wasn't looking forward to the discussion.

When he entered the room, he noticed immediately that the mood felt different. He looked at the people questioningly. There was a unified energy, almost as if electricity was in the air. He had the feeling that he could almost touch it. He smiled as he felt a glimmer of hope.

As soon as Steve saw Peter he blurted out, "Damian, Liam and I have shared our engineering knowledge and now know what we need to do to make the journey to Earth in the escape pods safe." He grinned knowingly. He'd desperately wanted to be the one who said it.

Peter looked at the three of them sitting together and just raised his eyebrows to elicit more information.

Without looking at the other two, Steve responded, "We don't have the parts to be able to build a new escape pod, but we do have heat shields and the other necessary spare parts in stock to be able to reinforce the existing escape pods." He nodded at Paul and Filip. "They checked in the stores for us."

Steve paused for a moment and smiled to himself. He was enjoying the attention.

Damian was nodding approvingly. Liam was staring at Steve without showing any enthusiasm. Steve was ignoring both of them.

Steve continued, "We'll be able to strengthen the shields to keep them more stable when entering the Earth's atmosphere. This gives us a better chance of survival on landing because the escape pods with be more intact after the braking manoeuvre." He added, "And we are going to take the time to think about other possibilities to make the journey safer."

Damian took the opportunity to speak. He sounded a little disappointed, "We won't be able to make the changes before December, and accepting the risk of meteoroids, we've decided to wait until June next year." He looked down.

Steve sounded upbeat, "Then we'll have time to modify all the escape pods."

Peter smiled wryly. This was good news and he needed some good news, but he knew there was a problem with the plan. He looked at them and bit his lower lip briefly before he carefully summarised his thoughts, "We can strengthen the escape pods, and it is a good idea, as then we'll be able to send people back safely. But we can't just send two people back. We have four rescue pods each with three seats. We can't make a plan that means that someone has to be left behind. We have to provide an escape route to everyone living on the Moon." Peter looked at them questioningly. "If Damian and Filip fly back, we need a volunteer to fly with them."

In a small voice, Paul asked, "Why are there three seats in an escape pod?"

Without prompting from Peter, Europa answered, "It is more energy efficient to have three people in one pod, and much easier for Columbus to find the Moononauts when they land together on Earth."

Paul nodded gently and smiled nervously. He thought Europa was really smart.

Beatriz changed the subject, "Have you thought about oxygen? There's a limited supply of about sixty-three hours of oxygen in the escape pods."

Liam sounded interested as he replied, "The escape pod starts at a perigee and not an apogee. We intend to fly when there is the minimum distance between the Moon and the Earth." He looked puzzled at Beatriz, "Why do you ask?"

Beatriz breathed in deeply before she said, "Columbus are offline and won't be able to correct the trajectory if there's a deviation."

Damian nodded, "We've thought of that, but we don't have a definitive solution yet. Maybe we convert carbon dioxide into oxygen or take extra oxygen tanks with us."

Beatriz smiled. The three of them seemed to be working well together.

Steve butted in, "The launch conditions are not the same here as on Earth. We'll need less fuel for the launch. Don't forget the Moon's gravity is only sixteen percent of the Earth's gravity, and this means that we have some flexibility with the take-off weight. If we want, there's also the option to create an external Art Feldmann's field to help us launch."

Everyone nodded, his suggestion sounded sensible.

Steve was enjoying the attention. John looked apologetically at Dervla, she glanced at him and nodded before averting her eyes. His voice was steady and calm as he said, "I'll volunteer. I want to go home as soon as possible."

The tense atmosphere in the room eased. Damian stood up, walked over to John's seat and shook his hand. Filip followed his father's example before they happily took their seats again. Peter smiled at the show and then announced, "Okay, we have a plan. The three of you will return together in June next year and before then we'll make some improvements to the escape pods."

The statement felt like a solution to Peter, but he knew that the meeting wasn't over yet, there were a few other topics to discuss.

Beatriz asked, "Has Meichun found anything new?"

They all heard the hesitation in Peter's voice, "The improved Re-Do Recycle machines could have caused problems. Some scientists had claimed that the upgrade could be dangerous. But there's always an opposing opinion to progress." He shrugged his shoulders. "Meichun suggested that we use the satellites to look at Earth outside the optical spectrum." He looked at Liam.

Liam responded thoughtfully, "We don't have direct access to the satellites orbiting the Earth. The signals are sent straight to Earth. I'll think about it, maybe there's something we can do." He looked at Europa. She must have an idea. Europa ignored him. She seemed to be thinking.

Paul broke the silence a little nervously, "If Meichun doesn't know, how about making suggestions? I mean, maybe there was a new antibiotic that caused a zombie apocalypse."

Paul smiled as he heard the laughter.

Maria joined in and sounded playfully serious as she spoke, "Or, a geological catastrophe with volcanoes and earthquakes combined."

Peter smiled broadly and looked around.

Filip wanted to play too, "Or maybe a giant meteor." Then he added a little disappointed, "but that wouldn't have affected the other side of the world so quickly." He breathed in quickly. He wanted to add another idea, "Or maybe there were extreme solar flares, they would have destroyed all the electronics with a gigantic electromagnetic impulse all over the world." He smiled satisfied with his speculations.

Nobody was taking any of these suggestions seriously and they all laughed together. It helped ease the stress a little.

Europa stopped laughing first, "A coronal mass ejection would have destroyed the satellites around the world, and that is not the case." Her seriousness made the others keep on laughing.

Peter watched them relax. He liked that. He raised his right hand and felt his chin. The beard was still there. He wasn't ready to shave yet. He got up and put on his captain's hat, "We'll meet again in a week to discuss the progress."

Final Meeting

Date: Monday 5th December 2140 – 10:56 CET
Location: Alpha 12 – Moon Base

The lights turned on automatically as he opened the door of the meeting room. He noticed the flash of light and blinked. He was first. He walked slowly over to his seat at the head of the table and put his captain's hat down. The chair moved out for him, so he could sit down. He sat down slowly and leaned back gently to relax his back. He waited a few seconds until the chair adjusted to his body. He smiled. He had a good feeling. The team had a common goal and wanted to work together. He expected everything to run smoothly.

He stroked his beard and thought about how quickly you can get used to new realities when you work together and have something to hope for. He heard the artificial squeak of the door opening and turned to watch as they came in cheerfully.

First on the meeting's agenda was the progress report on the conversion of the escape pods. He waited until they were all sitting down and then he began, "We've agreed on our preferred date and that one of the escape pods will launch on 4th June next year." He nodded at Damian and John. "Before then, the reinforcement work on the escape pods needs to be finished." He looked at Damian and Liam and smiled, "How's the work going?"

Damian glanced at Liam, who nodded his agreement that Damian should speak, "We're coming along nicely with our computer simulation programs and we're certain that we'll have made all the necessary reinforcements on the escape pod by June." He leaned back in his chair with a satisfied smile but only for a short moment, before leaning forward to take a closer look at John and Filip and saying, "I'm really happy that we are flying home."

Steve interrupted the ensuing silence, "We haven't given up trying to find a way to build another escape pod. We try when we have a little spare time. But so far, we haven't had any success." Despite the lack of success, he seemed self-satisfied.

Dervla ignored Steve's comment and changed the subject. She said in a quiet, calm voice, "I've been looking through the recent genetic publications for clues, and I think I've found something. A new variant of influenza emerged in recent months in East Asia. They're not sure how contagious the virus will be, and there's some evidence that it was artificially created." She paused and looked at John before continuing, "Maybe it's not safe to return."

Damian responded quickly, "We're returning anyway."

Filip and John both nodded in agreement.

Beatriz asked mercilessly, "Why doesn't Meichun know about this virus?"

Peter, who had grown fond of Meichun, felt the need to defend her, "Meichun only has access to the publicly available information. Those publications are private. Maybe we should give Meichun access to Dervla's genetic publications." He turned to Liam, "Could you manage to do that?"

Liam nodded.

Peter looked suddenly disheartened as he said, "I'm probably asking Meichun the wrong question. I asked her why the Earth is dark. Maybe another question would be more appropriate. But I'm not sure how to ask." He looked at the table in front of him. He just couldn't ask a question without assuming that something really bad had happened to people on Earth and possibly to his wife.

The ensuing silence was broken by Maria asking, "After they leave, who is going to take over their responsibilities?"

Charlie answered immediately, "I'm not going anywhere. I'll help." And he pushed his left hand slightly across the table towards Maria's right hand.

Maria raised her hand from the table and held her necklace. She started twiddling with it as she said, "But we are going to lose a scientist, an engineer and a technician. Someone who is qualified will have to do the work."

Peter thought she doesn't want to cause any trouble, she is just worried. He looked directly in her eyes and with a soft, measured voice, he replied, "I understand what you mean, and I've thought about it as well. Liam will be able to take over Damian's tasks and if necessary, Steve can support him. The geological experiments are being scaled back and John is working alone, and Steve can take over when he has finished working on the modifications for the escape pods." Peter looked over to Paul, "And Paul will be able to take over Filip's work."

Peter assumed that there were going to be no new deliveries coming from Earth, and that was going to reduce Paul's workload. He didn't say anything about this as he didn't want to remind them that there was no contact and therefore there would be no deliveries. He took a deep breath and thought of his mantra, "Just keep going." He knew that when people were busy that they didn't have time to think and then they wouldn't panic. He understood that the general nodding of heads indicated that there was nothing left to discuss.

Peter stroked his beard thoughtfully before he stood up and put on his captain's hat. He informed them, "In the future there will be a progress report meeting every week. Whoever has something to say or just wants to listen is welcome."

He went from the meeting to his private quarters and went straight into the bathroom. He let his hands rest on the basin, slumped a little and looked at himself in the mirror. He searched in the reflection of his eyes for an answer. Was he ready for the responsibility? He didn't expect any contact from Columbus any time soon. He could see the sadness in his eyes and the down turned corners of his mouth. There wasn't going to be any help from Columbus. There wasn't going to be a first report after the Leonid closure. Resolutely he took his razor in his hand, glancing at it briefly before he began to shave.

First Return

Date: Sunday 4th June 2141 – 20:03 CET
Location: Alpha 12 – Moon Base

With their helmets in their hands, the three-person team were standing together fully suited up in the entrance area and they were laughing. Peter couldn't help giving a gentle smile. Everywhere people were grinning and joking. The escape pod was ready. They'd managed to finish reinforcing the protective shields and increasing the stability of the cabin. Peter heard Damian saying, "I'm sure the landing will go well even if we touchdown on land." Peter observed the people gathered. He could feel and see the excitement and thought, "There's hope here." They believe that they are going to find out what has happened on Earth. He hoped they would find out. He relaxed and let the light-hearted mood carry him along and he felt the stress melting in his chest. He smiled with the others, but his smile didn't fully hide his worry. At every launch there was a risk that something could go wrong and today was no exception. He didn't share his concerns. He didn't want to spoil the mood. It had been a long time since he had seen them so happy and hopeful. They'd waited six months for this day, and now it was time for the launch. He wished the team good luck, stepped back and took one last picture of them in their orange spacesuits. He could feel the mood doing him good and enjoyed the calmness growing in him.

Art Feldmann's statue was looking down at the group. Peter thought he could feel her gaze and glanced up. She remained an impressive sight. He smiled at her and looked almost relaxed. He wondered if she was wishing them luck and then he laughed silently. He turned around and looked back at the team, watching them saying goodbye and hugging each other, which he considered a great achievement in those bulky spacesuits.

Peter stood a little way away from the others, but close enough to hear them. The people who were staying had formed a kind of circle around those returning. Peter looked at Liam, who was holding back from the group and trying to avoid eye contact with the returners. Damian didn't want any of Liam's bashfulness and forced Liam to shake his hand while giving him a friendly slap on the back. Liam forced himself to smile and managed a half-hearted attempt while he accepted Damian's thanks. As soon as it was appropriate, without being an insult, he withdrew his hand. Peter heard him reminding Damian that he should report as soon as he landed safely. Liam reminded Damian that the satellites orbiting the Earth had roughly the correct trajectory, and at least one of them should still be functional. Peter thought Liam seemed a little worried, but he wasn't sure why. He watched Liam, whose expression was tense and serious, as he listened to Damian's reassuring answer and his grinning promise that he would try his best. Liam nodded coolly, then he looked at Filip and John, who were busy saying goodbye to the others. Liam had already told them, "Have a good trip." He lowered his head, muttered an apology and returned to the control centre.

As Liam passed by Peter, Peter nodded appreciatively. Liam returned the gesture and with a slight movement of his head let it be understood that he was in a hurry. Peter turned and watched Steve, who was in a very good mood, joking, "Don't forget anything important, it's not easy to fly back and fetch what you forget." He heard him laughing at his own joke as he put his arms lightly around them and shook their hands firmly. Peter heard him wishing them good luck and watching Steve, whose arms were swinging at his sides, as he walked enthusiastically, following Liam towards the control centre. Peter didn't move when he passed by, and Steve didn't seem to notice him standing there.

Her eyes were tearful, and her voice was tight as Beatriz asked them how they felt and if they had everything. She reminded Damian of his mother as she was saying goodbye. He didn't know why, but it something about the way Beatriz warmly embraced them and forced them to promise that they would try to sleep as much as possible during the journey. Damian smiled as she reminded them that this would save oxygen and sleep helped their bodies to stay healthy. He could see the worry in her face even though she knew that they were taking extra oxygen cylinders to alleviate the risk of running out of oxygen if there was an extended journey time. He knew that she was worried because Columbus wouldn't be correcting any trajectory discrepancies.

Beatriz tried to smile, to say goodbye. She'd said enough. She managed a sad smile as she stepped back and went over to where Peter was standing. As she joined him, she turned to him and nodded reassuringly. He returned her gesture with compassion. She turned back to the others and tried not to think that there would be no rescue mission from Columbus.

Europa observed everything and everyone very closely. She wanted to behave correctly. The hopefulness was infecting her too, but she wasn't really convinced they had a good chance of surviving the landing nor was she convinced that they had a good chance of surviving even if they had a successful landing. She had a bad feeling about the undertaking. From her point of view, there wasn't enough evidence that life on Earth was still possible. Untroubled, she shook their hands, she glanced down at her hand puzzled by the brief physical contact and added in a conciliatory tone, "I did an analysis of the Sun spots this morning and there shouldn't be any solar flares to fry you during your journey home."

John's mouth fell open as he frowned. He looked at Europa while shaking his head and thinking that's supposed to be encouraging. He was still shaking his head, but he managed to close his mouth, as Damian, who had had more experience of talking to Europa, grinned and thanked her for helping and wished her all the best for the future on the Moon.

Europa, pleased that she could help, took a step back. Paul put his arms around Filip's bulky spacesuit and hugged him as tight as he could. Paul had tearful eyes and a sad mouth. He whispered, "Goodbye." He knew he was going to miss his mentor, his work colleague and his best friend. He could feel the emotion deep in his chest. He tried to smile but only managed a grimace. He could sense his sadness had highjacked his facial muscles and knew his expression clearly reflected his wretchedness. He so wanted to appear light-hearted for Filip and felt even worse because he couldn't.

Filip saw despair in his friend's eyes and hugged him as best he could in the bulky spacesuit before he leaned back, looked him in the eyes and then kissed him lightly on the cheek.

Damian and John noticed that Paul was almost crying and did their best to stop him. They shook his hand with a firm grip and slapped him hard on his right shoulder. Paul coughed a few times and sniffed deeply. He managed a weak smile as he stepped back to let someone else say goodbye and thought he could cry later after they'd left.

John smiled at Charlie, and he realised that no matter what he did, Paul was going to cry. Charlie was crying quietly, but probably only because Maria was crying. None of the returners had worked closely with Charlie or Maria. John didn't quite understand why they were both crying. He wasn't surprised when Maria and Charlie hugged him at the same time and he returned the hugs as best he could.

Both Damian and Filip seemed rather surprised with the impromptu group experience.

After they let John go both Charlie and Maria stepped back and joined Paul. The synchronised wiping away of their quiet tears and the following faint smile, seemed to Paul, who had tears quietly rolling down his cheeks, almost as if they'd planned it.

Dervla had stood back and watched the others saying goodbye. She was still waiting, and she looked sad. First, she hugged Filip politely and then hugged Damian but closer. John looked at her briefly before glancing at the floor. He couldn't look her in the eye. Dervla wasn't put off, it didn't bother her that he wasn't looking, and she didn't hold herself back. She held John tightly and let her lips touch his cheek lightly. He felt her tears on his cheek, but he didn't cry. He felt guilty, but he wanted to go home.

Peter watched Dervla hugging John clumsily. He thought she seems to have put on a little weight, and he wondered if he should tell her discretely about the tip that Meichun had told him of being able to enter a maximum size for her clothes.

Damian nodded first to his son and then to John. They nodded in return. Damian turned to Peter and said, "We're ready. We've waited a long time, and we don't want to miss this perigee." They put on their helmets together, stood next to each other in a straight line before simultaneously taking a step forward. They walked into the airlock, turned around and waved at the others through the hatch. Peter imagined that they were smiling and thought he could feel their optimism.

John waved one last time in Dervla's direction. She smiled faintly, and quiet tears ran down her cheeks.

Peter stood in front of the window wall, he was staying to witness the launch. He noticed Dervla following Charlie and Maria and he assumed they were returning to work. He knew that Maria was feeling sad and when she was sad she liked to spend her time in her beloved gardens.

He half-turned to Europa and speculated, "Would it be possible to see one of the space platforms floating near the Earth with a telescope?"

Europa sounded rather annoyed, "I haven't been able to observe any for months, and they'll probably end up in the sea anyway."

Peter spoke gently, "Could you follow the escape pod on its journey with your telescope?"

Europa took a deep breath, she wasn't happy, "I have my research and don't want to interrupt it."

Peter looked at Europa, "Please."

"Okay, I'll run some computer simulations, then we'll know where they'll land, and I'll point the telescope there when the time comes. But I can't help it if there are clouds." She wasn't happy and was even beginning to feel a little guilty.

Europa sounded frustrated and annoyed as she complained, "This year's shortest perigee is on 14 December. It was foolish to travel now. December is only six months away. Why didn't they wait?"

"Filip explained to me that there are only thirty-three km between June perigee and December perigee. It doesn't make much difference to the duration of the trip, does it?" There was a conciliatory tone in Paul's voice.

Europa replied annoyed, "I know." Before she turned abruptly and left them without saying goodbye.

The three remaining paid little attention to Europa as she left the entrance area in a huff. They were concentrating on the launch site. After a short while and without speaking to anyone in particular, Beatriz said, "I examined their bone and muscle strength. There weren't any problems, they'd all prepared well and done the official returning exercise routines."

Peter seemed pensive and continued watching the launch site, "John was one of our replacement pilots. We're losing a replacement pilot. If we ever need to fly home, we'd only have Steve as our pilot." Peter snorted briefly of course Steve was trained as a pilot. He'd learnt everything he could. He'd been determined to get to the Moon.

Peter turned to Paul and asked seriously, "Would you like to be trained as a replacement pilot?"

"Really? That'd be great." Paul's enthusiasm showed clearly in his grin and shining wide-opened eyes.

Peter could almost hear the eagerness dripping from his voice. Peter nodded, and his smile came from deep within him as he said, "Then let's do it." Peter knew that they didn't need pilots for the escape pods, they were pre-programmed to fly to Earth, but he thought it wouldn't hurt if they had more pilots just in case Columbus sent a shuttle. He returned his attention to the window wall and the launch. He noticed odd bits of debris surrounded by Moon dust blowing in the exhaust. The escape pod's ignition sequence had started. It occurred to him how quiet it was. It was quieter than the launches he had witnessed on Earth when he was a child. Peter's eyes followed the ever-smaller escape pod. He could feel the balance of his emotions tipping towards worry as the hopefulness of the returners got further and further away.

Paul was looking at the launch site, and pointed before saying, "Look, part of the launch stabilising equipment has fallen over. I'll tell Liam. We can send the robots to see what's going on."

Peter nodded and thought for a moment how fragile the Moon Base was. Liam had already told him that the Moon Base wouldn't last forever and that they needed to keep up with the regular maintenance. Peter knew that they had enough spare parts in stock to last for years, and they even had some equipment for a larger base, for the Mars Base. Really the Moon Base was just a staging area. Peter asked with an empty voice, "Do we have everything in stock?"

Paul smiled, "I don't know, but I know that we have forty-year-old whisky."

Peter responded to Paul's smile, "What kind of whisky?"

Paul frowned and shrugged his shoulders. His voice had a higher pitch than normal, "I just know it's forty years old." He shook his head and looked a little lost as he continued, "I don't know."

Peter laughed softly, "No problem. Go and get some and we'll meet in my office in half an hour."

A smile radiated from Paul as he scurried off to the warehouse.

Beatriz looked at Peter and said, "That's good of you."

Peter nodded. She could see he was busy with his thoughts. She listened attentively as he said, "There is nothing else to do but wait." He stopped and looked at her, "Perhaps, they'll be able to send a report, or maybe they won't." They looked at each other knowing that they must be prepared for the worst. Peter wondered if Beatriz knew how to prepare because he knew he didn't.

Beatriz gave Peter a careful warm hug. He looked like he needed a hug. For a few comforting moments she listened to his rhythmic, calming breathing and she hoped hers had the same calming effect on Peter. Beatriz slowly freed herself from his strong arms and gently with the palm of her hand she felt his smoothly shaved cheek. He hadn't been crying. She smiled caringly and told him in an encouraging tone, "Go back to work. Nothing will happen for two or three days."

Peter took her hand, squeezed it lightly and thanked her. They didn't know who smiled first, and it wasn't important to them either. Then Beatriz turned around and left.

Peter stood there alone, looking at the empty launch site. He wondered what was going to happen to the escape pod. He was worried for them, maybe there was nothing to go back to. He suppressed his negative thoughts and concentrated on the launch site. It was taking longer than on Earth for the fine Moon dust to fall back to the ground. Peter watched the dust settling patiently, and as it occurred to him that it was time to go and join Paul, he stroked his cleanly shaven chin, and thought maybe he should grow a beard. If they made it, he might need to do a first report. He smiled hopefully and skilfully suppressed his doubts.

First Wait

Date: Monday 12th June 2141 – 09:07 CET
Location: Alpha 12 – Moon Base

Meichun was attempting small talk with Peter, who was only half-heartedly listening. She was chatting about the weather on the Moon and whether they had weather on the Moon as there was no atmosphere, but they did have solar winds. Every now and then he'd say an encouraging word. He wasn't quite sure why an AI Program would want to learn small talk.

Relaxed and leaning back, he was sitting comfortably in his chair, staring at the ordinary white ceiling. His coffee cup was within reach and he was wondering if he should have another sip before the coffee got too cold. He glanced at the coffee and saw that his captain's hat was next to the coffee cup. He had already brushed and cleaned it this morning. It was reassuring and relaxing when he cleaned it himself, but that didn't stop him from letting the Sauberbots clean it once a month.

Absentmindedly, Peter touched his chin and felt his eight-day beard, which had already been growing four days too long and reminded himself that today he should really bring everyone together and officially discuss the lack of contact from Damian and his team. He slipped down in his chair and held his face in his hands as he sighed and thought it was his duty to lead the Moon Base. He sat up a little. He should take action, but he was enjoying the excuse of waiting. When he announced that the waiting was over, there would be nothing left to hope for. He felt deflated and knew he needed to stop himself before the depressed mood took over his thoughts. He thought of Steve and wondered if he had already started pilot training with Paul. They had a lot of computer simulations to start practicing with. He grinned. Maybe he should try it himself.

He stroked his chin and felt his beard, ignoring Meichun he closed his eyes and imagined himself cleanly shaved. Maybe he should shave before the meeting. He moved his centre of gravity and the chair tilted forward. He pulled himself up and reached for his coffee cup. His eyes opened wider. The hot liquid was wobbling. He stared at the surface of the coffee. The small waves became stronger and faster. One word popped into his mind, "MOONQUAKE!" The lights in the room switched over to the emergency lighting. He grabbed his captain's hat and automatically put it on before hiding under the table.

It was cramped under there and he was squashed up awkwardly. It took him a few seconds before he realised what he had done. He shook his head at his behaviour as he realised that his kindergarten earthquake training had taken over. He could feel the Moon Base still shaking and he wondered, was it necessary to hide under the table during a moonquake. The Moon Base was secure. He felt a little embarrassed that he'd forgotten his Moononaut training and looked at the clock on the wall. He hadn't looked at what time it began. He didn't know how many minutes or seconds had passed. He guessed that it hadn't been that long.

It was now four minutes since he looked at the clock and the Moon Base was still quaking. He reassured himself that, he wasn't in a hurry and decided to stay under the desk. After five minutes he started to get the feeling that it was lasting too long and could feel beads of sweat forming on his forehead. His breathing got quicker. He'd only experienced earthquakes that lasted up to around two and a half minutes. This was going on too long. He focused on his breathing. He didn't want to lose control and panic. He slowed down his breathing and stopped gasping for air and tried to regain control of his body, but the sinking feeling in his stomach remained.

At six minutes, he could taste the sinking feeling in his stomach and he wondered did he have quake sickness, was it just him shaking, was he imagining it? He heard something fall over on his desk and it jolted him out of his growing panic. It wasn't just him. It was still quaking. He concentrated on his breathing and tried to calm down.

At eight minutes he'd got used to the shaking and started to feel a little silly. He lowered his eyes and looked at the ground. He would have liked to believe that if there was an emergency, that he would behave like a superhero, but here he was sitting under the table with a suspected case of quake sickness. At least he was wearing his captain's hat. He felt ashamed of himself, but at the same time he did wonder whether quake sickness was a real illness.

Peter felt suddenly dizzy. Then he realised that the moonquake was over. He glanced over at the clock. Nine minutes. He looked to his left and right before he crawled out from under the table. He held onto his chair as he pulled himself up and stretched his back and arms. He glanced around the room. Everything seemed to be intact. Except his wife's picture had fallen over. He lifted it up and put it gently back in place. Otherwise there seemed to be no damage in his office. He felt relieved as the normal lights came back on.

As he sat down in his chair he considered the situation, they had often experienced moonquakes in the Moon Base, but never one as strong as this. Most of the time he hadn't even noticed anything was happening. The previous moonquakes, and there'd already been eight major ones within the last twenty months, often took place on or around the Moon's day-night cycle. He pondered for a moment, he thought they weren't due for the next change from day to night. He frowned. He wasn't sure. The other moonquakes had been smaller. He'd only noticed two of them, and then hardly at all, he'd been impressed by how efficiently the damping behaviour of the Moon Base had worked. It worked so well that he'd slept through the other six. He hadn't even thought about them until today. He knew that the Moon Base had been built to withstand strong moonquakes. But this quake was stronger, bigger and had lasted a lot longer than the previous moonquakes and it made him feel uneasy.

He turned to look at Meichun, he knew it wasn't necessary, but it just felt politer, "How are you?"

"Shaken, rattled and now rolling." Meichun sounded happy.

Peter frowned. It annoyed him that she sounded happy. He saw no reason why she should sound so positive. Still stood up, Peter called Liam, "That was a moonquake, wasn't it? Is there any damage? Can you run the Moon Base diagnostic?" He barely paused enough to breathe, "Paul and Charlie should do a visual inspection before we send the drones to perform a more detailed structural inspection."

Liam waited briefly until he was sure that Peter had babbled everything he wanted before emphasising, "There's no reason to panic. The quake was at a shallow depth of about 22 kilometres below the surface, and only a few kilometres from the Moon Base. The seismometers show exactly what happened."

Peter remained silent, and let Liam convince him that everything was okay. He felt the stable, reassuring tones in Liam's voice calming him.

"The Moon Base was designed to withstand even stronger quakes. We shouldn't feel anything at all when it is lower than five on the Richter scale. Although, if the quake exceeds a certain energy, the emergency systems switch on automatically and start trying to dissipate the energy. Then we feel the base moving a little. Today's event only lasted about ten minutes. However, we feel the effects for a few minutes afterwards as well." Liam looked at the seismometers, "Actually, the Moon is still quaking. The damping system of the Moon Base can contain the lower energy levels." He smiled at Peter. "So, we can't feel it anymore."

"The emergency lights came on."

Liam kept his voice level. He could still remember his first big moonquake, "I've experienced such incidents several times over the last six years." Liam looked at Peter who was still pale and continued explaining, "The lights dim, and the emergency lights come on because the Moon Base is trying to save energy. It needs it to dissipate the quake energy through its damping mechanism. You haven't experienced anything like this yet because it doesn't happen often. It's just a safety system."

The colour slowly returned to Peter's face.

Liam continued, "There are a lot of moonquakes. We don't notice most of them because they're too small and our Moon Base is very stable."

Peter managed a weak smile, "We'll get together in twenty minutes, and thank you for understanding. I think I'm still a little shocked."

Liam nodded glad that the conversation was over.

Peter sent a message to everyone at the Moon Base. "In twenty minutes in the meeting room. Please."

Peter sat down again and took a few deep breaths. On autopilot, he made a few notes and sent them to the meeting room. He looked around, did he have everything? He reached up and touched his hat. Well, at least he had his captain's hat on. He got up to leave and paused. He wanted to stop by Liam's before he went to the meeting. He looked around again, had he forgotten something? As he left, heading towards the communications area he didn't notice his still warm coffee sitting on the desk.

Liam showed Peter the Moon Base seismometers. It was reassuring to look at the scientific measurements. Peter knew it didn't change the facts, but it felt better, as if he had more control of the situation and he was able to smile again. He asked Liam if he wanted to walk to the meeting with him. Liam nodded with a small amused smile.

Peter entered the meeting room and announced to the assembled group, "That was an adventure. First, I'd like to determine the damage assessment." Nobody was listening to him. They were standing around Paul and laughing. Frowning, Peter looked over at what they were looking at, what on Earth was that? It looked like a toolbox with wheels.

Peter cleared his throat. Maria smiled, turned briefly to Peter and ignored him as she pointed at the toolbox and said, "Look at him. Isn't he cute?"

The light, carefree atmosphere in the room stood in contrast to his state of mind, and he felt the tension melting away. His curiosity was piqued, "Okay, what is it?"

Paul smiled broadly, stood up straight and said, "A gift from Filip." Grinning, Paul looked at the others, and explained for the tenth time, "It's a toolbox with wheels and it behaves like a dog."

Peter shook his head.

Paul's voice sounded cheerful and he gobbled his words as he continued with his explanation, "I had no idea that Filip had left a present for me. I didn't find it until yesterday. There was a riddle that I had to solve before I could find it." He straightened his back proudly, "He wrote, if I solved it I would get a present."

Paul was finding it almost impossible to contain his excitement. He wanted to show them his new toy. He ordered his toolbox, "Stay." Then Paul walked quickly away from the toolbox. The toolbox stayed where it was. Paul giggled, "Isn't it fantastic."

Steve mocked, "What's so special about that. A toolbox doesn't move. That's normal."

Paul went red. Steve's comment wasn't fair at all. He was insulting Filip's present. Paul glared at Steve then he ordered the toolbox, "Heel." The toolbox turned on its tiny wheels and slowly rolled to Paul's heel. Paul looked at Steve and gloated briefly, before he held out his hand and said to the toolbox, "Stay." Then he walked to the other end of the room and said excitedly, "Come here." The small wheels of the toolbox clinked as it moved towards Paul. When it got there Paul, with a broad smile, patted it and said, "Good dog." The toolbox's wheels squeaked as it turned quickly, and Peter thought, it sounds as if it's having fun.

Maria clapped her hands, laughed and enthusiastically said, "He needs a name."

"Okay, sit down, please." Peter tried to sound serious.

Still boisterous and joking, they all obeyed reluctantly, except Paul, who remained standing to attention.

Peter shook his head slightly from side to side and smiled as he answered Paul's pleading look, "Yes, he can stay."

Paul jiggled a little from pure excitement and smiled broadly as he ordered the toolbox to come directly next to his seat. As discreetly as possible, Paul leaned slightly to the side and patted the toolbox gently.

Peter noticed Paul's movement and guessed what he was doing. It made it very difficult for him to be serious as he tried to call the meeting to order and said, "The moonquake was an adventure." He briefly looked at them to see how they were doing before he continued, "This was our first moonquake above 5.5 on the Richter scale and I'd like to determine if there was any damage."

Peter nodded in Liam's direction for him to take over, "I've experienced several quakes over the last six years. There wasn't anything unusual this time." He glanced over to Peter, "The Moon Base is built to regulate itself. Mostly you never notice the quakes, because the system works efficiently, but occasionally with high energy levels it needs to shake a little to disperse the energy. I will still send the robots to be extra thorough during the normal weekly structural inspection."

Liam looked over to Charlie, who smiled and looked at Maria, "At first, I was a little worried during the moonquake." He smiled at Maria again, "But I knew the Moon Base was very stable and we were safe. I haven't noticed any damage from the preliminary checks."

Steve shifted in his seat and sat up straighter in his chair, before he looked at Europa smiling almost coyly, "I was in the lab and the seismometers there and the ones we have at various site locations went crazy. It was really cool, and I was able to collect a lot of data." He grinned. "Too bad John missed it." He looked over to Peter, "We've had seismometers all over the Moon for over a hundred and twenty years. We know exactly what to expect." Steve smiled as he noticed the interested attention from everyone there.

"The seismometers are part of an ongoing project that is now my responsibility. Today's quake was unusual. Polar moonquakes occur less frequently than their equatorial cousins. We only get about a fifth of the quakes near the Moon Base that you get at the equator." He looked at Peter, who nodded encouragingly. Steve continued, "As you will have noticed moonquakes differ from earthquakes in that they last much longer. Often you can feel them for over ten minutes." He was enjoying the attention, "Today's quake was one at a shallow depth just below the surface, and not very far from the base. That's why it felt so strong."

Liam was trying not to look bored.

Peter let Steve finish. The others wanted and deserved to know.

"At the equator, there are about five quakes per year that measure over five on the Richter scale." He looked at Europa to see if she was impressed by his knowledge.

Europa didn't seem that interested, but Steve wasn't about to give up so easily and was still trying to impress her, "There are four different types of moonquakes. The first three types are mostly harmless. The first of these are the so-called deep moonquakes, these are about seven hundred kilometres below the surface. The second type are caused by the vibrations of meteors impacting." He glanced around the group, "The third kind of the harmless quakes are caused by the thermal effects of the expansion of the icy crust when the Sun returns after a two-week moonlit night." He looked at Europa for a reaction, "And the fourth type that we normally can feel are the shallow depth quakes that occur approximately twenty or thirty kilometres below the surface." He looked at Europa again and smiled confidently.

Peter thanked Steve for the explanation. It helped when he knew the science about what had happened. Although he kept quiet about hiding under his desk during the quake.

Europa wasn't smiling, "It quaked, and?" She wanted to get back to work and had no patience for such nonsense,

"Statistically speaking, it was going to happen at some point during our five-year shift." Her voice sounded bored.

"I was worried about the plants." Maria seemed deadly serious, "If I could only find the appropriate music for a moonquake, the plants would think they were dancing."

Peter wasn't quite sure if she meant it.

During the awkward silence that followed, Beatriz explained, "I thought it was very different from my experiences on Earth." Then she admitted, "After about four minutes, I did start to worry." She glanced into the distance and added, "I was in Tokyo in 2129 for a conference when the devastating 7.0 magnitude earthquake struck." She remembered a comment that she'd heard repeatedly over the years, "Admittedly, it wasn't as bad as the quake on January 19th, 2038, but it was still bad." She had a sad expression as she remembered and the mood in the room dipped. She looked down at the table.

Peter knew that she had lost some friends that day and changed the subject. He asked Dervla if everything in the lab was okay.

"It was quite a shock, but there is no damage, the machines have a built-in emergency mode."

Peter looked at Paul. Paul seemed uncertain, "I didn't really notice it. I was out with the dog in the hall." He laughed a little embarrassed.

Peter laughed hard and thanked Paul for his honesty before grinning and admitting, "Actually, I hid under my desk."

The others laughed and didn't believe him, except Beatriz, who still seemed worried.

Peter looked at their faces, they were happy. He liked that. He found it difficult to return to a more serious expression as he started speaking, "Damian and his team haven't been in touch, and there is no word from Columbus either. We followed the journey as far as possible, but because of the weather, we couldn't see the landing. We don't know why the communication didn't work." He had no trouble looking serious as he finished. He took a deep breath and couldn't look at anyone as he said, "The question is, does anyone else want to go home? Granted, I don't know what would be best. But I suggest that we carry on as normal. We all had our reasons why we came, and we can stay and finish our five-year shift."

They started nodding, pleased with the suggestion that was probably the least frightening of their options. Peter assumed that the five scientists would want to complete their research, and he suspected that the others, except Paul, had their reasons to stay.

Unsure, Paul watched the others before deciding to join in the nodding.

Peter relaxed. He was glad that the subject had been settled for now, but he knew there were still a few things to discuss, "Liam is still trying to contact the Mars Base. Unfortunately, that's not as trivial as it sounds. The satellites communicate through Earth, and so far, we've had no luck accessing any of the satellites. Maybe it could work if the satellites were properly aligned. I'll let you know when we have any further news." Peter forced a smile. He hadn't given up hope and wanted to keep up the illusion for the others.

Maria took her necklace and held it in her hand as she looked at Peter. She had something to say. He nodded formally at her to give his permission.

"I am going to organise a yoga course. Yoga is very relaxing, and I think we should do yoga in a group." Her whole face radiated. She was looking around for interest from the group. Charlie volunteered right away. Who could say no to Maria?

Dervla turned to Maria and asked in a quiet voice, "Is it safe for expectant mothers?"

Maria's eyes flicked automatically to Dervla's abdomen. How could she have missed it? Maria smiled with understanding, "Certainly."

Peter was glad that he was already sitting down. He smiled and nodded with his eyebrows raised. He didn't trust himself to say anything. It took him a few seconds before he wondered who the father was. He watched how the others reacted happily and congratulated Dervla on her good news. After a few moments, he managed to congratulate Dervla too before he jokingly reminded them about their work.

After the meeting was over, Beatriz went with Peter to his office. When they got there, he asked if it was okay if Meichun listened in on their conversation.

Beatriz didn't object, and they sat down happily.

"I assume we can no longer contact and get any deliveries from Columbus." Peter sounded thoughtful as if he was thinking aloud.

Beatriz didn't react, she didn't think he was talking to her.

He turned to Beatriz, "Do you feel lonely?"

She smiled understanding, "Yes, of course I feel lonely, but let's not think about it. It's not going to help us."

With a soft voice Peter asked, "Are you also wondering what happened to the landing team?"

Slowly and firmly Beatriz replied, "It's not our fault."

Peter nodded as he handed Beatriz a scientific magazine, "I've been reading about the Re-Do Recycle machines. The so-called plastic eaters. I wanted to understand how they work." Peter seemed suddenly older and said forlornly, "The data mining techniques I've used with Meichun have come up with nothing. Which is a disappointment as I would so love to know what happened on Earth."

Beatriz nodded. She'd like to know too. "Since the flight last week, I've had a low-level sickness in my stomach. Actually, since contact with Earth couldn't be restored." She looked Peter straight in the eye, "Keep calm and carry on, keep going as if nothing has happened." She dropped her eyes and looked at the magazine.

Peter offered Beatriz a whisky. He still had the rest of the bottle Paul had brought and it was a good one. He smiled with his mouth but there wasn't enough energy in his expression to reach his eyes.

Beatriz looked at her watch. It was early in the day, but she nodded. She liked whisky, but not too much and without ice, "If we lied to ourselves that everything could be all right, we'd be happier." Her voice sounded both sad and amused.

After he'd poured the drinks, he agreed and added a little glimmer of hope, "It could be worse."

Beatriz laughed quietly, "Yes, fortunately nobody's sick."

They sipped the whisky and enjoyed the drink in silence.

Peter put his glass on the table and asked, "While we're talking about illnesses. Is moonquake sickness a thing?"

Beatriz hid her amusement, "I've never heard of it."

Peter nodded thoughtfully before asking, "And what are we going to do with a baby?"

Omega 13

Date: Monday 2nd October 2141 – 10:17 CET
Location: Alpha 12 – Moon Base

Holding his captain's hat in his hands behind his back, Peter walked purposefully across the large common room, the canteen. The energy-saving lights switched on and off as he passed under the sensors. He was concentrating on keeping his steps regular as he crossed the room in a shorter time than normal. His pedometer, which was built into his shoe, beeped quietly and interrupted the silence, "Target reached." He ignored it and carried on walking. He didn't care how many steps he walked today.

He got to the window wall that overlooked the main garden, and hesitated. He swapped his captain's hat between his hands and began to turn it around slowly. This time he didn't turn around immediately, instead he seemed to be waiting and looking through the window. The large illuminated garden was surrounded by the dark, never-ending sky. To the right of the garden, he could see part of the outline of the main laboratory, which had very few lights switched on. He murmured quietly. Dervla hadn't worked there today, and that was fine. He looked at his feet, turned around and walked back where he had come from. The room was big enough for him to get a good pace up before he collided with the opposite wall. Once more he stopped and relaxed his arms, which now hung aimlessly by his sides. He pulled himself together and with renewed determination he turned ninety degrees to the right and went to the door. He stood waiting in the doorway. He was listening to the conversation between Steve and Charlie while Steve was cutting Charlie's hair. Steve was a qualified hairdresser, a sought-after skill on the Moon, that he'd learnt while studying for his first degree. A little jealous, Peter wondered how he could have had the time and ambition to learn so many different skills, but then Steve would have done anything to get to the Moon.

Peter could hear the gushing praise in Charlie's voice as he thanked Steve for a job well done. His gratitude was so genuine that Peter thought he could almost touch it. Even so it didn't cheer Peter up. Nothing was freeing him from the brooding feeling that hung over him.

As Charlie left the hairdressing area, he saw Peter in the doorway. Charlie posing like a model showed him his new hairstyle. Peter knew that Charlie, who always wanted to look good, believed that Steve was a marvellous hairdresser, so he nodded without really looking at him and said in a lacklustre tone, "It looks good."

Charlie beamed and replied, "Thanks to Steve, we all look good."

Peter thought, yes, he's right, compared to the previous Moononauts, they looked really good, and they had Steve to thank. Steve kept his own hair under control with a hair clipper.

Charlie was in a very good mood and sounded almost flirtatious as he said, "There might be photos today."

Peter grunted in agreement. He didn't know what to do with himself and went in to the gym that was next to the small hair salon. Maria sat there alone and was lifting weights now and then. It wasn't intensive training, yet the effort showed up in her red cheeks, and the beads of sweat on her forehead proved that she was trying.

She noticed Peter and greeted him with a single movement of her head that made it clear that she had nothing to say. She returned her concentration to her training.

The corners of Peter's mouth were turned down, and his eyes were focused on an imaginary distant point. He didn't really notice Maria. He was thinking about the infirmary that was next to the gym. In particular, he was thinking about Dervla and Beatriz, who were there. He could pop in and see how everything was, but decided not to, he didn't want to intrude, instead he wandered back to the canteen. It annoyed him that the others called it a canteen, and it especially annoyed him when he said canteen by mistake. It was a common room. They didn't just eat there, there was also entertainment. He looked at the video corner, and then at the computer games area. Only then did he notice Paul and his dog, who was sitting next to him. Paul was playing on the computer game console. Peter looked at what he was playing. It was "Asteroids". Peter smiled a little as his innocent childhood memories returned. His smile lifted his gloomy feeling a little.

He sat down in the canteen and put his captain's hat on the table, while he without interest watched Paul playing. The chair felt too small, too uncomfortable. Something was wrong with it. His legs were twisting under the chair. He just couldn't sit still. He picked up his captain's hat, put it squarely on his head, and stood up decisively.

Peter glanced at Paul, but Paul paid no attention to him. His fingers glided easily and swiftly over the control mechanism, and his gaze was fully focused on the screen.

The common room offered Peter no sanctuary. He decided to go to his office. He moved on automatic pilot taking one step at a time trying not to think. When he arrived at the door, he stood for a moment, perplexed that he was already there.

Before he sat down in his chair, he fetched himself a cup of coffee, and then put his captain's hat next to it on his desk. The coffee smelled good and he carefully tasted the hot liquid. He felt the warmth on his lips, and it calmed him a little. He leaned back in his chair and tried to relax. After a while he asked Meichun if she was busy. If she had time to talk.

With a compassionate tone she replied, "I am always there for you."

"I never wanted children. Even as a child, before I knew I couldn't, I didn't want any."

Meichun agreed, "Children are a lot of work."

Peter thought about his wife. His favourite picture of his wife formed in his mind's eye. It was early autumn, and she was standing on the veranda, smelling the bouquet of flowers she was rocking in her arms, the late afternoon Sun shone on her hair, and made the subtle but fabulous colours dance in the light. She raised her face. Her eyes were looking for him. As soon as she recognised him, she smiled sweetly. He was still sitting in his car waiting, his muscles weak. He couldn't get out of the car. He didn't want the moment to end.

"Jean, my wife, knew from the beginning that there wouldn't be any children. It didn't bother her. She thought there were already too many people on Earth. Nine billion is enough."

Meichun encouraged Peter, "Yes, that's right."

"We could have had children, but only with serious medical intervention. And we didn't want that. We didn't want to risk losing our dignity."

Meichun attempted a supportive comment, "It could also have been dangerous."

"At first you don't realise that you won't have grandchildren either."

Meichun conciliated, "I wouldn't have thought so either."

"I sometimes wonder what it would have been like if I'd have been a father. While I was working on Earth, I never thought about it. We had each other, and we both focused on our careers and our life together."

Meichun tried to keep giving appropriate answers, "Work is important."

"I hope she's all right, and that she can handle the situation there, that someone is there to help her. You know, if we'd had a child, they would be with her, and she wouldn't be all alone."

The pain on his face was easy to see as he said, "It's been almost two years since the lights on Earth went out."

Meichun replied, "Two nice years."

Peter sat up and looked at Meichun. Today he just couldn't explain to Meichun why they weren't nice years. His thoughts were too distracted, too moody. He couldn't concentrate properly. He drank his coffee and returned to the canteen.

Paul was still playing "Asteroids". It was distracting him from the situation. He was giving the game his full attention. Peter sat down in the canteen and thought the chairs were still uncomfortable. He considered eating something to distract him.

Then they heard a baby crying.

Peter stood up abruptly, his chair tilted backwards and rattled to the floor. He didn't hear the noise. Paul turned around, his game forgotten, they looked at each other. Was it time? Paul carefully put his game console aside, stood on unsteady legs, and walked towards Peter. The wheels of the toolbox next to him clattered. In a deep, firm voice Paul said, "Stay." There was no doubt in the tone.

They stood nervously next to each other, and they walked, gingerly at first, the few steps to the infirmary. Each of them encouraged by the step of the other, and they walked the rest of the way with more confidence. They didn't hear the chair righting itself behind them.

In the infirmary, Dervla was half-laying half-sitting on the bed with the baby resting on her breast. Dervla looked tired, but she managed to smile faintly when she noticed Peter and Paul.

Concerned Peter asked, "How are you?"

Dervla whispered, "Good." She didn't want to disturb the baby.

Beatriz replied quietly, "We are waiting for some test results, but otherwise everything seems to be in order."

Paul, who suddenly seemed nervous, said, "I've made a cradle. I can bring it here if you want. I hid it upstairs in my room."

Dervla smiled faintly but gratefully, and she managed to say, "Thank you."

Peter contacted Liam and told him, "The baby is here."

Beatriz interrupted him, "Tell him to make an announcement for the whole Moon Base."

Peter nodded. He didn't have to, because Liam had already heard Beatriz. They heard Liam's announcement a few seconds later.

As Paul went to get the cradle, Maria and Charlie hastily arrived. Maria thought the baby was sweet and Charlie smiled but stayed in the background. Maria said, "We've made some baby clothes." She reached in her bag and showed Dervla some small colourful pyjamas.

Dervla showed her gratitude with a little smile. Beatriz, who was being protective, noticed how tired Dervla was and ordered the others to leave and let her rest. The three of them left without arguing and went into the canteen.

Liam and Europa were waiting there. They'd heard Beatriz's command, and decided to go and wait in the canteen. Neither of them wanted to disturb Dervla. Europa had chosen to sit on a chair and was reading her book, while Liam was looking out the window seemingly lost in thought. When they heard the others, they looked at them expectantly. The atmosphere in the canteen was light, excited but mostly relieved.

Charlie and Maria went over to Europa. As they arrived, Charlie said, "A baby isn't it great?"

Europa, who didn't particularly like children, managed nonetheless to react politely, "In my culture a child brings great hope and joy."

Liam came and joined the others as Peter and Beatriz sat down at a nearby table.

After a minute or so Steve came rushing into the canteen and said a little annoyed, "The door of the infirmary is closed." He didn't seem sure if he should be doing anything or not.

Peter laughed softly, finally there was something he couldn't do. Obstetrician wasn't one of his qualifications. It must be a profession he hadn't had time to learn.

Beatriz, who had just joined them, answered Steve, "She wants to be alone, she needs a little rest. You can talk to her and see the baby later."

Steve went over to the others, and watched Maria show more of the baby clothes creations she and Charlie had made.

Beatriz was tired and still wound up, but she was trying to relax. She looked at Peter and told him, "It's a healthy boy. His weight and size are good. I've done the normal blood tests and they all came back fine." Beatriz whispered, she wanted to be sure that only Peter heard, "I even counted his fingers and toes. I was worried about the spikes in radiation. They could have had a negative effect on the baby's DNA." She bit her lower lip softly and looked at Peter seriously, "Dervla refused a DNA test for the baby."

Paul's metal crib looked professional and very shiny. He put it on the floor in front of the group, and in the quiet they watched it rocking gently. Paul reached into the cradle and with a big grin he took out a bottle of whisky, "Let's toast the baby."

Steve nodded and went to fetch some glasses.

Paul poured the whisky into the glasses and offered everyone a drink. They toasted the baby and Dervla. Both Steve and Maria pulled a disgusted expression at their first sip of whisky. Paul laughed at their faces. Apparently, they weren't impressed by forty-year-old whisky.

Maria put her glass down and enthused, "I think the baby is very sweet." She tilted her head to the side and then shrugged before smiling as she wondered with amusement, "We may need to increase the daylight hours in the garden to compensate for the carbon dioxide from the baby. Does anyone have any thoughts about this?"

They looked at each other questioningly and shook their heads.

Maria muttered, "I need to research this." She smiled. She liked the feeling that she had something very important to do.

Charlie, who was watching Maria, asked curiously, "Do you want a child?"

Maria didn't answer.

Liam looked at the enthusiasm of the others and decided to take a step back, he didn't really want anything to do with the baby. He glanced at the time, finished his whisky in a simple gulp and said noncommittally, "I have something to do" and left. Nobody took any notice of him. They were busy with their thoughts, and they were enjoying the happier mood after months of darkness. They finally had something that they could celebrate.

Peter, who felt responsible, thought maybe that's what it feels like to be a father, but at the same time he wondered if the baby would resemble John. Or, perhaps, one of the other returners. He looked around at the men in the room and he realised he had no idea who the father was. He wondered if anyone other than Dervla knew and thought, we could do a DNA test. The results of the Moononauts were already available, it would be an easy comparison.

Steve, who was in a good mood, joked, "We were Alpha 12. Twelve people living on the Moon Base. With the baby, we've become Omega 13." He laughed ominously and said, "This can't be good."

Europa looked at him contemptuously, "I haven't seen the baby, but it is certainly not a devil's child, and don't be stupid. There are only ten of us."

Paul was smiling, he was simply glad that he wasn't the youngest anymore. He raised his glass and said, "To Dervla and the baby." They all raised their glasses to drink a sip of whisky, but Steve and Maria only pretended to sip.

Europa had annoyed Steve, and he wanted to get his own back, to get a reaction from them, "We don't have enough space in the escape pods, nor are they designed for babies or toddlers."

Everyone ignored his comment.

There was a lull in the conversation and Charlie wondered aloud, "Does anyone know who the father is?" As soon as he said it Steve and Charlie looked at each other before turning to Paul and looking at him questioningly. Paul wasn't paying attention to them as he was still playing with the cradle, but when he looked up, he noticed their stares and shook his head worried that he had done something wrong.

Steve calculated in his head and thought, "If I did my maths right, the child wasn't conceived during yearly close down."

Charlie was thinking, "Liam's not here. Does that mean anything?" He sipped his whisky absentmindedly.

Maria tried to change the subject, "Has Dervla chosen a name yet?"

Beatriz, who'd been observing the conversation, replied immediately, "His name is Patrick."

They nodded and sipped on the whisky. No one was sure what to say.

Peter, who'd been lost in his own thoughts, filled his whisky glass and took a sip. He wasn't sure if he should do something about the baby. There hadn't been any training for this at the Moononaut Academy, "Do we have baby food?"

Beatriz turned to Peter and looked at him puzzled for a moment before she explained, "We've had a few months to prepare in our very well-equipped laboratories. We've been experimenting making a baby formula. I think we'll be able to make enough," and she half smiled to cover her concern. She hoped Peter was okay.

Peter's voice was higher than normal, "And nappies, has someone thought about nappies." Peter trying to remember everything he knew about babies.

Beatriz replied patiently, "We're making the nappies out of T-shirts. Steve created some for us. With many helpful suggestions from the Happynet."

Everybody laughed. Somehow the thought of Steve making nappies from T-shirts was funny.

With the end of a laugh still sounding in his voice, Charlie said quickly, "Let's take some pictures."

Steve looked sceptical.

Charlie insisted, "It's a special event. The first baby born on the Moon." He looked for agreement before he added, "Patrick must be the first alien."

Paul nodded but the others looked at him surprised, what was he talking about.

Charlie continued, "If someone wasn't born on Earth, it means he's an alien because he's not from Earth."

Paul loved the idea, "You think Patrick is an alien."

Steve, who was rather unconvinced, objected with, "It doesn't count. We are only 384,000 kilometres from Earth. It's not far enough to be considered an alien."

Europa interrupted, "Actually, that's an average value. We're about 375,000 kilometres away today."

Steve looked decidedly annoyed at Europa's comment. He breathed in deeply and tried to remain calm, because he knew she was right.

Paul, who hadn't noticed Steve's reaction, speculated, "I mean, can he be an alien? Does it count, even if we are on a moon and not on another a planet?"

Maria, who found the topic amusing, joined in, "His parents are earthlings. It's not just about where someone was born, is it?"

Peter, who wasn't interested in the game, said to Beatriz, "I think a change is in order. Dervla and Patrick can move into one of the tourist suites when they get out of the infirmary. If a tourist comes, we'll have more than enough time to sort everything out."

Beatriz looked at him with a sad, worried look. He'd not yet accepted that there wouldn't be any tourists. Had he forgotten, they had no contact with the Earth? She felt almost angry with him, but remained quiet, she didn't want to destroy this happy, carefree moment.

Steve overheard what Peter had said and was immediately jealous. He deserved a suite on the top floor just as much has anyone else, "There's room for several people up there. I'd like to live in a suite too."

Maria wasn't alone in ignoring Steve. She thought, he doesn't need a suite. He's just jealous, so she changed the subject, "Well, now that the baby is here, maybe we should try to contact Earth again and find out what happened. We could try going over the theories again to see if we missed anything. Patrick needs our help for his future."

Peter grudgingly listened to Maria and didn't like her mention of the future. He thought, if we just live in the present day and exist day to day, we can cope with the situation. We all know that there is no future here. Peter filled his glass and raised it.

They toasted the future.

Paul had an idea. He spoke quickly and excitedly, "Perhaps we can try something new. Liam is helping me to learn some new inspection methods with the robots. We've already done thermal imaging, X-rays, 3D geometry mapping, and ultrasonic crack detection comes next." Paul beamed at the others and searched in their faces expecting to find the enthusiasm he felt echoed. He was disappointed. Nobody showed any real interest. His enthusiasm waned, and he scratched his left ear slightly when he said, "I thought we could use the technology for Earth analysis." His voice became quieter and slower as he continued, "Perhaps we can see if something has changed. I mean, how and where the plants are growing, when nobody is there, they get out of control very quickly." He was thinking about his garden at home, and he remembered his dog Astro. He looked around for Astro, who was still over in the games corner.

Maria suggested a toast to Dervla and Patrick in an attempt to change the subject, she didn't want to think about the plants on Earth.

Paul poured out whisky for everyone except Maria and Steve, who didn't want any more.

Peter, who was sitting across from Beatriz, smiled and looked full of energy. He wanted to organise something to try and sort out everything. He felt a new sense of purpose. He hadn't felt like this for a long time. With a puzzled expression and shaking his head, a little he asked Beatriz, "Do we have everything we need to live?"

Beatriz didn't know where he was going, so she made a list for him, "Water, salt, sunlight, food, sleep, exercise, mental stability." The last phrase was a question.

Peter nodded. He seemed satisfied. He hadn't really heard the list. He'd already thought about it and had already read in the Intellinet what they needed to live and found out what they had available on the Moon Base. "I don't think we have liquid soap and moisturiser and you need that for a baby. We can't make them on the Moon Base either." His expression turned serious. "There's a danger of explosion if you make them."

When Paul came over to pour some more whisky, Peter asked if he could check in the warehouse to see if they had any soap and moisturiser for babies.

Paul smiled and agreed. He was pleased to have something to do. As he left, he took Astro with him. He didn't need to go, he could have used any computer console to find out, but he just wanted to get away for a while and to move.

It wasn't long before Paul and his toolbox dog were back. He returned with an answer to Peter's question, "We've plenty of soap, and baby soap. It is stored under optimal conditions." It said this on the storage notes, he didn't actually know what these were. "They're due to be sent to Mars at some point." He laughed with amusement, "I guess they thought there would be babies on Mars." Paul opened the top shelf of the toolbox and grinned at the others as he got out a bottle of whisky. Then he said, "Maybe there's already a baby alien on Mars." Paul looked suddenly sad as he said, "Then Patrick won't be the first alien."

Peter's curiosity was aroused, he hadn't expected baby stuff in the stores, "Is there anything else when it comes to baby equipment?"

Paul shrugged his shoulders and replied, "Yes, it was a long list. There are inflatable cots, nappies and some other stuff that I didn't know what it was."

Charlie wanted more whisky, and he called Paul to come over and bring the whisky with him.

As soon as Paul was gone, and Peter thought that the others weren't listening, Peter spoke very quietly to Beatriz, "The Earth's satellites are falling slowly out of orbit. Their self-correcting orbits were regularly checked and adjusted by Columbus, and there now haven't been any corrections in two years. We've no way of adjusting them from the Moon Base. Liam is trying to hack into the satellites to adjust their positions, but so far without any success." He started shaking his head. "I don't know if we'll ever make contact again."

They looked at each other briefly and then avoided each other's gaze. Sipping the whisky served to distract them for a while before Peter added, "I'm assuming that there will be problems in three years."

Beatriz looked puzzled, what did he mean?

He added, "When the employment contracts come to an end."

Beatriz didn't know what to say.

They toasted Patrick and Dervla one last time. Peter placed his empty glass on the table and looked for his captain's hat. He looked down at the table. Where was the thing? Had he left it in his office?

Contract Renewal

Date: Monday 26th October 2144 – 09:00 CET
Location: Alpha 12 – Moon Base

Peter was looking at the large calendar displayed on the wall of his office, his eyes flicked over it slowly counting the days from the beginning of the month and stopped abruptly at the red dot on today's date. It was a reminder that the five-year contracts were due for renewal. He stared hard at the red dot, half hoping it would disappear as it occurred to him that they'd been waiting for today. He shook his head, no that wasn't the case, they weren't waiting, they'd put off thinking about the rest of their lives until today. It'd made their lives bearable. He glanced at the wall clock and thought about what he still had to do. He'd got half an hour to prepare before the first of the end of contract reviews. He bit his lower lip, tasted the salty dried saliva and thought about whisky. He shook his head and frowned, he needed to keep his thoughts clear.

He reached over, and resting his arm on his desk, caressed the frame of the small professional portrait of his wife with his index finger. Today would have been the day that they travelled back to Earth. He felt a wave of sadness and laid his hand next to the picture and concentrated on it, if only they hadn't lost contact.

His computer beeped a reminder that the meetings were due, he turned and looked at the list of possible return dates for the Moononauts displayed on his screen. It was a list of dates with the minimum distance between the Moon and Earth for each month and it had been calculated many years before by Columbus. The predicted return dates that coincided with the end of a five-year shift were marked with an asterisk. It was never exactly five years per shift, normally a few days either way. He looked at their date, it didn't have an asterisk, but the previous month's date did. He reached out to it but didn't quite touch the display. He'd delayed long enough. He slid his chair back, hugged his arms around his waist, closed his eyes tightly while leaning as far forward as his stomach would let him. He rocked gently before suddenly sitting upright, he felt slightly sick. They were approximately at the end of a five-year shift and the date had to be before the Annual Closure. He laughed quietly to himself because he knew that Columbus double checked the dates for suitability and they wouldn't be pleased that he'd delayed a month. Nobody here seemed to mind. They mostly thought that the calculation was about as complicated as calculating Easter and just wanted to be given a date.

He scrolled down the list before him and looked at the last entry. It was for fifty years in the future. He felt empty inside as he stared intensely at that date and wondered would it be far enough in future to cover their stay on the Moon. He raised his hand and with his finger scrolled back to the beginning of the list. He didn't want to think about the future.

He looked over at his wife's picture again and his smile was genuine, as he realised that today was a near-Earth date. He liked near-Earth days because he was physically closer to his wife than normal. He wondered if she felt closer to him on these day than on others. He hated the thousands of kilometres that lay between them. He wondered, did she know he was close by, did she know that he was thinking of her, and he hoped that when she looked up at the Moon she thought of him.

Meichun announced, "Five minutes to go. Are you ready?"

A look of mild panic crossed Peter's face and he forced himself to concentrate on the task at hand. He put both hands face down on the desk in front of him to help him and he focused on the even spaces between his fingers before deciding that he'd offer everyone a contract extension. He raised his right hand and chewed on the thumb nail hoping it was a wise decision to attempt to carry on as if nothing had happened. If they accepted that they were all going to get an extension, he was sure that everything would be fine.

He glanced at the door and breathed in through his nose feeling his chest filling with air. It was going to be tricky. He was anxious about how each team member was going to react. The stern voice in his head told him it would be fine and, "just to get on with it." He knew that extending the contract for another five years might not be easy for them to accept and the dialogue was going to force them to think about how scared they were about returning home, a topic that they'd all been avoiding for the last three years. He was worried. He hoped they would pretend that the contract extension was what they wanted and their choice. They knew that there wasn't any practical way that they could refuse the extension, well unless they returned in one of the escape pods, but he didn't think they would. They felt the same as him. They found it difficult to stop worrying about their families and whether or not there was anything or anyone left on Earth for them to return to. They knew that after a five-year shift away from home that things would have changed, not everything would be how they left it, but were they prepared for the possibility that there was nothing left for them, nothing at all. He shuddered and wished he knew what was happening on Earth.

"Meichun, can you help me? How do we make everything appear as ordinary as possible?"

Meichun asked, "What's ordinary?"

Peter thought for a second about what he really meant before clarifying, "How do we make it look like it was five years ago?"

Meichun replied, "You changed the picture of your wife."

He rested his hand on the handle of the top drawer, where he'd hidden his favourite photo of his wife. It had been over two years since he had hidden it. He opened the drawer slowly and reached in carefully. He turned the photo over as he took it out of the drawer and placed it on the desk next to the other picture. He smiled but felt her absence as a sharp pain in his chest as he told her, "Today we are going to pretend that nothing has happened." She was beautiful in the picture, and he realised how much he'd missed her. He looked closely at the photo and wondered about the passage of time and if the last five years had been kind to her. When she smiled, she'd have new wrinkles, maybe more grey hair. He liked the idea that she was older and that she was still living at home, in their home. Her existence formed an almost physical connection to the Earth and it made him smile.

He placed the portrait back in the top drawer and closed it with a click as he prepared himself mentally for the meetings. He'd read the personnel reports, which had been kept secret until the renewals were due. The personnel reports were only released if there was approval from Columbus or the contracts were up for renewal. They were then released automatically in case the Moon Major needed them for any decisions about the next shift. He'd already known everything about the Moononauts he'd travelled with. There hadn't been any surprises there, but the information about Liam's past was new to him, and he'd not yet decided how he was going to deal with it.

He had thought a lot about who to invite first and whether someone would find meaning in the order of the meetings. He didn't want to offend anyone. He smirked and shook his head. When he was honest with himself it wasn't everyone he was bothered about. It was just Steve. He didn't want to offend Steve. He didn't think that the others would notice or that they would even put any significance on the order of the meetings.

He looked at the wall clock. It was time. He put his captain's hat carefully on his head, glanced in the wall mirror and smiled encouragingly. He looked the part. He was going to play a major role in the game and he wanted to present himself both confidently and convincingly. He said to his reflection, "Harmony and a comfortable life. That's all I can offer."

Paul was first up and arrived punctually for his meeting. He came alone.

When Peter noticed that Paul hadn't brought Astro he was a little disappointed but managed to hide his feelings well.

Paul didn't see Peter's welcoming smile he was still looking at the floor. He stood there trying to stand still but fidgeted awkwardly. Then he cleared his throat involuntarily and blushed deeply.

Peter nodded at one of the chairs and suggested he sit down. He knew it was Paul's first employee appraisal, and Peter had the feeling that Paul felt he'd done something wrong. Peter smiled to himself as he remembered how nervous he'd been for his own first appraisal. Then he wondered what Paul could have actually done wrong anyway.

Paul looked at the chair before sitting down carefully and then avoided looking directly at Peter.

Peter stared at him with a furrowed brow. He had the feeling that Paul was looking at the wall behind him and wanted to turn around and see what was there. He resisted the temptation and wondered how he could help Paul relax. He seemed so tense and nervous. Peter asked him kindly, "Are there many bottles of whisky left in stock?"

Paul looked at Peter and smiled gratefully. His voice was cheerful as he answered, "There are hundreds of bottles. They must have planned a really big party, or there wouldn't be that many, would there?"

Peter laughed briefly and nodded approvingly, "Yes you are probably right. Shall we get started?"

Paul fidgeted again and looked away from Peter.

In a friendly tone Peter said, "I think your work is excellent and if you want to extend your contract of employment, there are no concerns on my side." It was true that Paul's work was excellent, but Peter thought even if it wasn't, there was little else could he have said at this point. Peter observed Paul's reaction. He seemed to relax a little. At least he wasn't sitting so stiffly anymore, and he was even leaning back. Peter asked, "Do you want to renew your contract of employment for another five years?"

Paul nodded in agreement, but somewhat subdued and without enthusiasm.

His reaction was good enough for Peter to continue as planned, "That means you get a fifteen percent pay rise and because you are working a double shift and we save the fuel from the return flight, you automatically get credits on your environment and social responsibility account." Peter looked pleased for him. They both knew that these credits had a lot of value, they represented how much respect you had earned, and for a twenty-four-year-old it was impressive that he had built up so many credits representing his social competence, his environmental friendliness and his long-term vision of the future.

Paul hadn't expected such good news and looked surprised as he grinned. He proudly tapped his chest and said the word, "I," before his voice trailed off, he was still smiling as he frowned.

Peter had known Paul would be pleased. He wanted to be someone who cared for future generations, not just for himself. The environment and social responsibility credits meant even more to Paul than most people.

Paul, who had completely forgotten his nervousness, let the doubt in his mind crept across his face before he said in a small voice, "I thought I could only stay for one five-year shift."

Peter had known that the question would come. He smiled reassuringly and explained, "It was recommended that you only do one shift because of your existing DNA damage. We have treatments available now that can keep the situation under control. Beatriz has done the analysis and says everything is okay."

Paul nodded but seemed a little worried.

Peter pulled himself up in his chair, leaned forward and looked meaningfully at Paul, smiled ironically and said, "And you know what, it would be pretty difficult if you wanted to go home." Peter watched him closely for his reaction. He knew Paul wasn't an idiot. Paul knew what had happened almost four years ago and understood the situation. The question was whether he was more willing to play along.

Paul nodded slowly, understanding.

Peter exhaled with relief. Paul was going to play along. Peter held his breath as Paul started to speak, "If we stay here another five years, it will probably be too long for my dog. I left Astro at home with my brother Andrew. He'll not survive another five years." Paul stared at the table. His voice sounded smaller, "If there is a way to fly home within the next five years," he looked up, "I'd like to take it."

Peter smiled and nodded, "I understand. No problem." Peter wrote something down before handing Paul his thank you for all the good work letter.

Paul took the letter from Peter and thanked him before he got up confidently and went readily back to work, closing the door behind him.

Peter sat back in his chair and smiled to himself before getting up to fetch himself a cup of coffee. He'd earned it, the first meeting was over. When he sat down again, he double checked whether he'd given Paul the correct letter. Then he went and opened the door and waited for Dervla and Patrick. Beatriz had offered to look after Patrick, but Dervla had refused. She wanted to bring him, and Peter didn't mind. Patrick was a sweet kid. He'd just had his third birthday three weeks ago. Peter smiled as he remembered the little birthday party and shook his head as he remembered the delicious cake Steve had baked. Peter had wanted to give Patrick something special but hadn't managed to get the present ready in time. Now it was finished, and Peter wanted to give it to him today.

Patrick came running into the room and skidded to a stop nearly dropping what he was holding. Peter smiled broadly when he saw him. With his green eyes and short reddish-brown hair, Patrick was a good-looking boy. Peter wondered where the reddish-brown hair came from, it wasn't from Dervla with her brown hair. Dervla's arrival brought him back and he offered them seats.

Dervla sat on one of the offered chairs, but Patrick didn't want to sit on a chair at all. It was much more comfortable on the floor, where there was enough space to play with his new toy. Paul had given him a mini toolbox with small wheels for his birthday and he was still holding it in his arms. As soon as

Patrick sat on the floor, he saw a marvellous hiding place. Patrick shuffled along on his bottom until he was under Peter's desk and then started playing quietly with his toolbox. Dervla looked apologetic, but Peter just shrugged his shoulders, if Patrick wanted to play under the desk, it was perfectly fine. Peter looked under the table and checked to see exactly where Patrick was. He didn't want to accidentally kick him.

Before Peter could say anything, Dervla spoke, "You don't understand my work. Do you think you can judge it?"

Peter was momentarily stunned, but he managed to quickly recover, "To be honest, you're right. I have no idea about your work. I assume you want a contract of employment extension to keep going with your research?"

She nodded. She was glad she would have the opportunity to continue her research.

Peter asked seriously, "How much raise do you want?"

Dervla thought briefly before she said, "Does it really make a difference?"

Peter silently pleaded with her to play along with the situation. She didn't respond so he said, "Please. It's a game. Play along. Imagine that fifteen percent could mean something when you live at home again." He waited a moment for a reaction. She seemed to be thinking, so he added, "And because you are working a double shift, you also get credits on your environment and social responsibility account."

Dervla nodded gently and watched him.

Peter was satisfied with her response, "And I have something for Patrick too." He looked under the desk to see if Patrick had heard. He didn't seem to have noticed, so Peter said louder, "I have a belated birthday present for someone."

Patrick looked up and turned around excitedly. A present. His face lit up. Peter put his hand under the table and handed the brown paper packet to Patrick, who grabbed it out of Peter's hands and then quickly ripped off the wrapping, which he threw carelessly to the side. He recognised the colour of the soft fabric immediately and laughed gleefully before trying on the cute little captain's hat. With a huge grin, he jumped up to proudly show his mother, unfortunately the cap was a little too big and the jumping caused the cap to fall over his eyes, Patrick laughed again and pushed up the cap, so he could see again.

Dervla laughed with him and told Patrick that he looked good before she bent down to pick up the thrown away wrapping paper.

Peter smiled and shook his head, "Don't worry about the wrapping paper. I'll take care of it." And he watched as Patrick ran out of the room to go and show his new present to his friend Paul.

Laughing, Dervla followed Patrick out of the office. As she walked through the door, she looked at the tracking device to see where he was going. She left the door open behind her.

Beatriz was in a good mood as she arrived punctually. She came straight in without knocking and closed the door behind her. They both nodded and smiled warmly. She sat down directly opposite from Peter and smiled before saying, "I can't believe five years have passed."

Peter saw no reason for small talk, not with Beatriz, "Do you want to hear the offer?"

Beatriz let out a brief loud laugh, "Not really, but I suppose I should pretend it is important."

Peter forced himself to use a professional tone and said, "You'll get an employment contract extension for another five years, a salary increase of fifteen percent and because you are working a double shift, you automatically get credits on your environment and social responsibility account."

Seemingly unimpressed, Beatriz thanked him briefly before she changed the subject, "I suggest that we conduct additional medical examinations. I'm worried about the effects of cosmic radiation."

Peter agreed, "Yes, especially for Paul."

Beatriz suggested, "Liam could increase the cosmic radiation deflection field. It costs more energy, but we can afford it, and no one is monitoring our budget." Ironically, she added, "We don't want to get Moon Madness."

Peter nodded and remained quiet. He didn't like the thought that no one was monitoring them.

Beatriz continued, "We have DNA-targeted drugs that are a kind of immune system booster, but you can't use them all the time, otherwise they could attack the body, similar to an autoimmune disease."

Peter nodded. He thought it was a good idea.

Beatriz continued, "Liam has already helped me, and we have installed a Robotician in the infirmary. None of us are getting younger."

Peter was pleasantly surprised, "One of Robotician's new models. They're as good as an eye check at the opticians."

Beatriz smiled, "Yes, and I suggest that everyone undergoes a thorough five-year health check. Including a session with the Robotician."

Peter was pleased. The conversation had gone perfectly well. He handed her the letter and said, "Thank you. They're great suggestions. Can you make sure it happens?"

She agreed and thanked him for the contract extension.

He watched her leave. He hadn't expected any problems from Beatriz and she hadn't disappointed him, however he couldn't say that about Steve, who was next.

Steve was standing right outside, already waiting as Beatriz walked out, he almost pushed past her to get into the room. He sat down without being invited and demanded to know what the significance was with the order of the meetings.

Peter sighed he knew this was coming but he'd considered the consequences if he had given Steve the first meeting. Peter tried to assure him that there was no significance to the order of the meetings. The list had been put together by chance.

Steve didn't look like he believed Peter and insisted, "Why was Paul before me? Does he have precedence?"

Peter defended himself in a quiet, controlled voice, "Liam is scheduled after you. Does that mean you have precedence over him?"

Steve ignored Peter's reply, and he changed the subject. He had something else he wanted to argue about, "If you are giving me a new employment contract, I want a raise, and a promotion."

Peter sensed his growing impatience with Steve. He was always looking for trouble, where it didn't exist. Peter replied in a tired slow voice, "You can have whatever you want."

Steve lent forward and said in a quiet calm voice, "It's part of the game," and then he almost pleaded, "Please play your part. Otherwise it's no fun."

Peter nodded and understood immediately. This was Steve's game. This was how Steve was trying to keep himself sane. He thought, people try and control their world in different ways. Peter looked stern and said, "Your work is satisfactory, and we would like to renew your contract of employment for another five years. Would you like to extend your contract of employment?"

"Yes."

"I'm offering a ten percent pay rise, and because you're working a double shift, you automatically get credit on your environment and social responsibility account."

Steve leaned his head to the left, stroked his chin and said with a harsh tone, "Fifty percent pay rise and thank you for the credits."

Peter played along, "I can go to fifteen percent and not a penny more."

Without smiling, Steve suggested, "Thirty-five percent."

Peter looked him directly in the eyes and shook his head gently from side to side while mouthing no.

Steve looked at him for a few seconds before saying, "Twenty-five."

Peter smiled and nodded relieved. They had an agreement and shook hands amicably.

Steve relaxed in his seat and became friendly almost chatty as he suggested, "I mean if we are staying longer, I could increase the cosmic radiation deflection field. We don't want to get Moon Madness. Although, I think some people might already be affected." Steve didn't say he meant Europa.

Peter already knew his opinion and decided not to react to the provocation and quietly thought that Steve had got the idea about the radiation deflection field idea from Beatriz. Peter made a note to avoid having to say anything.

It annoyed Steve that Peter hadn't commented on his excellent idea. He sounded bitter as he added, "We're only living for today and never think about the future. We know that there are only three escape pods each for three people that means nine people can return, and with Patrick there are ten of us." His expression was hard, "I want you to assure me that I belong to the nine who will get the chance to return. I'm not giving up my chance of getting back."

Peter wanted to laugh, but he managed to stay serious, "I understand, I'll put your name on the returners list." Peter didn't have a list and wasn't going to make one, but that seemed to pacify him.

Steve seemed satisfied and even sounded upbeat when he said, "I suggest that we start a new custom. Every fifth year there should be a celebration, with food and wine. I could cook something special if you want."

Peter struggled to smile in agreement. He knew that Steve was a trained cook and was good at it. It was also a great proposal, but the implication that they would remain another five years worried him.

Steve accepted the responsibility of organising the event willingly and got up smiling. He nodded politely and said pleasantly, "We'll meet again in five years." He closed the door behind him.

Peter glanced at the clock on the wall. The meeting with Steve hadn't lasted as long as he'd expected, and that meant he now had a few minutes to himself. He tried relaxing, but it wasn't working. He was worried about the upcoming meeting with Liam. He folded his arms and shut his eyes. He tried not to worry. He looked at the clock again and noticed it was time. He checked the door camera if Liam was there. He wasn't. Peter opened the door remotely and waited patiently, but Liam didn't come. He was late. Liam was never normally late. Peter wanted to get this meeting over and done with. He wondered if something had happened and decided to go and get him. When he got there Liam was working. He stood quietly behind Liam and waited to see if he would notice him.

Liam's head remained perfectly still while he stared at one of the monitors. He could feel Peter's presence and was trying to ignore him. It didn't last long before Liam said, "I wanted to see if we can increase the cosmic radiation deflection field."

Peter's voice was gentle but firm, "Are you coming?"

Liam got up slowly and followed Peter to his office. Peter closed the door firmly before going to sit in his chair. Once there, he leaned forward a little. He wanted to reduce the distance between him and Liam. He looked squarely at Liam and kept his face friendly. His arms were on the table and his hands were touching with the palms showing, "Your work is excellent. I honestly don't know what we'd do without you. Would you like to renew your contract of employment for another five years?"

Sounding both tense and defensive, Liam asked, "Do I have a choice?"

Peter's deep fatherly voice sounded caring, "Not really, but it's probably easier if you believe it's your decision."

Liam leaned forward, his expression hardened, and he straightened his back as he said slowly and deliberately, "If it's my decision. I never want to go back."

Peter held his body still and without smiling, nodded once, "I know."

Liam looked defiant, as if he didn't believe Peter.

Peter forced himself to speak with a steady neutral voice, "The personnel files were automatically released as the contracts came up for renewal." He looked at Liam closely, "I alone have read them, no one else."

Liam remained quiet and watched Peter closely.

Peter's gaze flicked between the desk and Liam as he lowered his voice to hide both his nervousness and his awkwardness as he said, "I know you're a paedophile and you were in prison for four years."

Liam sank a little in his chair, he seemed smaller and didn't look at Peter as he answered, "I did part of my Moononaut training in prison." He looked briefly into Peter's eyes and then turned his gaze back to the desk.

Peter went red in the face. He didn't want to, but he had to say it. He was responsible for order on the Moon Base. He felt uncomfortable and it was reflected in his voice, "Patrick is only three years old. He should be able to grow up unharmed."

Liam froze, his facial muscles became rock-hard and his words were spoken slowly, clearly and deliberately, "I've never touched Patrick and I've no intention of getting anywhere near him."

Peter was watching Liam closely. Trying to decide if he was a risk to Patrick.

Liam's voice was quiet and sounded both pained and honest, "After prison I came to the Moon because there aren't any children here." He looked at Peter defiantly, "I want to stay here. I've found peace here. A peace I will never again find on Earth."

Peter remained silent and looked at Liam. He didn't know what to say.

Liam continued talking quietly, "I moved as far away from children as possible." He paused, plagued by the pain of admitting his guilt, then he looked at Peter directly and said, "Yes, I'm still a paedophile, but I've decided never to act on it again."

Peter looked at him closely. He still wasn't sure what to say.

Liam felt angry and challenged Peter, "It wasn't my idea for a child to come here." His brief anger spent, he became more appeasing and his voice sounded softer, "I'll never do anything against the law again. I realise it doesn't matter what I do, everyone will always hate me. I've come to terms with that." He looked down into his lap and whispered, "I just want to be left alone."

When they looked at each other, Peter could clearly see Liam's remorse and sadness.

Peter was curious, "Before we lost contact, did you control the flow of information?"

Liam turned his chair to the left, "Yes, but there was nothing to control during your shift."

"And during your previous shift?"

With an open gesture Liam nodded, "I'm not an idiot."

Peter looked at him closely.

Liam looked Peter directly in the eye and said, "I just wanted to protect myself. I still have morals. I know the difference between good and evil." As he spoke, he sounded more and more desperate. Liam looked at his hands, wrung them, and breathed deeply in and out before he said in a soft serious tone, "I have no intention of hurting anyone to make myself feel better." The determination and clarity of his statement was unmistakable.

However, Peter believed that it was necessary to warn Liam, "Sometimes it gets very hot in the Moon Base. We sit ninety percent of the time in the Sun. It can get way too hot in here without temperature control. I'm in charge of temperature control. Can we work together?"

Liam understood Peter's indirect reference and recognised the mollifying note in Peter's tone, "Yes, we can, but I don't want anything to do with the child."

Peter handed Liam his letter and they both said a respectful goodbye before Liam returned to his work.

As Peter watched Liam leave his stomach rumbled and reminded him that it was time for a break, and to get something to eat. He fetched something small from the canteen and returned to his office, closed the door firmly and turned to Meichun and asked, "How are you?"

Meichun's attempts at small talk were improving and Peter enjoyed the distraction while he ate his lunch. He avoided thinking about the meetings. He could do that later.

Europa came after his lunchbreak. She was, as he'd expected, punctual and before she came he'd opened the door. She walked straight in and glared at him for a few seconds. Looked pointedly at her watch and then at Peter. She raised her eyebrows to signal that they should start.

Peter smiled, he liked the simplicity and predictability of Europa, "Thank you for coming. Is it okay if Meichun listens?"

She nodded uninterested.

He refrained from commenting on her work and deliberately avoided any small talk, "Do you want to extend your contract of employment for another five years?"

Europa's expression was serious and her voice level, "I welcome the opportunity to continue my research."

"That's good. Do you want to know about the terms of the contract?"

She bowed her head and without enthusiasm said, "Yes."

"You'll get a fifteen percent pay rise, and because you are working a double shift, you also get credits on your environment and social responsibility account." Peter avoided smiling.

Europa nodded satisfied and changed the subject, "I thought about the cause of the loss of communication. There might have been a gamma-ray burst from Betelgeuse supernova. It could have destroyed half the atmosphere. This is only speculation."

Peter was pleased, "Meichun can integrate this into their search program. Maybe we'll find something. Is there anything else you want to say?"

Europa looked concerned, but her voice remained steady, "Yes, the next international vote will take place soon and I'd like to cast my vote."

Peter hesitated before asking, "You know it's not possible?"

She bowed her head, "My sister Callisto probably has a proxy vote."

Peter looked at her a little perplexed and realised this was what she needed – this was her game. With a serious expression he replied in a deep voice, "Yes, probably."

He passed Europa her letter. She took it and got up, signalling that the meeting was over.

Peter thanked her as she left and wished her lots of fun with her work. He thought that she had almost smiled as she'd left.

Peter stood up and walked around the office. He needed to stretch his legs. Something about Europa's demeanour had disturbed him. He couldn't put it into words and found it frustrating as he tried to work it out. He didn't noticed Maria when she arrived. He heard as she sat down. He looked at her and smiled but Maria's sadness took away his smile. He let her talk.

She didn't look at him and spoke quietly, "I miss my family. Especially my sister. Another five years away from home will be hard."

He nodded and waited.

He listened to her confess to both of them, "I don't want to fly home in one of the escape capsules. I'm scared."

Peter felt sorry for her but knew he needed to do his job, "Do you want to know the terms of the offer?"

She shook her head and shrugged her shoulders.

He tried to make the offer sound exciting, "You get extra credits on your environment and social responsibility account and a fifteen percent salary increase."

She smiled a little and nodded accepting the terms.

He'd thought she'd be pleased about the environmental credits. She seemed so sad and he wanted to cheer her up but didn't know what to say. He tried, "You have a new necklace."

She looked down at her necklace and smiled a little, "It's the same one Beatriz gave me. I've just adjusted the shape and colours."

He thanked her for the good work and handed her the letter.

She thanked him and holding the letter against her necklace, stood up to leave. As she opened the door. Peter saw Charlie already standing there. Peter watched as Charlie whispered something to Maria who nodded and continued on her way without saying anything.

Peter welcomed Charlie into the room. Pleased to see him and not only because he was the last one.

Charlie came in smiling broadly and sat himself down with a plump across from Peter.

Peter was pleased that it didn't seem to bother him that he was the last.

Charlie remarked, "Maria smiled at me. She seemed in a good mood."

Peter's impression had been different, but he didn't contradict Charlie, he just asked him, "How is everything going with you? Any complaints, problems?"

Charlie shrugged his shoulders and pulled an ambivalent face, "I'm very happy."

Peter smiled and thought, happy that he has more time with Maria. Peter explained to Charlie about the raise and the credits. And asked him if he wanted to extend his contract.

Charlie grinned and said enthusiastically, "Of course. The offer is more than I'd expected. I would have been satisfied without a raise." He put his hand to his mouth and looked as if he wished he hadn't said that.

Peter laughed and asked him about his work with the drones.

Charlie had just finished some improvements with the drone control system and explained that they seemed to be working much better than before, but unfortunately not yet when Maria was around.

Peter listened to him carefully and laughed at Charlie's jokes.

Charlie chatted about how he liked working in the gardens, and now and then he helped Paul. He thought work was going well and his life on the Moon was just great. He was smiling the whole time he talked.

Peter enjoyed Charlie's positive energy and when he stopped talking, he gave Charlie his letter and thanked him for the good work.

After Charlie had left, Peter sat up straight and breathed in and out deeply. He'd made it. The fifteen percent had worked out brilliantly. Nobody had expected so much, because most of the time they got between 0.5 and 1 percent. Although Steve always wanted more. He hoped that he would never have to justify his decision to Columbus.

He felt good that the reviews were over for another five years, and he hoped that they could carry on with their daily lives. He took off his captain's hat, put it on the desk, leaned back in his chair, closed his eyes and relaxed.

Moonday Six

Date: Monday 2nd October 2147 – 06:07 CET
Location: Alpha 12 – Moon Base

Patrick's heavy eyelids fell back shut as he tried to open them. His mouth fell open and he dribbled as he turned his head while trying to lift it off the pillow. His eyes flickered registering the regulated early morning light, but his head wobbled unsteadily as he tried opening his eyes again, it felt like a dead weight on his straining neck muscles. His head was still too heavy with sleep. He let it fall gently back onto the soft pillow of his mother's bed before turning onto his side and snuggling up with his face under the duvet.

The top of his head was poking out and something was interrupting his warm cosy world under the duvet. He could hear soft, gentle music and could feel someone touching his hair, someone gently and lovingly stroking his hair, he tried opening his eyes again, and he wasn't sure if he'd managed it. He turned over and forced his eyes to open enough to make out a blurred picture of his mother. He recognised her beautiful smile, and the familiar curves of her face before sleep took over again. He turned towards where his mother was sitting and put his arms around her.

Dervla wasn't mad at Patrick for sneaking into her bed during night. For once, it was all right because today was his sixth birthday. She smiled and tousled his hair again while saying his name softly a few times and trying to remind him that it was time to get up if he wanted to meet Maria before sunrise.

She knew he wanted to wake up and go to the main garden with Maria. With his eyes still shut, he began to move his arms and legs jerkily. She turned him onto his back and wiped his drowsy face with a small damp cloth, and then she watched the heaviness of sleep begin to leave his face. His eyes opened, and he smiled sweetly at his mother and heard her say, "Happy birthday my son," as she put her hand gently on his cheek.

She opened the drawer of the bedside table, and, like she did every year, took out a little wake up present for Patrick. He sat up wide awake, wanting to open the gift immediately. The wrapping paper flew to the side and he stuffed the candy greedily in his mouth.

Dervla helped him get up and sent him to the bathroom to brush his teeth. After a few minutes he came back with toothpaste all around his mouth smiling broadly. He ran back to his mother, who was lying on the bed, and gave her a hug. Dervla laughed quietly and motherly. She got up, wiped Patrick's face again and said to him, "What are you going to wear today? Go to your room and choose something sensible."

He returned a short time later with a colourful pile of clothes and dropped them to the floor in the middle of the room. On top of the pile lay his captain's hat. He took a big step backwards, put his arms on his hips and smiled proudly as he looked at his great work of art. She reminded him gently about getting dressed. He looked at the pile a little puzzled he wasn't sure where he was supposed to start.

Dervla watched him in his indecision lovingly for a few moments before saying, "Get dressed, as I showed you." Her voice sounded gentle and caring.

Patrick looked at her in confusion.

"Choose your vest and underpants."

Patrick rummaged through the pile and chose his clothes, letting the others fall in a pile to the side. He clumsily took off his pyjamas and dropped them on the floor and needed a few attempts with the underwear.

Dervla watched his clumsiness and smiled. The colour mixture fascinated her. His choice of clothing was a startling mixture of blue, violet and white. He was particularly fond of violet and bright white clothes. After dressing himself correctly, he proudly stood up straight and showed her the result. She laughed spontaneously at his seriousness.

Dervla affectionately reminded him, "Put on your captain's hat."

Patrick picked up the hat and put it on his head with great satisfaction. He was big enough now, and it fitted him really well. It no longer fell over his eyes when he moved his head.

"Should I come with you or do you want to go alone to Maria?"

In reply to her question, he ran out of the room to go and look for Maria in the main garden. He ran down the flights of stairs, continued running through the Moon Base towards the main garden. Maria had promised him that if he could get up early enough, she would show him a wonderful natural spectacle for his birthday and he couldn't wait.

She was waiting in the garden surveillance station. She had been relaxing with a cup of coffee in her hand and looking at the monitors as she slowly came around. She'd delayed sunrise by half an hour to give Patrick a better chance of getting up on time.

Maria had increased the daylight hours in the garden after Patrick had been born. At first, they'd had an extra hour of daylight in the gardens, but it turned out that it wasn't necessary. People preferred more daylight, but her plants didn't. Plants also needed to sleep, and Maria wanted to keep them healthy. They had discussed the issue a few months later, and everyone had agreed to twelve and a half hours of daylight. She'd thought about delaying sunrise for longer this morning, she knew she could do that without damaging the plants, but she didn't want to, because they didn't jeopardise the plants' metabolism and anyway it was more exciting for Patrick to have to get up early.

Completely out of breath, Patrick stopped in front of Maria and grinned. She saw the excitement in his face as he jumped up and down on the spot a few times. He pulled a face when he landed the last time, as if he was in pain, but it was only brief, not long enough for Maria to react to her momentary concern. He could barely stand still as he looked around searching for his present. He wanted to know what it was.

It warmed Maria's heart when she saw him and felt his unquestioning enthusiasm. This was his present to Maria and she loved him for it.

Maria stood up and pointed to where they needed to go. Patrick walked up to her and slid his hand into hers and they walked together through the shadowy moonlit garden. The artificial moonlight was created by a row of white lights mounted high on an arc in the ceiling. The row of lights allowed her to create the impression of a moving moonlight. The last light in the row was illuminated. It was just before moonset.

Soon they stood in front of the moonflowers exhibition, which were blooming at this time of night, or more precisely in this light. The white climbing plants were impressive with their fifteen-centimetre diameters, and Patrick thought they looked like little moons. He told Maria that they looked like the pictures of the Moon that Paul had shown him the day before. Maria glanced at him as he marvelled and pointed excitedly at the flowers, and it occurred to her that he'd never seen the Moon in the sky, that he'd never even seen real moonlight.

These were some of Maria's favourite flowers and she knew that he'd only seen the flowers during the daytime when they were closed. She asked Patrick, "The white flowers are beautiful. Aren't they?"

Patrick smiled and replied, "I like the white and violet colours."

Maria looked at him to see if he was serious. The flowers were white. She didn't want to spoil the mood and chose not to correct him.

Maria pointed to one of the low laying flowers, "Look, the blossom is bigger than your hand."

Patrick lay his hand on it and giggled, the petals tickled his palm.

"Moonflowers can only endure daylight for about twelve hours a day. If there is too much light, the seeds don't form." Maria smiled as she explained, "Plants need to relax in moonlight to survive." Maria looked at Patrick to see if he was listening.

He was listening avidly.

"They don't like direct sunlight either, so we use the filter windows." She pointed up to the dome ceiling. The filter windows were closed to keep the sunlight out, "The filter windows can reflect the sunlight back completely or only partially and imitate the conditions of clouds."

Patrick seemed confused.

Maria reminded him, "Paul showed you the film about the weather on Earth there were clouds, they bring rain."

He still looked puzzled.

"Rain is when water falls from the sky." She was looking at him to see if he had understood.

He nodded and seemed to understand.

Maria continued, "They grow in the shade of the trees which is best seen during the daytime. You've already seen them during the day, do you remember?" She smiled at Patrick and continued, "If they get too much light, the flowers don't feel very well, and they don't produce any fruit." She showed Patrick one of the moonflower fruits. It was a small, conically shaped capsule. Maria took it and placed it on Patrick's hand.

He looked at the fruit curiously before carefully poking it with his finger.

She showed him how to open it, so he could see the black seeds inside. Patrick laughed and squashed the fruit and seeds on his hand. It felt spiny and cold. After a while Patrick looked at the mess in his hand and gave it to Maria. She had a small compost bag in her pocket and while smiling, she packed it away before putting it in her pocket, "We'll take it to the compost heap later."

Patrick nodded excitedly.

Maria touched his cheek gently and said, "You're my beautiful moonflower. You're so sweet and cute."

Patrick grinned. He liked Maria.

Charlie was hiding in the garden with his robots, listening in on the conversation between Maria and Patrick, and he couldn't believe that he was jealous of a six-year-old child. He tried to get his emotions under control. He needed to be calm otherwise he wouldn't be able to control the robots and he'd promised Maria that he'd do a special robot show for Patrick's birthday. He was pleased that he had pre-programmed the robots just in case he wasn't able to think clearly. He saw Maria's signal and started the automatic program. Then he stood back and watched as the robots flew out of their hiding places. He watched as Patrick clapped his hands with joy. The robots took their positions and with their lights shining they formed in the shape of a giant flower.

Patrick wriggled and squeaked with glee. The robots held position before one after the other they started to fly in a figure eight and do a celebration bee dance. While they danced, the song "Happy Birthday" started played in the background. Patrick grinned and held Maria's hand while he pulled her to come and look in the bushes for Charlie. Then Patrick stopped and looked. One of the robots had broken formation. It flew close to the moonflowers and picked a single beautiful flower and flew over Patrick's head before dropping the flower at his feet. Patrick grinned as he picked it up. He looked up at Maria wondering what he should do next.

She took the flower from his hand and attached it to his lapel, "You're my moonflower."

Charlie couldn't help himself and was glad that the robots had parked themselves safely, without him having to use the emergency park button. He felt jealous again. He rushed to go to Maria and Patrick and when he found them he forced himself to smile politely. The three of them stood together and watched sunrise over the garden. They watched as the light from the last of the large round, white moonlight lamps gradually faded away, and the filter windows slowly opened and let the strong sunlight come in.

Maria suggested that they go to the compost heap to dispose of the rest of the moonflower fruit. On the way there, she explained how they reused or recycled everything in the gardens. She said this as she placed the plastic bag into one of the Re-Do machines. Then she added thoughtfully, "We don't want to pollute the Moon, not like they did on Earth in the past."

Patrick was confused, "But why do people pollute the Earth? Don't they want to go on living there?"

Maria looked at him and with a forced smile unsure how she was going to answer. It seemed somehow inappropriate to show Patrick an angry reaction on his birthday. She was relieved when she saw Paul walking around the corner.

Paul went straight to Patrick, bent down and shook his hand, "Happy birthday Patrick. Are you hungry?"

Patrick's eyes opened wide and he grinned and nodded energetically, "Yeah, yeah, yeah."

Paul grinned, glanced at the others checking for any objections and said, "Then let's go to the canteen." Paul poked Patrick gently on the shoulder and said, "Are we playing tag on the way there? Or are you too grown-up now?"

Patrick tagged Paul and ran as fast as he could without saying anything.

Paul watched him go. He wasn't worried about finding Patrick, who couldn't keep quiet and whose giggling always gave his position away, and if Patrick didn't give himself away Paul could track his clothes. He looked at Maria and Charlie, "See you in the canteen. I'll chase him there." Then he shouted, "I'm coming to get you!"

Patrick was crouched behind a bend in the path and held his hand tightly over his mouth trying to stop the sound of the giggling. When he saw Paul's shadow appear Patrick held his breath and stopped giggling. He thought briefly about running away but only managed to turn his body undecidedly left and then right. Paul appeared and towered over Patrick, who looked up at him in panic.

As Paul slowly bent down to tag Patrick, he jumped up and ran off towards the canteen.

Paul shouted after him, "You're too fast for me." Then started running after him.

Out of breath both Paul and Patrick arrived at the canteen almost at the same time. Patrick looked at Paul and defending himself with his hands said, "Time out. Time out."

Paul agreed, and they went laughing into the canteen. Maria and Charlie were already there and had started preparing breakfast. They all sat down at one table together. As Paul sat opposite Patrick, he noticed the flower barely clinging on to Patrick's lapel. Paul thought, it looked pretty limp. Although, he considered it could have looked worse after their little game. He snorted and thought but not much worse, at least the flower was still hanging in there. He smiled cheerfully, pointed at the flower and asked, "Where did you get the flower from?"

Patrick sat up straight, wriggled his shoulders up and forward, and with a smug tone he said, "It's a moonflower, and Maria gave it to me."

Paul wanted to laugh, but managed to look disinterested and teased Patrick, "It looks withered."

"Moonflowers only open and look beautiful when there is artificial moonlight," and with a serious look and sounding very grown-up, Patrick recited Maria's lesson. His expression changed completely, and he grinned as he said, "Maria showed me moonflowers in bloom in the moonlight for my birthday."

Charlie teased Patrick, "You're usually asleep and miss the moonflowers."

Paul laughed suddenly as he realised that today was Monday, the day of the Moon. His voice sounded soft and slow as he thoughtfully said, "Today is a Monday and you saw the moonflowers." His brow furrowed, "You were born on a Monday, weren't you?"

Patrick's full mouth opened a little as he nodded, and a little piece of food fell onto the table top.

Paul didn't notice it and continued, "This means we can say that today's Moonday."

Maria and Charlie looked at him funny.

He added quickly, "It is a mixture of moonflower and Monday. And I think it's good."

Paul watched while Charlie pulled a serious, thoughtful face and nodded in agreement, and while Maria's eyebrows moved to convey her more sceptical opinion. Paul took a deep breath while he thought and said, "If the first Moonday took place six years ago, we've now had six Moondays." He smiled and looked at the others waiting for them to say how clever he was.

Patrick laughed and announced very loudly, "I have the same birthday as the Moon."

It occurred to both Maria and Charlie what Paul had badly explained and they liked the idea and they all laughed together as they continued with their breakfast.

After breakfast, Paul and Patrick went hand in hand to the next part of Patrick's gift. Astro was already waiting at the Re-Do machines in the second laboratory. Paul tried to sound as suspenseful as possible as he explained, "Today I'll show you how to empty a Re-Do machine. Usually the Sauberbots do it, but today we're going to see how the machine looks and works from the inside."

Paul knocked gently on the top of the Re-Do machine, the hydraulic control system responded and opened the lid smoothly and silently. Paul lifted Patrick up, so he could see inside and gave Patrick the small piece of plastic, that he had brought with him and with a warning that he should watch out for his Pulsera, he told Patrick to drop the plastic into the machine. There was a clang as the plastic hit the bottom of the machine.

Paul joked, "Now the nanobots have something to eat."

Patrick laughed and then Paul began with his explanation of the machine's workings, "The nanobots are going to eat the plastic we dropped in, and they will turn it into an oil-like liquid, which is normally a mixture of different types of plastic. The machine then sorts out the dyes and fillers separating them between metallic and non-metallic."

Patrick was listening intently.

Paul felt encouraged by his interest, "The fillers mostly consist of materials like carbonic lime and they belong in the non-metallic group. After the sorting the next step of the recycling process, is to separate the materials on a finer level so they can be prepared for reuse." Paul looked at Patrick again, who seemed to have lost interest and was looking at something behind the machine.

Paul tried another way, "Do you want to close the cover?"

Patrick nodded eagerly.

Patrick pressed the cover gently. You didn't need much force to close the lid. You just needed to trigger the hydraulic system. The protective cover closed tightly over the machine and a warning light flashed as the machine started. Paul put Patrick down on the floor and they listened to the Re-Do machine as it worked.

Paul explained, "Closing the lid wakes up the nanobots and we're waiting for them to finish eating the plastic. They won't go back to sleep until they've eaten all the plastic. After they have gone back to sleep we can open the protective cover again." Paul looked seriously at Patrick, "Never try to open the protective cover while the machine is running."

Patrick looked worried and sounded scared, "Are the nanobots dangerous?"

Paul sounded undecided, "Yes, but don't worry, they are carefully locked up and the warning light flashes when the machine is running." Paul smiled at Patrick, "And you know what, I've never heard of one malfunctioning."

The nanobots didn't need long and as soon as the warning lamp went out Paul opened the top cover and then he knocked on the side of the machine to open it. He pointed to the bottom left of the inside of the machine and said to Patrick, "Look, there are the containers for the metallic and non-metallic materials. You can pull them out like drawers."

There was a larger container next to them and that contained the plastic raw material. Paul took the empty and cleaned containers out of the cabinet next to the Re-Do machine and replaced the drawers before explaining to Patrick that full containers needed to be taken to the warehouses where the Sauberbots would empty and store the materials, before cleaning the containers and bringing them back to the cupboard.

Patrick was curious, "Can we make something out of the plastic?"

Paul looked disappointed, "It's not that simple. Most of the time we store the raw materials to be sent back to Earth. We could reuse some of it, but the dyes and fillers have to be further processed before they can be reused."

They loaded the containers on an equipment cart and left them there for the Sauberbots to transport to the warehouses. Paul looked at his watch, "We have to go and see Beatriz and your mother will be waiting there for us."

As they arrived in the infirmary, Beatriz was speaking sternly to Dervla. As soon as she saw Patrick, she stopped and smiled him. She beckoned him to come over to her, "Happy birthday and that means today is your birthday medical appointment." Without letting Patrick see, Beatriz cast a quick glare at Dervla.

Patrick waved happily to Paul as he left to go to the canteen.

With a practised carefree tone Beatriz asked, "Does it hurt anywhere today?"

Patrick pulled a face and said, "Sometimes my knees hurt when I jump."

Beatriz asked Patrick to lay down and while he slid into a big white machine she said, "Stay as still as possible." She looked serious as soon as he couldn't see her anymore and she waited a minute before smiling at Patrick as he came out.

She had the result immediately on the monitor. Beatriz opened one of her drawers and took out a couple of prepared needles and injected the contents into Patrick's knees while she asked him, "Have you eaten cake yet?"

With a sad expression, he shook his head.

Beatriz's voice became higher than normal, "You haven't eaten any cake on your birthday. Should I believe you?"

Patrick denied it violently.

The medical examination was finished, and Beatriz sent Patrick to the canteen to join the others before she turned to Dervla and asked, "Did you do something with his DNA? It's very unusual that six-year-olds get an autoimmune disease like juvenile rheumatoid arthritis."

Dervla remained calm, "He is the first child to grow up on the Moon. We've no idea what this means for the human body."

Beatriz thought she didn't answer the question, but she felt obliged to respect Patrick and Dervla's privacy, "He can come for the injections whenever he needs them."

Dervla ignored her kindness and replied abruptly, "His Pulsera monitors the disease. If it gets bad, I'll know."

Beatriz's sounded a little worried, "What exactly are you monitoring?"

Dervla didn't answer and went to the canteen.

The birthday party in the canteen wasn't due to take place until lunchtime, even so all the others were already there and waiting for Beatriz and Dervla to arrive. Patrick was impatient because he could see the presents on the table and he wanted to know what he was getting. Paul nodded to the others and then took a step forward and dramatically lifted a black blanket from a small box shaped present. Patrick squealed as he saw a little mouse crouching in the corner of its cage. He was thrilled his mother had given him a mouse.

Mysteriously and in a scary voice Dervla announced, "There is something you should know. Could somebody dim the lights?"

Charlie was prepared. He turned off the lights and closed the filter windows. The canteen was completely dark until Dervla turned her UV torch on. Patrick giggled with glee. The twenty-eight-day-old mouse was glowing green under the ultraviolet light.

As soon as Charlie turned the lights back on Steve pointed out the cake he had made to Patrick. He had baked a special birthday cake. It even had a captain's hat on top. Patrick wanted to eat a piece right away, but Dervla insisted that he waited until he'd seen all the presents.

Patrick got birthday cards and a few small presents from the others, which he unwrapped quickly and put safely in a pile on the table. When he was finished Peter presented him with a certificate for a year's worth of good behaviour and completing another year of school. Patrick grinned as he took the certificate. He'd got his first certificate last year when he turned five and now he had two. The first one was already hanging on the wall in his bedroom. Patrick thanked Peter and took the certificate and placed it carefully on the table next to his other presents.

Peter watched him handling the certificate carefully and thought he's going to expect this next year. I've done it twice, and it's now become a custom.

Patrick looked around and asked, "Why didn't Liam come?"

Peter replied quickly, "He's got a lot of work and can't come today."

Somehow it sounded like a lie to the others, but nobody said anything. Paul distracted Patrick, "Who has the same birthday as the Moon?"

Patrick laughed amused and lifting his chest in pride, "I have the same birthday as the Moon."

Paul agreed enthusiastically, "And today is Moonday."

Patrick was enjoying the attention and was proud of himself, "I saw moonflowers with Maria. I had to get up really early."

Steve turned to Maria, "You could easily have been two hours late for sunrise in the main garden."

Maria replied angrily, "I know, but I don't want to confuse the plants. They're used to their daily routine."

Steve mocked, "There are solar eclipses on Earth, and they don't hurt the plants."

Maria countered, "Solar eclipses only last a few minutes and it never really goes completely dark, at most it resembles twilight."

This prompted Europa and she remembered her present, she announced to Patrick, "My present to you is a poster of our solar system, and I'll explain about the celestial bodies in our solar system if you want."

Dervla put her hand on Europa's arm and said, "He's too young for the cosmos explanation. Wait a few years."

Europa nodded and accepted Dervla's observation.

Peter suggested, "How about eating cake before lunch." Steve started cutting up the cake and Charlie passed the plates around. Everyone seemed happy to be there and eating cake.

Peter looked at the people around him and thought on such days it was fun to live on the Moon Base. And then he thought, "Today is Moonday." Then laughed as he dropped some cake on his front.

Moonday Eight

Date: Thursday 2nd October 2149 – 09:03 CET
Location: Alpha 12 – Moon Base

Standing behind Patrick, Beatriz put her hands firmly on his shoulders trying to get him to sit still. She held him for a short while trying to calm him with her steady breathing. As soon as she let him go, he started squirming in his chair.

He couldn't sit still. He was already bored of his birthday medical examination and wanted to go and find Paul. He looked imploringly at Beatriz. It was his eighth birthday and he was sure Paul knew about the presents, his presents.

With a wave of her hand that indicated Patrick could go, Beatriz gave up on the medical examination. She'd finished the necessary tests and knew she could finish up without him.

Patrick grinned broadly and jumped off the chair landing awkwardly before raising his arms and waving them madly over his head as he ran out of the infirmary looking for Paul.

Beatriz watched him go and observed his movements with her trained medical eye as he ran through the doorway. His balance and running style were fine. She was pleased that the rheumatism medication was keeping the pain in his legs and hips under control. Then she remembered his smile, he had John's smile. Beatriz smiled to herself and thought with each birthday he seemed to resemble John more and more, but she didn't know for sure, who the father was. That remained

Dervla's secret. It puzzled Beatriz because she couldn't believe that if John was the father how he could have returned to Earth before Patrick was born. She was curious but respected Dervla's privacy. If Dervla wanted to tell she would.

Beatriz turned to Dervla, "He's in good health. The drugs are working well."

Dervla was looking at the monitor and reached out with her hand almost tapping the display, "Are we running enough tests. I'm worried because we don't know all the effects of raising a child on the Moon."

Beatriz looked at her and tried to judge how serious she was before she nodded and agreed, "This is the first time and you're right we don't know what to look for, but we are monitoring his health and he seems to be developing perfectly normally."

Dervla didn't appear to be fully concentrating on the conversation, "I'd like to know if we could make some improvements to our DNA to make life in space easier."

Beatriz waited a moment before she answered. She had the feeling that Dervla might reveal something about her research. When she did answer she spoke slowly and as neutrally as she could, "Theoretically to achieve a better chance of survival in space, it would be good if we could strengthen bones and make the muscle mass more resistant to wasting away."

Dervla nodded still deep in thought, "And the ability to fight the effects of cosmic radiation, perhaps with an improved immune system. This could prevent cell mutation and improve the body's ability to heal itself."

Beatriz replied light-heartedly, "Unfortunately, we are not Superman." She continued watching Dervla, who seemed lost in her thoughts.

In a very soft tone Dervla said slowly, "I used artificial insemination for him, for Patrick." Then she looked at Beatriz.

Beatriz returned the look and nodded. She wanted to indicate that she had heard but didn't know how to respond. Thoughts were racing through her head: Patrick did resemble John, it was possible that John didn't know that he had a son when he chose to return to Earth. Her mouth opened a little and she stared at Dervla. She didn't dare say anything.

Dervla's voice remained quiet and deep and she looked down at the floor as she said, "I didn't want to miss the chance to have a child." She looked Beatriz in the eyes, "I wanted to make it happen and thought it wouldn't be possible without artificial insemination."

Beatriz kept her voice neutral and slowly asked, "Was it just one egg or were there others?"

Dervla replied factually, "There were several."

Beatriz was curious, and struggled to keep her voice steady as she asked, "How did you decide which egg to use?"

Dervla reacted calmly, "I have an electronic decision-maker that I used to decide which egg to implant. I froze the others."

"An electronic decision-maker." Beatriz's laugh hid her awkwardness and she felt obliged to explain, "I use a coin."

"Really?" Dervla's voice was raised and she looked amazed and curious.

"My great-grandmother gave me the coin, and I still use it when I can't make a decision." Beatriz smiled as she remembered the story her own great-grandmother had told her, "It's over a hundred years old. It was made in 1977." She put her hand in her pocket and held it in the palm of her hand as she showed it to Dervla while telling her, "It was made for the silver anniversary of the Queen of the United Kingdom and it's a collector's item." Beatriz tossed the coin high into the air, and let it fall back on to the palm of her right hand, then she skilfully placed the coin on to the back of her left hand.

Dervla was fascinated, "Can I hold it? I've never had a coin in my hand. I've only ever seen them in a museum."

With her eyes opened wide Dervla turned the coin over in her hands. She felt the hard, cool metal against her skin, and she asked naively, "You didn't ever use coins, did you?"

Beatriz grinned and showed her wrinkles as she shook her head and laughingly denied the statement, "I'm not that old." The lingering echo of her own words sounded like a lie and she suddenly felt old. She looked to see if she could see signs of aging on Dervla and thought they'd been here almost ten years, and none of them were getting any younger.

Patrick had found Paul and Astro in the main warehouse. He was chasing Astro because Paul had hidden Patrick's birthday card and a clue to the present inside his top box. Paul was watching them play and laughing at Patrick's antics in trying to get Astro to stay still.

"Sit. Heel." Patrick shouted and willed Astro to obey.

Astro went running off to hide among the storage corridors.

It took a while before an out of breath Patrick finally managed to get the card. He'd thrown himself on top of Astro and pinned him down. Paul laughed as he heard the tiny wheels spinning frantically. He said, "Game over." Astro stopped trying to escape and Patrick opened the top box and took out his birthday card. He closed the top box carefully and sat on Astro and opened the envelope. There was a card from Paul and an invitation. Patrick read the invitation slowly and then looked up at Paul and sounded worried as he said, "What time is it?"

Paul voice sounded reassuring and almost as if he was laughing, "We have enough time. Don't worry. We'll get there."

"But it's Europa!" Patrick looked and sounded a little scared.

"Let's go then." Paul held his hand out for Patrick to get up and then they both started running.

Europa smiled at them kindly as they ran through the door of the large meeting room. They both stopped out of breath and they greeted Europa politely. She was waiting patiently for them but couldn't resist looking at the clock just to see how many minutes they were late. She looked at them and ordered, "Sit down and pay close attention. Today's topic is moons of our solar system."

Patrick glanced at the chairs set in a neat row and at the desk. He could tell Europa had prepared for the class. He couldn't keep the disappointment out of his face as he said, "I thought there was no school on my birthday." His voice and his shoulders fell at the end of the sentence.

Europa announced, "It's not school. It's better than school. I've put together a special lesson for you and Paul. It is going to be fun." She looked at them sternly.

Paul shuddered involuntarily, sat up straight and started paying attention. Patrick looked at Paul and then at Europa, his internal struggle clearly playing out on his face. He wanted to do something exciting, run around, play catch, anything but sit in a classroom and learn. He was torn but it would be rude to refuse Europa's present. He looked at Paul's behaviour and with a hanging head, and sagging shoulders he sat down again reluctantly next to Paul.

As soon as Patrick sat down his shoulders slumped. Paul looked at him and smiled broadly before gently nudging him a few times as he reassured him, "It'll be fun. Relax." With the index finger of his left hand, Paul tapped on the piece of paper resting on the upside-down photo laying on the table between him and Patrick. Paul picked up the bit of paper and handed it to Europa, "We're particularly interested in these moons. It's a copy of the list I gave you earlier."

Europa glanced at the list of twelve moons and frowned. There wasn't any connection between them, the only fact of significance was that most of them had an almost perfectly round orbit. She was a little puzzled but for some unknown reason, they were important to Paul. She ignored the list in front of Paul and resumed the class.

Europa brought up the first slide of her presentation and cleared her throat before beginning, "The four giant planets Jupiter, Saturn, Uranus and Neptune each have large moons. The larger ones are comparable in size to our own Moon. We don't yet know exactly how these moons formed around their planet, but we do have a lot of theories."

Europa noticed Paul shaking his head.

She skipped to the next slide of the gas giants, "All of the giant planets in our solar system have many smaller moons that are irregularly shaped." Europa showed a picture of some of her favourite moons.

Paul interrupted Europa and asked, "Why are some moons not round?"

Europa seemed a little taken aback but replied respectfully, "If the mass of a moon is too small, then there will not be enough gravity to pull it into a sphere." She looked at Paul questioningly.

He smiled and nodded.

"Some of these irregular small moons are in very close orbit to their planets and are probably debris from larger moons destroyed by collisions or internal tides. There are other irregular moons that orbit much further away from their planet and it is assumed that these were former comets or asteroids that came too close to the planet and got caught in its gravity."

Patrick looked at the picture of the irregular moons on the slide. He didn't fully understand everything Europa said, and it didn't bother him, but he did want to know, "Can a moon have a moon?"

Europa smiled at Patrick. She knew it, he was interested in moons. Her voice sounded both understanding and excited as she explained, "Theoretically yes, but we don't have any in our solar system, however we do know that asteroids can have moons. Asteroid 243 Ida has a moon called Dactyl." She nodded at Patrick thanking him for his question and then smiled to herself before continuing, "The moons in our solar system are very different from each other. One of Jupiter's moons, Io, has over a hundred active volcanoes on its surface that are all full of sulphur."

As she mentioned Io, Paul turned the photo over and tapped on it. Patrick leaned forward to see what he was doing. Paul pointed to a picture of a young Steve. It was a copy of their first team photo. Europa was curious and looked to see what he was doing. Paul gave the list of moons and a pen to Patrick and told him, "Write Steve next to Io."

Europa didn't like the interruption, "What are you doing? Isn't my class interesting enough?"

Paul looked at her and answered apologetically, "I'm sorry, we just want to make a list of nicknames. I'm hoping that we can find a moon nickname for everyone. We won't interrupt, when we find something suitable, we'll quietly write it down." He pulled the most innocent face he could.

Europa breathed in deeply through her nostrils with her hands on her hips. Then she turned and pointed the next slide a yellow picture of Io, "Io is Jupiter's third largest moon, and it is a little larger than our Moon. Its peculiarity is extreme volcanism. Like the Moon, it has a bound rotation."

As Paul asked his voice sounded amused, "What's bound rotation?"

"When a moon is strongly influenced by the gravity of its planet, it rotates with the same side facing its planet." She answered succinctly and then she explained slower, "The orbit of Io is in a 1:2 orbital resonance to Europa." She showed Paul and Patrick a short video of the orbital resonance of the moons around Jupiter. The video showed the three moons, Io, Europa and Ganymede. She explained as the video played, "For one orbit of Ganymede, there are exactly two orbits of Europa and exactly four orbits of Io." She looked at them demanding interest. Then she continued, "The gravity of each of these moons has attracted each other and over millions of years they have slowly come to their perfect orbital resonance." She paused and smiled as she showed a picture of Europa.

Paul nodded, that was actually interesting. He pointed to Europa in the photo and said to Patrick, "Write Europa."

Europa wanted to know, "Where are you writing my name?"

Paul said placatingly, "Don't worry, you are getting the nickname Europa." He smiled nervously, "Otherwise it would be confusing."

Europa ignored him, "Europa is a young and icy moon. It has an ocean, that contains chemical energy and a weak magnetic field. Those are indications that there could be life." She paused and showed the next slide, "Callisto is another Jupiter moon and it is the second largest after Ganymede." Europa glared at them, "My sister's name is Callisto and she's not in your photo."

Both Paul and Patrick looked guiltily at the table.

Europa ignored their reaction and continued, "There are three moons in our Solar System that have enough liquid to give the possibility of the emergence of life a chance." She showed a picture of the three moons, "They are Europa, which we have already seen and two moons of Saturn Enceladus and Titan."

Paul tapped on the picture. Patrick smiled and picked up the pen and guessed Paul meant his mother, but he paused before writing.

"Enceladus, a Saturn moon, has an almost perfectly circular orbit and regularly sprays ammonia into space, showing that it is probably geologically active. The ammonia spray creates a thin atmosphere."

Patrick asked uncertainly, "Why my mother?"

Paul reassured him, "Because there is a very high chance of life there and it's a nice moon."

Patrick relaxed and smiled as he wrote Mother on the list.

Europa was in full flow and wanted to clarify, "The volcanic activity on this icy moon provides evidence of liquid water and this means that Enceladus is considered to be one of the possible places in the solar system with favourable conditions for the formation of life."

Paul nodded encouragingly to Europa indicating that he was listening as he looked at her and he gave her an exaggerated smile.

Europa moved on to the next picture, "Titan is an icy moon and the second largest moon in the solar system after Ganymede. It is the only moon with a dense gas shell and it has lakes and seas of liquid methane."

Paul tapped himself on the photo. Europa waited patiently.

Patrick looked at him questioningly.

Paul smiled and said, "Because I'm so tall."

The next picture came into view of a small irregular moon. Europa looked at the picture for a few moments before saying, "Prometheus has a very low orbital eccentricity. The orbit is almost exactly on the equator of Saturn." She looked at Paul and explained, "This means that the orbital distance to Saturn hardly varies." Europa's voice became flat and emotionless, "The orbit is circular and not elliptical like our Moon."

Paul tapped Liam on the photo and whispered, "He's good with technology."

Europa waited for the game to finish before adding, "Prometheus is also known as the so-called shepherd moon because its gravity helps to hold the rings of Saturn together."

Europa showed a picture of Uranus with seven of its most important moons, "Uranus has over thirty moons, most are small and are probably captured comets or asteroids. However, the first two Uranus moons, discovered in year 1787 by astronomer William Herschel, were large moons and they are Oberon and Titania." She showed a picture of William Herschel's telescope, and then a photo of Titania and Oberon, "Titania is the largest Uranus moon and has an almost perfectly circular orbit."

Paul tapped on Maria in the photo. He didn't offer an explanation to Patrick why Maria was called Titania.

Europa ignored their game, "Oberon is the second largest moon of Uranus. It is only about fifty-five kilometres smaller than Titania and it also has an almost perfectly circular orbit."

Paul pointed to Charlie, and Patrick put his name on the list.

"Oberon has an icy surface that is obviously very old and has little geological activity because it is littered with craters. Both the number and size of the craters on Oberon are much higher than on Titania or Ariel but it cannot be compared to the number on Miranda."

Europa clicked to a new slide, "Miranda is one of the great moons of Uranus and has an almost perfectly circular orbit. This moon is easy to recognise by its particularly complex surface. It shows extraordinary distortions, that are up to twenty kilometres deep and it's got an irregular shape, which is unusual for a moon of this size."

Paul seemed eager as he tapped on the photo, "Beatriz - write Beatriz."

Patrick responded excitedly and wrote Beatriz in his best handwriting as Europa waited patiently but still managed a look of disapproval.

Europa pointed to a photo of Ariel in the next picture and said, "Ariel." She saw Paul move excitedly and waited for Paul to finish.

He tapped on the photo and said, "Write John."

Patrick wrote and then looked up.

Europa continued, "Ariel is the fourth largest and brightest Uranus moon. It's bright because it has the largest albedo of the Uranus Moons."

Paul asked innocently, "What is Albedo?"

Europa kept calm and replied, "Albedo is what we call surface reflectivity. Interestingly, Enceladus has an even higher surface reflectivity than Ariel."

As Europa said Enceladus, Paul suggested Dervla before he realised, they'd already written it. They both laughed about his mistake.

While they were still laughing Europa selected a new image, one that showed Mars with its two small moons, and then she explained, "Phobus and Deimos these are the small irregular moons of Mars." She looked at Paul, raised her eyebrows and waited.

Paul suggested Damian and Filip to Patrick.

Patrick started writing Damian next to Deimos.

"No Damian is Phobus."

"But why, D stands for Damian and Deimos."

"Damian is Filip's father and Phobus is bigger than Deimos."

Patrick shrugged his shoulders and wrote what Paul wanted as he asked, "Okay. But why are Damian and Filip Phobus and Deimos?"

Paul explained kindly, "Because they are not far away, and they are still together."

Europa pointed to the picture and continued, "Like our Moon, Deimos has a bound rotation, that is, it always has the same irregular side facing Mars." She checked to see if they were paying attention to her before she showed the next picture.

"Our home, the Moon."

Paul said to Patrick, "Write Peter the Moon Major."

Patrick picked up the pen and nodded as he wrote Peter's name and smiled as he thought Europa's lesson really was fun.

Europa continued, "Our Moon has a bound rotation. It always shows the same side to Earth."

Patrick interrupted her, "If we stand on the other side of the Moon, can people on Earth see us?"

Europa explained, "We call that the far side of the Moon, and you are right, no one on Earth will be able to see us there."

Paul smiled to hide his thoughts, that he didn't think there was anyone to see them on this side either.

Paul looked at Europa as he heard her say, "And that means that a Moon day and a Moon month have almost the same duration."

Patrick looked amazed and then puzzled before asking, "Why doesn't our Moon have a name?"

Europa looked at him perplexed and answered sternly, "The Moon's name is simply Moon because it was the first moon discovered."

Patrick nodded satisfied. Although, he wasn't sure if that was a reasonable explanation, but Europa's tone made sure he believed it.

Europa turned her back on the picture and looked at them, "And now for a short history of the Moon. The Soviet Luna 2 module was deliberately brought into contact with the Moon in September 1959. The crash site is near Mare Imbrium, that isn't so far from where we are, but unfortunately too far for a day trip."

Patrick opened his eyes wide and suggested in a small voice, "We could go outside and visit the crash site."

Europa quickly thought about his suggestion and replied, "It's possible to take a moonwalk when we find a spacesuit that fits you."

Paul interjected quickly, "Not yet you're too small for the spacesuits."

Patrick made a long face and looked at Paul with pleading watery eyes.

Paul could feel Patrick's disappointment stabbing him in his chest and knew he had to say something to comfort him, "Maybe next year, or the year after that, but soon, we just can't, not yet." Paul smiled and ruffled Patrick's hair.

Paul added slyly, "Maybe we can even play golf. Did you know someone has already played golf on the Moon?"

Europa was quick to reply, "Yes, I know. Do you know his name?" Europa knew it was Alan Shepard. She was testing Paul.

In an unsteady voice Patrick asked, "What's golf?"

Paul replied in a flash, "It's a great game. Let's play it together sometime." And then he grinned before tapping on the one name on the moon nicknames list without a moon next to it.

Patrick looked at him forlornly.

Paul turned to Europa and asked her, "Which is your favourite moon?"

Europa responded immediately, "Ganymede."

Paul looked at her and asked, "Please, can you tell us why?"

Europa was both surprised and delighted by their sudden interest and answered almost smiling, "Ganymede is my favourite because it's unique and very big. It's even bigger than the small planet Mercury. If you want to know how big it really is, then imagine it as three-quarters the size of Mars. I don't have a picture, but I can find one and show it to you later."

Paul smiled and nodded as he enthusiastically said, "Good idea."

Europa wasn't finished, so she continued, "Ganymede is the only moon that has a strong magnetic field and it also has a very thin atmosphere. It was discovered a long time ago in 1610 by Galileo." She looked at them intently, "This was a significant moment in history, it was the moment when Galileo realised that not everything revolved around the Earth. And he did it with Ganymede's help."

Paul thanked Europa for the lesson then he asked Patrick, "What about finishing the list?"

The name at the bottom of the list didn't have a moon. Patrick looked at the list and then at Paul before saying in a small voice, "I don't have a moon nickname."

Paul smiled as he saw how sad he looked because he thought he'd been forgotten. He looked him in the eyes and said, "So Ganymede what are we going to do about it?"

At first Patrick was confused and then he beamed. He was Ganymede, Europa's favourite moon.

Paul nudged Patrick conspiratorially, and said, "Here is a felt-tip, shall we write the moon names on everyone's room doors?"

With a worried expression, Patrick looked up at him trembling and sounded short of breath as he replied, "Yes." Then it occurred to him, "But the Sauberbots will clean it off afterwards." He looked sad.

Paul nodded omnisciently, "No problem. We can reprogram them, and they'll think it's modern art." Both he and Patrick laughed out loud as they ran off to go and do their best writing.

It was lunchtime, and everyone had gathered in the canteen for the birthday party. Peter looked around and smiled. He nodded to the others appreciating that they were there. He liked Patrick's birthday. It was a day where they could forget everything and step out of their daily routine and come together to celebrate. Peter had told Liam that he should come this year and Peter was pleased that Liam was there. Peter had felt guilty about not inviting Liam and hadn't enjoyed excluding him. Since Liam had kept his promise and stayed away from Patrick, Peter saw no reason not to invite him, but he was still a little concerned.

When Paul and Patrick turned up at last, both with ink on their hands, Peter gave Paul a knowing look. Then he started the little ceremony to give Patrick his certificate, proof that Patrick had been good for a year.

Patrick beamed as Peter gave him his certificate and congratulated him on his Moonday birthday. To end the ritual, Peter touched his captain's hat and nodded appreciatively. Patrick reached up and tried to do the same but realised too late that he had forgotten to put his captain's hat on. He looked lost before Beatriz started shaking his hand and congratulating him. He soon forgot his mistake, and everyone took turns at wishing Patrick happy birthday and shaking his hand. As Liam stepped up, Peter watched him very closely. He didn't want to, he wanted to trust him a little, but he just couldn't.

While they were eating the cake, that Steve had baked, Peter asked Paul and Patrick, "Were you upstairs? Someone has graffitied on the room doors. Do you happen to know anything about that?" Peter laughed as he watched the two of them running into the distance and laughed again with the others as they heard the distant laughter. Everyone seemed happy today. Positive enough that they had forgotten about the upcoming contract renewals. He tried not to think about the discussions that were going to take place in a couple of weeks. He wasn't looking forward to them.

Second Renewal

Date: Saturday 18th October 2149 – 10:00 CET
Location: Alpha 12 – Moon Base

"Thank you for coming." Peter looked at the familiar faces of the team. The remaining eight of the original team had, over the years, found their favourite places to sit, and they would probably always sit there. It simplified Peter's life because he always knew where to turn his head without thinking about it. The tense expressions showed that they were worried about their uncertain future. Before he came, he'd looked at the old team photo, examined the faces, and wondered what they were thinking and feeling back then. Eight of them were now sitting before him, they were older, more experienced, but probably not wiser. He certainly didn't feel any wiser, but they expected him to offer them a solution for their uncertain future that he didn't have.

He was nervous and had a low-level feeling of sickness at the bottom of his stomach. He looked seriously at them and explained, "I thought, if we all got together, maybe we could understand the situation better." He paused, his eyes flicked around the group and he waited for a reaction. None came, and he took off his captain's hat and laid it on the table, as he slowly lowered himself to sit down. All eyes were following the hat. He looked around, they still expected him to have answers, which was, as always, not the case.

He broke the silence, "First of all," he turned to Paul, "please explain to me why there's still graffiti on everyone's door."

Paul glanced away, blushed, opened his mouth as if to say something before closing it and deciding not to say anything.

It was only with difficulty that Peter kept a straight face. Paul looked completely guilty, which Peter thought was funny.

Maria looked concerned and explained, "I like it. I would even like to have a picture of Titania painted on my door."

Charlie thought it was a great idea, "I'd love a picture of Oberon." When he'd found out what nicknames he and Maria had been given, he'd been very pleased. They thought they were a couple, and he'd beamed then as he was beaming now.

Raising his hands in a gesture of giving up, Peter withdrew his half serious comment, "It seems as if you all like your graffiti."

Paul visibly relaxed and jokingly wiped his forehead with the back of his hand.

Steve laughed, he liked being called Io, and had also enjoyed Paul's discomfort.

Peter enjoyed the distraction, it delayed them talking about the topic at hand. He needed to ask, if anyone wanted to go home. They'd postponed the decision five years ago, and he knew it would come up again. Now it was time, and they were gathered together to discuss it. From what Peter could read in their expressions, he suspected that they weren't ready to talk about it.

Peter put his right hand on the table with his palm up, "The question before us today is: What do we want to do? Do we want to stay on the Moon, or do we want to go home?" Unconsciously, he clenched his fist.

Nobody said anything. They were all watching his hand.

Watching his fist, Peter gently tapped it on the table a few times before he looked up and decided to break the silence, "Let's stay for another shift and wait for new information, maybe Earth Base Columbus will get back in contact."

Steve's tone sounded peevish, "We don't know anything about what happened, and I don't think we'll ever know. We sit here and keep going through the same old theories. We don't have any new information."

Liam looked a little offended. He was doing his best, "We had a moment when I thought we'd made contact with the Mars Base, but it was only briefly, the satellites have now deviated too far from their course for it to be worth trying again."

Steve looked at him with contempt.

Liam shrugged his shoulders and pulled an indifferent expression. He didn't care what Steve thought.

The repeated, quiet tapping of Peter's finger nail on the table slowly drew their attention, one after the other they turned towards Peter. When he had their full attention he said, "If we stay here, everyone will get the same renewal conditions as last time." He smiled calmly, hoping it covered his nervousness, "Of course, there is also the possibility to arrange an appointment with me," he looked at Steve, "if you want to negotiate something different, or if you want to discuss anything." He glanced around at the others. There was no reaction. He looked around for confirmation. Their body language relaxed, and he could see a few little nods. He realised he'd been holding his breath and breathed out before adding, "As a reward for the good work, there will be extra credits added to your environment and social responsibility account." He smiled and waited while they considered the offer.

Charlie shuffled in his seat and sat upright. He opened his mouth to say something and then quickly shut it. He tried again, "Before we came, I registered to take part in a Citizen Science project. The first phase of the project ends next month." The volume of his voice dropped at the end of the sentence and remained quiet as he added, "I thought I'd be back by now."

Peter looked at him compassionately and could feel tears welling up in his eyes. He put his hand up to his face and covered his mouth, feeling the warmth of his palm on his face, and the warmth of his breath on his hand, and it calmed him. He looked at them, they all had their reasons why they wanted to return to Earth and also why they weren't yet ready to return.

Steve asked mockingly, "What project would have you?"

Charlie, who had seemed distant, ignored Steve's tone and explained, "It's a hundred years long project studying how people develop spiritually over time. I've been doing it for twenty years. My brothers are involved as well."

Steve snorted before saying, "Spiritual development. You. You're just crazy. Didn't they have a minimum intelligence requirement to participate?"

Charlie didn't look at Steve. He didn't have enough energy to respond to him. His feelings and thoughts were with his brothers and the memory of them promising each other that they would never give up. His gaze was on the cold dregs in his coffee cup on the table in front of him, "I've filled out the questionnaire every year. I thought I'd be able to take them back with me." He looked at Peter, "I never quit the project."

Beatriz's tone was kind as she said, "You can still take them home when you return. I'm sure they still want to know what you've recorded." She stressed, "Your results are really valuable. No one else in the project has spent part of it on the Moon."

Charlie noticed the nods of encouragement from the others and smiled. He thanked them for the support. It was a comfort to him.

Bored, Steve interrupted the supportive mood and in an angry voice asked, "Are we going to avoid the real issue forever?" He looked first at Peter and then at Dervla directly in the eyes, "We don't have enough room for all the people in the escape pods."

Everyone remained silent, and they avoided looking at each other.

Steve continued to make his point, "We can't all go back because there aren't enough escape pods. Only nine people can fit in the escape pods, and Patrick is probably too young for the journey."

Dervla turned to Steve. She had a very determined expression, "If it needs to be, Patrick can have my place." Her voice sounded clear and firm. Her determination hid her uncertainty about whether it would really come to that.

A few seconds later Beatriz added, "I'm not so young anymore. Let's wait and see, you never know what could happen to one of us."

Liam didn't want to draw attention to himself, but he also wanted to relieve the burden on the others, so that they'd be less worried, "Maybe someone doesn't want to return. That's another possibility."

Peter suddenly remembered, "Where is Patrick?"

Paul smiled and said softly but firmly, "He's playing with Astro. He wanted to come to the meeting and was upset that he wasn't invited. He's waiting for us to finish."

Peter nodded and gave a sign that he'd apologise to Patrick after the meeting.

Absentmindedly, Maria suddenly added, "I have to take care of the gardens, without me they'll have problems."

Paul looked at Maria and said, "I'd like to take Astro when I return. If it is possible."

Steve almost exploded with contempt, "There is not enough room in the escape pods for all of us, and you want to take your toolbox instead of a person?"

Paul looked embarrassed but also indignant, "No, of course not."

Peter distracted them by asking Europa, "Do you have any feedback from the infrared Earth observation?"

If Europa was honest, she hadn't been making any regular Earth observations for a while because it would interfere with her real work. She looked Peter straight in the eye and made an educated guess, "The observations show an unexpected growth in the intensity of vegetation."

Maria was interested, "What do you mean unexpected?"

Europa closed her eyes briefly and let her mouth open a little as she thought. She breathed in and out deeply before explaining, "There is a greater than normal vegetation cover in the cities." That was true, or at least it was when she'd recorded the Earth during the last observation window.

Maria seemed satisfied, but the others looked concerned. Paul was worried and asked, "Have people stopped living in the cities?"

Europa frowned, "I don't know. There may be another explanation, or the instruments might not have been working properly." She was getting the feeling that she was going to have to redo her observations after all.

Steve changed the subject back, "Are we stuck here simply because Patrick's too young to travel?"

Peter reacted calmly, "We can fly home in the escape pods any time we want. Of course, only if it's a near-Earth day, and you're right. Patrick is too young to return."

Steve interjected, "Then it's no return for Patrick."

Peter ignored Steve's comment, "My impression is that you all would like a contract extension." He smiled at them and continued in a friendly tone, "To be honest, I've gotten used to life here, and I'm starting to like it." He still missed his wife and wanted to go home, but he knew it wouldn't help if he mentioned it. He had the feeling that the mood was increasingly turning towards going home. Peter added, "We've no hurry to go home. We have enough supplies for years. We can wait for Patrick to turn sixteen and be old enough to travel."

Peter looked at them to see their responses. The small smiles and gentle nodding gave him the impression that they liked his suggestion. It was a decision that meant they didn't have to change anything and could continue on as normal. Peter smiled and thought we're all a little afraid of change. He was pleased the meeting had gone better than he'd expected. Peter slid his chair back away from the table.

Beatriz knocked gently on the top of the table with a clenched hand and said, "Before you go. I just want to say, that you are all welcome to come to the infirmary for your annual medical examination." She looked over to Europa and Peter before adding, "Liam has helped me set up a Robotician that was destined for Mars. This means we can do better eye tests." She smiled proudly and took something out of her top pocket before saying, "We can even make improved glasses and contact lenses." She put on her glasses and glanced over to Maria. Then she nodded before adding, "Your necklace is beautiful."

Peter picked up his captain's hat and held it in his hand as he went back to his office. He sat down at his desk, put on his captain's hat and waited for who would come. He didn't have to wait long and was surprised when it was Liam who stopped by first. He only stayed briefly and thanked Peter for inviting him to Patrick's birthday party and trusting him. Peter nodded and smiled. He remained quiet because he was unsure what to say.

As Peter expected, Steve came after Liam had left.

Still standing Steve announced, "I want a bigger pay rise. I don't think you are offering enough." He had a serious expression on his face.

Peter smirked he understood Steve's game this time and replied, "You need to justify why you deserve a bigger pay rise?"

Without pausing Steve answered, "I work harder than the others and achieve more. I'm qualified enough that I can do most jobs on the base. I want you to give me an incentive to want to stay."

Peter asked, "How much do you want?"

Steve looked him straight in the eye and said, "An extra ten percent."

Peter didn't flinch and countered with, "Five percent."

Steve nodded he was satisfied with five percent, but Peter could see there was something else bothering him.

Steve sounded unsure as he asked, "What's happened to the list of returners? You haven't mentioned it lately."

Peter reassured him, "It exists, and your name is on it." He made a mental note to write a list.

Peter sat there looking at the door waiting to see if anyone else came. He was just about to give up waiting and get on with something else when Beatriz came by.

She walked into his office and explained, "Sorry, that it took me so long to get here. I needed to plan a couple of medical examinations." She smiled at him. "The terms of the employment contract are fine, and I have no problem with it."

Peter was relieved, and she said, "I just came by for a little chat."

Peter nodded and shut the door automatically. He offered Beatriz one of the chairs, and she made herself comfortable before she asked, "Have you ever thought that Patrick might be colour-blind because his choice of clothes is sometimes unusual."

Peter looked thoughtful as he replied, "He doesn't have any influence from other children or from fashions. Maybe it's perfectly normal."

Beatriz replied, "Well he isn't colour-blind. I did an eye test and the results were a little surprising. He has a wider visual range at the violet end of the visible spectrum." She looked at Peter to see if he had anything to say. He remained silent, so Beatriz added, "I was just thinking that maybe we might need to give him contact lenses. John was red/green colour-blind. That's why I asked Dervla for permission to test him."

Peter nodded in silence, looked at his watch and poured himself a glass of whisky. Beatriz shook her head, she didn't want any.

Beatriz watched him sip his whisky. She hadn't trained as a dentist, but over the years she had to learn more and more, "Liam and Paul have finished building a new automatic dentist. We installed the machine yesterday. I wanted to mention it in the meeting but forgot." She smiled and continued, "It was destined for the Mars Base. We also have a good supply of self-building peptides for tooth enamel repair and a hydrogel, which has similar mechanical properties to a natural tooth."

Peter wasn't really interested, yet he managed to smile politely and replied, "Does that mean I can eat more sweets?"

Beatriz laughed politely, but sounded a little stern as she explained, "It's been ten years since we arrived, and your enamel reinforcement coating will not last forever." She looked sternly at him in a motherly way.

Peter didn't notice, his thoughts were elsewhere, "Do you ever think about what you'll do when you get home?" He looked at her.

She kept silent. She wanted to know where he wanted to go with this before she answered.

Peter sighed and spoke quickly, "Who you'd hug, what you'd eat, whether you'd go swimming in the sea? Or even go for a walk barefoot so you can feel the grass between your toes when your feet touch the ground?"

Beatriz observed Peter carefully. She was a little concerned.

He continued, "Patrick has only ever breathed cleanly filtered air. Never the variety on Earth." Peter looked at Beatriz and stressed, "He was never ill. He's never been vaccinated." He thought briefly, "Maybe there are vaccinations destined for the Mars Base that we can use for Patrick."

Beatriz smiled. She was becoming less worried about Peter, "There certainly are."

Peter turned serious, "The supplies are now over ten years old. Isn't there an expiry date for vaccinations?"

"If the drugs are stored at optimal temperatures and conditions, the expiration date can be prolonged, and the vaccinations don't lose their effect."

Peter nodded, thinking briefly before asking, "Will Patrick's muscles and bones be strong enough to withstand gravity on Earth?"

Beatriz shook her head, "In that respect he won't have any problems. His muscles and bones are stronger than normal."

Peter nodded and leaned back in his chair, then he sat upright, and his eyes lit up as he smiled. Then he said, "He sounds like Superman. Stronger than normal and with a broader visual spectrum." He laughed softly at his joke. The comparison made Beatriz laugh too.

The laughter helped them relax, and Peter sipped his whisky enjoying the flavour and thinking of what he would do when he got home. He turned to Beatriz and said quietly,

"Can you remember how air smells and feels when you can see a rainbow? I think I've forgotten." He looked sad and went silent.

Beatriz was worried. It seemed that today had hit Peter hard. She wished she could help him.

He just sat up straight and said, "Everyone seems to be getting along well. The meeting went better than I thought it would." He looked distant.

Beatriz felt worried, "You know, most of the time everyone is either taking antidepressants or anti-anxiety medication. Sometimes both. And if we're not taking medication, we've found our own way to deal with our emotions." She looked pointedly at his whisky bottle.

He smiled half-heartedly and looked a little guilty.

After Beatriz had left, Peter sat alone in his office. He'd requested Meichun remain inactive. He wanted to be left alone. The captain's hat was on his desk, and Peter was looking at it. It's getting old, too. It's over 11 years old and still looking good. He smiled. He took good care of his hat. He tilted his head to one side and thought the cap hasn't put on weight and doesn't need whisky to get through the day. He poured himself another glass and drank it in one, then twisted his body on his chair and it occurred to him that it was time to increase the maximum size setting in his clothes again.

Moonday Ten

Date: Saturday 2nd October 2151 – 09:30 CET
Location: Alpha 12 – Moon Base

Beatriz was sitting in the sick bay staring at nothing on the wall. She felt like she'd forgotten something and was frowning. She massaged her temples with her fingers and felt the pain as she pressed down harder. It bothered her. She wasn't used to forgetting anything.

Patrick came skidding into the room and came to a stop when he hit the wall. He straightened himself up and greeted her with a big grin.

She looked surprised to see Patrick and gave him a friendly smile before asking him, "What are you doing here?"

He grinned broader. He'd pulled himself up to his full height and sounded very proud as he said, "It's Moonday 10. My birthday." His eyes lit up and his shoulders led his body into a mini-wobble dance manoeuvre. Beatriz couldn't help smiling at his antics.

Was that what she forgot, or was it something else? She suppressed the uncertain feeling and nodded in a way that matched the severity of the situation, "Of course, let's start right away. Sit yourself down." As soon as he had sat down, she started the examination. Like every year she measured his weight directly in the chair, and then got him to stand up, so she could measure his height and scan his muscle and bone strength. The results of the tests were available immediately and came as no surprise to Beatriz. Every year, the results were above average for his age. She congratulated him on how well he was growing and told him that he was stronger and taller than an average ten-year-old boy.

He grinned proudly, and his eyes shone. He was enjoying the attention. Beatriz thought he behaved like a normal boy. Being the only child didn't seem to have damaged his development. She laughed softly as she thought probably because Paul acts like a child most of the time, and it was good that they had a lot in common. Patrick also had a similar body size to Paul, she wondered if it had something to do with the fact that they spent so much time together.

After the examination was over Beatriz noticed a package with a note stuck on it sitting on her table. She turned to Patrick, and before he ran away to find Paul, who was organising something special for Patrick's birthday, Beatriz put her hand gently on Patrick's arm. He looked at her questioningly. His muscles were tense. He was trembling a little. He wanted to go.

"I have something for you." She ripped off the note and put it in her pocket before she handed him the little package. She thought he looks cute when he's confused.

"A gift, but I thought the examination was my gift?"

Beatriz declared affectionately, "This year you're getting something extra."

Patrick beamed and took the package and asked, "Can I open it now?"

With twinkling eyes Beatriz advised him quietly, "Wait for the party. And another thing. Don't forget that the asteroid belt lies between Mars and Jupiter."

Patrick promised not to forget and ran off. He ran into the large meeting room, but when he saw Paul he stopped abruptly and dropped the package. Paul laughed, it looked like he'd run into an invisible wall. Paul tilted his head and smiled at Patrick before asking gently, "Is anything wrong?"

Patrick looked disappointed, "I thought I was getting a present, but there are so many people here."

"Yes, and so you will." Paul's tone was understanding, and he pointed at the package on the floor and added, "Pick up the package," as he continued speaking you could hear the laughter in his voice, "This year the theme of Europa's lesson is so interesting that the others wanted to participate as well." He nodded towards Maria and Charlie.

Patrick smiled, visibly relieved, he picked up the package and sat down excitedly between Paul and Maria.

Maria tapped gently on the top of the parcel and raised her eyebrows as she said, "I hope nothing broke."

Patrick looked at her suddenly worried. He picked up the package and shook it next to his ear concentrating hard to see if he could hear anything shaking.

Paul shook his head and let it fall into his hands in an attempt at disapproval, but he couldn't hide his smile, "Stop shaking it. You'll only make it worse."

Full of energy, Europa walked into the room. She glanced at the CET clock on the wall and nodded to them before smiling at her audience, which scared Paul a little because it was so unusual.

"Today's topic is the difference between celestial bodies located in our solar system." She pulled up a huge picture of the solar system on the visual display, before pointing at the picture and explaining, "We see here the eight planets and Pluto-Charon, which is the nearest thing we have to a double planet system in our solar system." Europa liked the Pluto-Charon double planet system, she thought it was somehow romantic. Europa turned to her students and looked sternly at them, "We'll start with a test. We have eight planets in our solar system, two belts, and a cloud. You need to name them all." She looked at Patrick, "We'll ignore the dwarf planets."

Patrick grimaced. He was a little scared and covered his face with his hands. He was sure he wouldn't know the answers. He looked at Paul nervously and then started chewing his thumbnail. Patrick's eyes were wide and watering, and without making a sound, he was moving his dry lips uncertainly. Paul saw him and smiled before patting his hand.

Europa suddenly turned and faced Charlie. She hit the table with her flat of her hand making a loud banging sound.

Charlie jumped, sat up straighter, paying attention and looked scared.

Europa asked, demanding, "The first planet from the Sun is?"

Charlie sounded insecure when he barely audibly whispered, "Mercury." He looked at Europa questioningly. He was worried that the answer might be wrong.

Without smiling, she nodded and left him with the feeling that if the answer had been wrong then he would know about it. She turned to Maria and asked just as sternly, "The next planet is?"

Maria felt a shiver run down her spine and forced herself to relax before answering in a confident voice that hardly quivered, "Venus." She managed to smile half-heartedly.

With a severe expression, Europa looked at Patrick. Her voice sounded softer but not much, "And the third planet from the Sun?"

Patrick visibly relaxed and even smiled as he sat up straight, pulled his shoulders up and answered, "The Earth."

Europa nodded and said, "Correct. Well done."

As Patrick beamed and relaxed, Charlie looked over jealously.

Europa turned to Paul and abruptly asked, "And what's the fourth planet called?"

Paul shook his head lightly from side to side as he looked at Europa and thought she's enjoying this.

Europa raised her eyebrows.

He answered hurriedly, "Mars. It's Mars." He knew the answer was correct, yet he could feel the beads of sweat forming on his forehead.

Europa turned to Charlie and demanded, "What lies between Mars and Jupiter?"

Charlie bent his head and looked at the table. He apologised and stuttered, "I don't know."

Patrick breathed in quickly. He knew the answer. He almost jumped up in his seat. He wanted to answer, but wasn't sure if it was allowed or not. Excited and uncertain, he looked questioningly between Paul and Europa.

Paul smiled encouragingly and nodded exaggeratedly with both his head and with his eyebrows.

Patrick started wriggling and twisting in his seat. He raised and lowered his arm. Would she see him? Was he allowed to answer? He was so excited, and the words burst out of him, "I know it. I know the answer. The asteroid belt lies between Mars and Jupiter."

Europa smiled and congratulated Patrick on being so clever. He knew something Charlie didn't know. She looked at Charlie disapprovingly.

Charlie blushed. He'd not expected that the game would go so far. He leaned over to Maria and whispered, "I know the answer really."

Europa once again pointed to the picture, "The next four planets are Jupiter, Saturn, Uranus and Neptune." She paused for a moment and smiled as she said, "And then comes the Pluto-Charon double planet system."

Europa turned to Maria, looked at her directly and asked, "Beyond the orbit of Neptune and the orbit of the Pluto-Charon double planet system is what?"

Maria was determined not to be intimidated by Europa, "The Kuiper Belt."

Without acknowledging that this was the right answer, Europa turned to Paul, "And what is outside the heliosphere and in inter-stellar space?"

Paul had known the answer, but he was still glad he had prepared, "The Oort Cloud." His voice sounded calm and steady. He even managed a smile.

Europa seemed impressed, "Well done. Now comes the second part of the lesson. The first part was just preparation. The date August 11, 2140. Anyone know why it's important?"

Uncertain Charlie suggested, "Was it the closest approach of Halley's comet?" He held his breath.

Europa was happily surprised that he knew, "Yes, well done." She showed a picture of Halley's comet traveling with its long comet tail across the southern night sky.

Charlie breathed in and out deeply, smiling relaxed and started enjoying the lesson again. He had rescued his reputation in front of Maria.

Europa looked at Patrick and explained, "The picture was taken on Earth before you were born." She turned to the picture and smiled at it before turning around and saying, "I'm sure you all want to know the differences between comets, asteroids, meteoroids, meteors and meteorites."

They all nodded eagerly.

"A stone that originates in space can have many different names depending on what it is made of and where it is located." She showed a picture of a few celestial bodies.

"Comets are usually made of stone and can form a comet tail of ice, methane, or ammonia as they get warmer when they approach the Sun. This means that comets are not just made of stone they are also made up of ice, methane, ammonia and other compounds."

She looked at her audience. Did they understand? She looked closely at Charlie.

He noticed what she was doing and went red from suppressing his anger.

Europa announced, "Comets come from two different sources. There are comets with a long orbital period, these have an orbit that has a duration of more than two hundred years to go around the Sun, these originate from the Oort cloud. There are also short-period comets that take less than two hundred years to orbit the Sun, and these come from the Kuiper Belt."

She looked at Paul questioningly. He nodded encouragingly.

Europa pointed to an asteroid in the picture and explained, "Asteroids resemble comets, but they are not so interesting. Asteroids are usually larger rocks coming from the asteroid belt between the orbits of Mars and Jupiter. There are between 0.7 and 1.7 million asteroids with a diameter of 1 km or more."

She looked for a reaction.

Paul opened his eyes wider, nodded his head once and seemed to be generally impressed.

Europa was pleased by his response and continued, encouraged, "Sometimes the asteroid orbits become disturbed by mutual impacts and some of the asteroids change course and come closer to the Sun and thus closer to the Earth and the Moon, but this doesn't happen very often. We are far more like to see small meteoroids than a large asteroid." She pointed to a picture of a small meteoroid and explained, "Meteoroids are considered space debris. A meteoroid is a piece of interplanetary matter smaller than an asteroid. So less than a kilometre in diameter, and they are often only millimetres big."

Europa pointed at what looked like nothing on the picture and explained, "There are the smaller Meteoroids. You probably can't see them." She ignored the problem presented by this explanation and continued, "Most Meteoroids entering the Earth's atmosphere are so small that they evaporate completely before they reach the surface of the planet." She paused for thought, then turned around threateningly, looked at Paul and asked, "And when they enter the Earth's atmosphere, they get another name, and what name do they get, Paul?"

Paul was prepared for it, but still he felt scared, "Shooting star, or meteors."

A smile flashed across her face, "Yes, exactly. A meteor causes a flash of light that we see in the earthly night sky when a small piece of interplanetary debris burns in the mesosphere and evaporates." She checked whether they were still paying attention, "But if the friction caused by the air in the atmosphere isn't strong enough, the debris doesn't burn completely, and the space debris manages to land on Earth, and then it is called a meteorite." She turned back to the picture, looked at it for a moment as if she had forgotten something before turning to look at Charlie and saying, "To put it as simply as possible, comets are mostly made of ice and stone, asteroids are usually rock, meteoroids are space debris, meteors glow, and meteorites kill you when they fall on your head." She smiled sweetly.

Charlie felt like he was burning up inside.

Europa showed a photo of her heroine, Art Feldmann, and explained, "And to the third part of today's lesson. Art Feldmann's field and why it's so important to the Moon Base." She smiled before continuing, "Art Feldmann discovered the ability to control gravity. This knowledge was fundamental to building the Moon Base. We can generate an Art Feldmann's field that is strong enough to easily distract meteoroids, but when asteroids come, it becomes a bigger risk. For example, when a Leonid meteor storm comes, we close the shields for protection," she looked at Patrick, "and we take our annual vacation. Art Feldmann's is not a strong field, but it has a long-range effect. This means that as asteroids approach, the effect becomes increasingly stronger. Asteroids that are initially only slightly deflected feel an ever-increasing repulsive force as they approach."

Paul was prepared and asked, "What kind of field is Feldmann's field exactly?"

Europa seemed thoughtful as she replied, "Simply put, it is a kind of colourful flowing of anti-gravity energy."

Paul wanted to know more, "What happens if a comet comes directly at us?"

Europa nodded, "To reflect comets, we can use the entire mass of the Moon to help us generate a stronger field. We have built this mechanism into the protective shields of the base."

As Europa turned off the display, they all thanked Europa for the lesson, before standing up and going together to Patrick's birthday party in the canteen. They followed the same routine as they did every year. Steve had baked a cake, and Peter came in with a certificate for Patrick's good behaviour. Patrick beamed as he accepted the certificate and explained that he would hang it alongside the other four on his bedroom wall. As Peter saluted him, Patrick grinned and saluted back touching the brim of the now rather too small captain's hat. He enjoyed being the centre of attention and liked hearing the good wishes of the people around him. He didn't notice that Peter had been hiding a little package in one hand. As he handed it to Patrick, Peter smiled and raised an eyebrow as he said, "Guess what it is."

Without guessing, Patrick took the gift and ripped off the packaging. It was a new captain's hat. It was exactly like the other one but bigger. Patrick swapped hats and saluted Peter. Peter responded with an appropriate amount of seriousness.

Beatriz prompted Patrick gently, "Didn't you have another present?"

Disappointed, he looked down, pouting and shaking his head.

Maria nudged him and smiled as she handed Patrick the forgotten present.

He put his hand to his mouth and blushed. Then he took the package and opened it in a hurry. It was sunglasses. He seemed confused.

Beatriz smiled mysteriously and said, "You'll need it when you go outside."

Charlie patted Patrick on the back and said, "We'll meet at the Art Feldmann statue in thirty minutes. Don't eat too much cake beforehand, or you'll get sick."

Patrick was curious and immediately wondered if two pieces of cake were too many, or if three would make him sick.

Before he went Charlie added, "And don't forget to bring the sunglasses."

Patrick's eyes were looking for Paul. He'll know what's going on. But Paul had already gone. Patrick turned his attention to the cake and forgot about Paul's absence. He managed to avoid the temptation to give Astro a little bit of cake and tried to follow Charlie's advice.

After the party Beatriz and Peter went to Peter's office together. They wanted to chat a little and relax. Moonday, or rather, Patrick's birthday had gradually become a holiday on the Moon Base. Nobody worked on that day anymore. After they arrived in the office, they both sat down and made themselves comfortable. Before Peter sat in his chair, he took off his captain's hat and commented, "I don't have much experience with children, but Patrick seems great for a 10-year-old child."

Beatriz, who was already relaxing in the visitor's chair, replied, "Yes, he is."

As he poured himself a whisky, Peter asked, "Do you want some?"

Beatriz looked at the time, "It's still too early for me." Then she pushed a glass towards him. Slowly and with pleasure they drank a couple of glasses. Without any hurry they enjoyed the familiar presence of each other and the taste of the whisky.

It was Beatriz, who broke the silence, "Dervla used artificial insemination."

Peter was surprised but not concerned, "Really?"

Thoughtfully Beatriz said, "I wondered who the father was. Patrick is definitely not a direct clone of Beatriz. His Y-chromosome genome must have come from somewhere."

Peter nodded, "Yes, he looks different from Dervla." He thought a little, "Maybe she spliced a Y-chromosome on her own DNA. Who knows? She's very talented. We probably have the equipment, and we don't have many regulations."

Beatriz seemed sure, "Patrick doesn't have the same mother and father. Dervla's not that crazy. The inbreeding coefficient would be too high."

Peter shrugged. He didn't know what she meant.

Beatriz asked Meichun, "What would happen if someone uses the same DNA for both the mother and father?"

Meichun's voice sounded almost friendly, "Since most hereditary diseases are inherited recessively, a high inbreeding coefficient can lead to the occurrence of unexpected hereditary diseases. If the same DNA is mixed twice, this is very likely to happen because there is no possibility for the DNA to use a healthy gene variant."

Peter thought, whisky and DNA don't mix with each other very well, but asked, "Do you know who the father is?"

Beatriz shrugged her shoulders and said, "I don't know."

As Patrick walked up to Art Feldmann's statue, he saw Paul and Charlie standing there. They were in their Moon Base outside uniforms but didn't have their helmets on. He looked and sounded amazed as he asked, "Are you going outside?"

Charlie and Paul looked at each other and smiled. Paul said, "We are all going outside."

Charlie added, "You're big enough for a little moonwalk. Did you bring the sunglasses?"

Patrick was thrilled and his whole face shone, "Yes."

Charlie suggested, "Then we need to outfit you with an outside uniform."

Together they walked past the statue of Art Feldmann towards the spacesuit locker room. Patrick could hardly restrain himself from jumping, and each of his steps came with a small excited suppressed leap. He was imagining trying on different suits until they found a suitable one. He could hardly believe it. He was going outside.

When they arrived in the locker room, Charlie chose one of the smaller suits. He assured Patrick it wasn't a woman's suit, even though Patrick didn't seem to care.

Charlie explained, "The smaller suits are for women and children, except for the size there is no difference between the suits, and each suit is assembled specially for each person. You don't just get a full suit. First we have to find the right parts for you."

Patrick let it all happen around him. He could hardly believe it and didn't know what he could do to help, but he did want to know, "Why are the suits white and purple?"

Charlie looked at the suit a little confused before explaining, "The suits are white so that they can reflect the Sun's rays easily. If we are in the Sun all the time the white reflects more heat and makes it easier to keep the temperature in the suit under control. The suits come with cooling units, but we don't want to overload them." He smiled pleased with his explanation.

Patrick nodded and agreed that he didn't want to get too hot.

Charlie kindly added, "Your young eyes will be very sensitive to the sunlight. Beatriz prepared the sunglasses for you to protect your eyes. You have to wear them." Beatriz had already explained to Charlie that Patrick needed special sunglasses that filter more UV light than normal if he was going to go outside.

Patrick was excited to be wearing the full suit. Paul and Charlie watched him as he moved around. They wanted to check that he could walk well without a helmet and that he was strong enough to move around independently.

Charlie warned him, "I know you are very strong for your age, but when we go outside of the Moon Base Art Feldmann's field, it becomes much easier to walk around. And that means you have to be careful."

Charlie said, "Sunglasses on, helmet on, and let's go." They went through the airlock together and started their short space walk. This was a test to see if Patrick could cope with the stresses of wearing a spacesuit, and to see if he was physically strong enough to wear it.

Charlie watched Patrick carefully as Paul showed him around the outside of the base. They only stayed outside about 30 minutes, and the time went by quickly. Even so Charlie was relieved when they got back inside, as he didn't feel directly responsible for Patrick's safety anymore.

Peter looked at the surveillance monitors and saw Charlie, Paul and Patrick returning from their moonwalk. He was relieved that Patrick was back safe and sound. He knew there wasn't any good reason to worry, but he was worried anyway. Patrick represented the future and held everyone together, a life without him would be unbearable.

Moonday Twelve

Date: Tuesday 2nd October 2153 – 09:45 CET
Location: Alpha 12 – Moon Base

Patrick came running into the infirmary almost bouncing with energy. He started sliding a little too late to stop himself elegantly, but he just about managed to stop before he hit the wall, although his captain's hat almost fell off. Luckily, he managed to grab it in time, and set it straight on his head. He looked around and said loudly and excitedly, "It's Moonday and my birthday. Where are you?" He sounded happy. He raced around the front office of the infirmary looking for Beatriz. He even checked under the desk to see if she was there.

He stood in the middle of the room and his shoulders fell as he realised that she wasn't waiting for him. Uncertain what to do he stood frozen to the spot. Then he decided to look for Beatriz. He smiled. It must be a game. Then his face fell. Or, had she forgotten. She was good at forgetting things. He laughed. It was his birthday. Then he looked around to see if he could see a present or a note but found nothing, and he wondered where she was. He looked under her desk again and then glanced at the door to the isolation room. He'd never been in there and wasn't sure if anyone ever went in. Could she have hidden herself in there? There was a window covered with a curtain next to the door. He could just peek through it and if she was there that wouldn't hurt anyone. Was she in there? He hesitated and looked around to see if anyone was watching. Was he allowed to look through the window? He moved cautiously towards the curtain, and at arm's length he lifted it slightly before letting it fall back. No alarms sounded so he tried it again and raised it a little more before letting it fall and looking around. Then he carefully pushed the curtain aside but only enough for him to just see through, and he dared himself to look through the window. He smiled as he noticed Beatriz. She was standing on one side of the bed, and her hand lay on Europa's forehead. Europa was very pale and laying on the bed.

Beatriz looked up as she noticed Patrick's shadow in the light of the opened curtain. She turned around and smiled at him. He watched her come through the door and take off the plastic gloves which she put in the Re-Do machine as she said, "Patrick, I'm so sorry, but we're going to have to postpone your annual check-up to next week."

Patrick looked visibly disappointed and said in a high-pitched voice, "But why?"

Beatriz explained patiently, "Europa is very sick. She's got a cold, and it's going to take her a few days to get well again. We don't want you to get sick on your birthday, do we?" She smiled at him. Patrick had never had a cold, and Beatriz didn't want to take any chances. She wanted to protect him. She wasn't sure how his immune system would react to a virus, and she didn't want to find out.

Patrick shook and nodded his head at the same time. He didn't want to get sick but wasn't sure if yes or no was the appropriate answer.

Beatriz's voice was compassionate and apologetic, "I'm sorry I couldn't let you know, but I was hoping that she might be well today." She smiled apologetically and promised him, "We'll do it next week when Europa is well."

Disappointment showed clearly on his face, but he tried to be brave for Europa. He looked at her through the window and said, "Her face looks thinner."

Beatriz explained kindly, "She hasn't eaten much for a few days, and she's been in bed the whole time."

Patrick looked concerned as he said, "If she's not eating that's not good. It's not healthy."

Beatriz answered patiently, "You're right, it isn't."

He asked a little worried, "How long will it last?"

Beatriz smiled, and thought he hasn't had any experience with colds or flu, as she explained, "I'm not sure, it could take up to a week."

Patrick's mouth fell open a little, and he articulated his words clearly, "A whole week." Then he looked disappointed as he realised, "There'll be no lesson with Europa today." He stared at Beatriz shaking his head. He wasn't sure what to do and where he should go next.

Beatriz noticed his indecision and suggested that he should go and look for Paul.

Patrick grinned and as he turned around abruptly to run away, he collided with Steve, who had sneaked up behind him.

Steve, with his strong hands, held Patrick upright and laughed. Patrick recovered quickly from the shock and laughed as well before remembering his plan to run away and find Paul.

Beatriz looked at Steve frustrated. She sighed and said, "Hello, Steve." It didn't sound welcoming.

Steve said neutrally, "I thought I'd stop by."

Beatriz was suspicious, "Are you waiting for something?"

He shrugged his shoulders and didn't answer the question.

She looked him in the eye and said, "I know what you did."

Steve took a step back and said in a low controlled voice, "I don't know what you mean."

Beatriz looked at him intensely and clarified, "The DNA sequencing of the virus didn't take long. It's not a virus that came with us and has reappeared." She watched him and waited for him to react.

He remained silent, but he seemed interested.

Beatriz's voice was serious, "The virus is new, and Europa has had an extreme immune system response to it. She's really very poorly."

Steve had enough decency to look concerned.

Beatriz sighed again, "There are only three people on this base who know how to create a targeted virus. I am one, Dervla is another, and she told me that you've been experimenting in her lab for months." She paused, maybe he wanted to confess something.

He looked at her apparently innocently.

She kept her tone steady, "I am very impressed that you learnt how to modify a virus if you have no official qualifications in genetics."

Steve casually explained, "There's a lot of good information in the Intellinet. You can find everything there."

Beatriz frowned, "Why did you do it?"

He pulled a face, as if he didn't care, "She was rude when she rejected me."

Beatriz was surprised but not really, "You developed a personal bio virus because she didn't want to have sex with you?"

He nodded calmly.

Beatriz had suspected the answer, but the confirmation nevertheless came as a surprise. She shook her head in disapproval as she said, "Well, that's a new kind of revenge. Come on, look at her." They went together to the window of the isolation room. Beatriz opened the curtain further and let Steve see how pale and thin Europa looked. "Her immune system is overreacting to help her body fight the virus. I assume that's not what you wanted."

He looked at Europa and then looked at the floor. He said in a small voice, "I didn't know it would be that bad."

Beatriz explained, "It's a dangerous game to play creating a targeted virus. Although if it doesn't mutate, at least no one else will get sick."

He sounded remorseful as he asked, "Is there anything I can do?"

Beatriz closed the curtain, and she said, "Haven't you done enough?" As soon as she had said those words, she felt guilty and regretted it. With a kinder tone she added, "I'll let you know if she needs anything."

Steve looked guilty as he turned around and left.

Maria, who was carrying flowers in a vase, noticed Steve's expression and wondered what he'd done.

Beatriz took the flowers from Maria and explained that Europa was too sick for flowers. Beatriz put them on the table, and said, "We'll put them in her room when she's a little better." Beatriz smiled at Maria soothingly.

Maria was concerned about Europa's condition. They both looked at Europa through the window as Maria asked, "Is she getting better? Can I go in and talk to her?"

Beatriz shook her head and assured her that it was only a matter of time before Europa recovered.

Patrick went looking for Paul and Astro. He found Paul in the warehouse playing with Astro. They'd invented a new game, and Astro was trying to find what Paul suggested. Patrick watched Paul for less than a minute and really wanted to play as well. Paul laughed and explained the rules of the game. Patrick told Astro what he should find and off he went and beeped when he had found it.

Patrick got bored with the game quickly because Astro couldn't bring anything back. He could only track it down. Patrick looked at his foot as he kicked Paul's desk gently and explained that Europa was in the isolation room and that he had to wait a week for the physical, and there wouldn't be a lesson today. Patrick looked disappointed and sad.

Patrick's exaggerated sadness made Paul laugh and he patted Patrick lightly on the back and said, "I've got a short film for you. Let's make our own lesson." He smiled, and Patrick couldn't help but want to join in.

They moved over to Paul's workstation, and Paul made sure that Patrick was sitting comfortably before starting the short film. The film was about the Orion constellation and showed where it was in the sky. Paul paused the film to remind Patrick that they'd seen Orion together and how they had followed the other stars to find it. Then he played the film again, and they watched what would happen if the 3D image of the Orion stars rotated. It started with the view of the stars that we see, and the image looked flat. Paul asked Patrick, "Are the stars the same distance away from us?"

Patrick shrugged his shoulders, "I guess so."

Paul smiled and said, "Wait and see."

The image rotated slowly and showed a sideways view of the stars. Patrick was amazed, and he looked at Paul as he realised how far apart from each other the stars really were.

Patrick was impressed, "I thought the stars were all the same distance away. This is great."

With sparkling eyes Paul replied, "But what's really good is that we can use the drones to reproduce this concept really well."

Patrick didn't know what he meant, but he was curious and wanted to find out.

Paul put on a BULcap helmet and grinned. He sent out four drones holding flashlights. They moved to different distances in a long corridor in the large hall where Paul und Patrick could see them. Patrick watched them move with fascination. The drones took their places, turned on their flashlights, and waited. Then Paul turned off the lights in the storeroom. They were in the dark, except for the flashlights, the points of light looking like a flat picture. Patrick laughed and pointed as he said, "It's great, but why did we use flashlights when we could have used the drones' headlights?"

Paul looked at him, laughed briefly and explained, "Because it's more fun with flashlights." He turned the lights back on and suggested that they visit Maria.

Maria was waiting in the main garden. She was looking at a tree and watching two birds feeding on a half-hidden bird feeder. As Patrick approached, she looked at him and put her fingers on her lips and whispered, "Super quiet."

He nodded eagerly and watched with her.

In a hushed voice she said, "Even though the two birds look the same, one is male and the other female. Can you tell the difference?"

Patrick looked closely at the birds then glanced at Maria. He seemed confused, "The vioviolet on the left looks prettier than the darker bird on the right."

Maria looked at him a little taken aback at his pronunciation of violet and answered as patiently as she could, "They're not violet. What do you mean?"

Patrick remained looking at the birds as he spoke, and was relaxed, "You can see the difference easily between the birds. They don't look alike at all. The left one has purple spots on the feathers."

Paul laughed quietly to himself.

Maria looked at Paul puzzled, and asked, "The sexual dichromatism of these birds is only visible under UV light.

Humans can't see any difference, only the birds themselves. Can he see ultraviolet light?"

Paul shrugged his shoulders and then nodded smiling.

Maria shook her head and told Patrick, "The bird on the left is female."

Patrick smiled and nodded, "She's more beautiful."

Peter was standing in his office, looking in the mirror watching himself put on his captain's hat. He smiled at himself and leaned closer to look at his wrinkles. He comforted himself with the thought that he looked younger than his fifty-five years, but he was feeling his age today. His muscles felt stiff, and he was low on energy. He hoped he wasn't getting sick. He felt in control as he flipped the switch to convert the wall mirror back into a picture, then turned around and picked up the certificate off his desk and went to see Beatriz. He wanted to go and see Europa before he went to the birthday party. For the last few days, he'd been to see her regularly to convince himself that her condition wasn't getting any worse. As he walked slowly, he felt helpless wishing that there was something he could do other than just wait. Beatriz had told him that it could last for another week. It was the first time that someone had become sick since he was in charge, and he didn't like it. He sighed and walked slower.

When he arrived, he stood in the doorway and looked at Beatriz. She saw him immediately and smiled, waving him in as she said, "I thought you'd come this morning."

He looked serious and nodded, "How is Europa doing?"

Beatriz replied softly, "No change, her condition remains stable." She looked over Peter's shoulder and to the closed curtain and said, "We've many automated medical treatments, but it still makes a difference when someone is there. Someone to take care of you." She looked at Peter, "I don't think any machine can replace a caring hand on your forehead."

Peter nodded in agreement. He could see the worry in Beatriz's eyes. She'd told him that it was just a virus, but he could sense how helpless she felt, and it bothered him. He asked, "Is she awake?"

Beatriz shook her head, "I don't want to wake her."

Peter nodded. He could understand that. Without looking at her, he said, "I'm going to Patrick's birthday party. Are you coming too?"

Beatriz looked towards the curtain and said, "No, I don't want to leave her. I'm sure Patrick will understand."

Peter nodded and still had a worried expression as he left to go to the party.

Peter was soon standing facing Patrick, they were both smiling at each other and wearing their captain's hats. He nodded to Patrick, the light reflecting from the black peak of his hat, as his head bowed in appreciation and respect to Patrick, who nodded in return but with too much force, and his hat slipped. It made them both laugh. Still half-laughing Peter congratulated Patrick and handed him his birthday certificate.

Grinning, Patrick stood up straighter to accept the certificate and then held it in his arms pressed against his chest. He looked proud, he had the feeling that he'd earned it. He thanked Peter warmly and promised that he was going to hang it up with the others.

As soon as Patrick finished speaking, Steve cleared his throat, everyone turned to look at him. When he was sure he had everyone's attention, he leant over the table and lifted the oversized cake lid to reveal his latest creation, Patrick's birthday cake. The sounds of awe reverberated through the room. The birthday cake was amazing. They moved in closer around the table to look at the details in the icing of the mini Moon Base. Peter looked at Steve and nodded appreciatively. He'd gone to a lot of trouble, and it wasn't unnoticed.

Steve enjoyed his moment in the limelight.

Patrick was pointing at the details of the main garden. He was a little too excited, and his unsteady hand got a little too near. Luckily Maria managed to push Patrick's hand aside just in time. Otherwise the main garden would have had a new skylight.

Dervla was looking at the cake from different angles and asked, "How on Earth did you even manage to bake such a cake? It's amazing."

Steve took a step up to the cake where the entrance to the Moon Base was and held a big knife in his hand, ready to cut into Art Feldmann's area.

Patrick looked worried and said, "Charlie's not here. We should wait for him before we cut the cake. Otherwise it won't be fair."

Steve looked at Patrick and smiled before answering, "If he wanted to see the cake he should have been here." Then he pushed the knife into the cake with a satisfied smile and started cutting it into pieces.

Peter watched him and was a little disturbed by Steve's apparent glee while cutting. He seemed to be enjoying destroying the Moon Base. Peter tried smiling at the others. He was hoping it would distract him.

Peter noticed Paul and Patrick standing next to each other and observed them as they raised their hands together and put the food in their mouths at the same time and realised that they had the same way of eating cake. He glanced at the other men in the room and wondering if any of them resembled Patrick. Was one of these men the sperm donor? He wondered if they had a picture of John when he was 12 years old. It could be that he looked like him. He heard a laugh and looked at Patrick and Paul sharing a joke. Patrick was getting on very well with Paul, maybe they have similar genetics. When Peter looked over at Steve, he shook his head involuntary. It wasn't Steve, they were just too different. He needed to remember to ask Beatriz why they still hadn't done a paternity test.

The quietness in the room proved how good the cake tasted as everyone was concentrating on eating. Maria was looking at the cake and considering eating a second piece as Charlie ran excitedly into the room.

He stopped near the doorway and didn't see the cake. In between trying to catch his breath he said, "There's a new Twitter message on my account." He looked around before adding in a voice barely above a whisper, "Someone from Earth has contacted me." His eyes were wide and almost tearful.

Steve sounded cruel as he laughed and sneered, "Don't be daft. Who would want to get in touch with you?"

Charlie turned to him and looked hurt. He put his arms on his hips and looked at him sternly, "I really have got a new message."

Everyone continued watching him, they didn't dare look at each other.

"What's Twitter?" Patrick asked puzzled about what was happening.

Liam's hand was itching to look at his mobile communication device that was hanging from his belt. He looked at Steve and resisted the temptation.

Steve started laughing but managed to say, "And you think the Twitter message is from Earth? After almost thirteen years without us hearing a word, you think that they'd choose your Twitter account to get back in touch with us?" He looked at Charlie and laughed at him.

Charlie seemed to grow smaller, "You think it's a trick?"

Steve mocked, "You're such an idiot. How could you believe it's real?" And with his words, he burst Charlie's dream, but it wasn't just his dream, for a short moment there had been hope that everything was normal again. Steve looked at their facial expressions and laughed as he took a piece of cake from the main garden.

Maria walked over to Charlie and hugged him before she held his head against her shoulder and stroked his back.

Peter turned to Steve, "We need to talk."

Steve nodded calmly, and they took a few steps away from the others. Steve continued eating the cake nonchalantly.

In a hushed tone, Peter asked him, "You know that it isn't acceptable to behave like this." He looked intensely at Steve, "What's the matter?"

Steve shrugged his shoulders, "Nothing. I guess, I'm just bored."

Peter looked closely at Steve and asked him, "Do you need a break? Away from the others?"

Steve immediately understood that Peter meant the Moon Base prison, "Aren't we already in a prison? Will it really make a difference if I spend time there?" He gave Peter a challenging look.

Peter kept his voice steady, "You're disturbing the others. Can't you see that?"

With a dismissive wave of his hand Steve said, "It was just a joke. Who'd have thought he'd believe it? How stupid can he really be?"

Peter nodded and thought for a moment before saying, "Then we'll let it go. I don't want to hear anything else about it."

Steve nodded and looked a little guilty as he left the party.

Peter looked him up and down as he left and thought, "Maybe it's Moon Madness. He's going a little crazy, or maybe he just needs a change, something new." Then he realised that they'd all been doing the same job for almost thirteen years.

As Peter returned to the group, Dervla was asking Patrick, "And what are you doing on your birthday afternoon?"

Patrick beamed with excitement and was almost trembling as he explained, "We're going outside this afternoon. My spacesuit has been measured and prepared, and we're ready for a moonwalk." With wide eyes he looked over at Paul and Charlie.

With a mock serious expression, Dervla asked him, "Have you asked your mother for permission to go on a moonwalk?"

Panic spread across Patrick's face and in a small, high voice he stuttered, "May I go?"

Dervla smiled jokingly and said, "Of course you can."

He sighed loudly, and his shoulders fell then he almost jumped up and said, "We are going to walk outside the Art Feldmann's Field. It can be felt up to twelve kilometres away. The field gets weaker and weaker the further we go, and when there is less gravity, it's more fun to jump."

Charlie smiled and laughed to himself on hearing how well Patrick remembered what they'd told him an hour ago.

Patrick smiled and looked around as he added, "We are taking one of the moon vehicles."

Dervla pretended as if she didn't know, "Indeed. And who is going to be looking out for you?"

Patrick looked serious as he answered, "Liam is going to watch our journey from the base and Charlie and Paul are coming with me."

Charlie stepped up and assured Dervla, "He's very tall and strong for a twelve-year-old, so he is ready to take a moonwalk."

Dervla smiled at Patrick's excitement. It was going to be the first time that he'd go outside Art Feldmann's area, and it was obvious that he was happy. Dervla reminded him, "You must behave well and don't do anything dangerous." Then she added, "And don't forget your sunglasses."

Patrick nodded eagerly but stopped as he remembered what he wanted to ask his mother. There was a photo in his mother's room, which showed Damian, Filip and John in their orange spacesuits just before they returned. He seen it almost every day and never really looked, but now he wanted to know why Damian and his crew were wearing orange spacesuits and not white and purple suits like his Moon Base spacesuit.

But it was Paul who replied, "When you fly back to Earth, you wear orange. Orange has a higher visibility, so the search team can find you easily."

Patrick nodded and asked, "Can we take Astro with us?"

Paul could clearly hear the pleading in Patrick's voice, and he didn't like having to disappoint him but had to explain, "Astro can only move around inside. He was never equipped for outdoor work."

Patrick looked sad but accepted the answer.

Dervla raised her finger and warned Patrick, "Don't spend too much time in the sunshine." She knew that Patrick liked the Sun and wanted to go to Earth to enjoy sunshine with the protection of an atmosphere.

The forming of a question showed clearly on Patrick's face before he asked, "If we are in the Sun, can we sunbathe?"

Paul shook his head and explained, "We can't sunbathe, we'll be wearing our spacesuits."

Charlie added, "The helmets have safety visors, and you'll need your special sunglasses too." Then he laughed and turned to Paul before asking him, "Which of the moon vehicles shall we take? Do you want to drive, or shall I?"

Paul and Charlie looked at each other and laughed before Paul said, "Are we ready? Let's go."

Peter came with them and joined in waving goodbye to the party. They walked towards Art Feldmann's statue together, well they would have if Patrick hadn't been walking a little too fast. On the way Charlie and Paul discussed the pros and cons of which vehicle they should take with them. Patrick was listening with fascination, while trying not to walk to fast.

With a sensible and serious expression Charlie explained, "We only want to drive about twelve kilometres. It's enough to use one of the normal lunar vehicles. We don't need to take an anti-gravity vehicle." He looked at Patrick and said, "The antigrav vehicles can travel up to 200 km/h, and they are equipped with a toilet and an autopilot." He smiled broadly, and Patrick laughed with joy.

Paul had an idea, "If we take a normal moon vehicle, Patrick can have a go at driving and try for his license."

Charlie objected, "He's not old enough to get a base driver's license. You have to be eighteen years old."

Paul countered, "He's tall enough to reach the foot pedals and strong enough for the gear stick. Why not, and who really cares how old he is? It's Peter who issues the licenses when we're done." He looked at Peter to see if it was okay.

Peter nodded in agreement, it wasn't a bad idea.

Charlie thought for a moment and realised that nobody was going to mind.

As they approached Art Feldmann's statue, they realised something was wrong. A brown liquid was dripping from the statue. Peter looked at it, wished the others lots of fun and said that he would pursue the matter with the liquid.

Peter took a closer look at the statue and knew immediately that Steve was responsible. Peter was annoyed and disgusted with him. How dare Steve disfigure the Art Feldmann's statue. He could feel the blood racing in his veins and his heart pumping, and he realised how angry he was. He actually enjoyed the feeling, the flow of energy in his veins. It had been a long time since he'd felt so alive and part of him was grateful to Steve. He looked at the statue for a while as he calmed down. He decided that he'd ask Liam to repair the damage. Peter shook his head. Steve had probably been bored and wanted to see what would happen to the beer and if it really would fall on her face if the statue moved too quickly. Regardless of why Steve had done it, Peter knew he needed to talk to him.

The air in the main garden always seemed cooler to Peter than in other areas of the Moon Base. He resisted the temptation to cool his head by taking off his captain's hat. He wanted to keep the feeling of authority. He breathed in and out deeply and enjoyed the smell of the flowers and plants. His step was slow as he walked towards the second lab, Steve's lab. Peter just wanted to make sure everything was okay with Steve. He pressed the buzzer to announce his arrival, but without waiting he went straight in, ignoring his own rule. He knew Steve wasn't doing anything dangerous, and he also didn't want to wait.

Steve had placed a map of the South Pole of the Moon on a huge table in the middle of the room and was leaning over it marking a spot as Peter walked in. Without looking at Peter, he explained, "I am looking for caves. I don't know if I'm going to find anything. It's my new hobby. I started with a map of craters, but nobody cares. No one on Earth cares what we're doing."

Peter said in a flat tone, "I've seen the statue."

Steve kept looking at the map, "I know, otherwise you wouldn't be here."

Peter said as compassionately as possible, "What happened?"

Steve deliberately misunderstood the question, "There was no beer in the glass, I shook the beer over her myself."

Peter was angry that Steve had dared to treat the statue so disrespectfully, "Someone has to clean the statue."

"That's what the Sauberbots are for." He looked at Peter provocatively, "I freaked out. I feel trapped, bored. I wanted to feel alive again."

Peter understood exactly what Steve meant, but asked, "Was it Moon Madness?"

Steve ignored Peter's comment, and his voice sounded practical and resigned when he asked, "Will there be a punishment?"

Peter replied, "No, not this time. Everything can be repaired." Then he smiled and added, "You've probably touched too many moonstones." He looked closely at Steve as he spoke, and wondered if Steve wanted to be punished or if he'd changed his medication.

Third Renewal

Date: Saturday 26th October 2154 – 10:00 CET
Location: Alpha 12 – Moon Base

Peter was late, he stood up abruptly, stamped his foot on the floor to rid it of pins and needles and swiveled his head around. He felt his neck click and tried moving his shoulders to ease the tension. He wasn't even sure what he was looking for. He gathered himself together and hurried out of his office. He didn't know why he was late. He'd started preparing early enough. Although he had a vague feeling that he'd simply forgotten to get out of his chair on time. He decided that he could think about it later, but now he didn't want to appear disrespectful to the others, not today, not the day of the renewal meeting. He concentrated on his breathing as he walked as fast as possible to the meeting room. Halfway there he stopped suddenly remembering that he'd forgotten his captain's hat. He looked behind him and then forward again wondering briefly if he should go fetch it before deciding he could manage without it.

Everyone was waiting as he arrived. He'd known they'd be waiting. Peter articulated every word as slowly and clearly as possible, partly because he was a little out of breath but also to hide his nervousness, "It is the beginning of our fifteenth year on the Moon Base and this means it's time to renew our contracts." He looked at them waiting for a reaction. None came so he remained calm and continued, "We are meeting for our annual get-together. The date was calculated in advance, as it has been every year, by Earth Base Columbus."

Europa interrupted him, "That is not true. This year the optimal perigee was June 24th and Columbus had calculated the shift change for that day. In October this year, the Moon is simply too far away for a shift change to be practical."

Peter forced himself to smile as he realised that Europa also had the Columbus list of return dates. He should have known. He nodded at Europa and then looked down at the table to hide his mistake. He didn't feel guilty about trying to lie about the date but was annoyed with himself for slipping up so easily. He'd deliberately delayed the meeting from June, delaying the confrontation for as long as possible and had won four months of peace for himself. He really should have known that Europa would have the list. Either she had it from Columbus, or she'd compiled it herself.

Peter forced his friendliest smile and looked at his attentive audience and explained, "We're used to meeting in October, I didn't want to disturb the cycle." He watched their reactions and felt a moment of relief as they nodded, not really seeming to care that they were meeting on the wrong date.

Peter was sure that their continued peaceful coexistence depended on his next sentence. He decided to keep his voice as calm and steady as possible, but he still breathed in deeply before he started the sentence and paused, before he rushed to say the words, "We can extend the contracts for another five years as we have done previously." He stopped and looked at them. He had the feeling that if he explained slowly, that they would better understand and be more likely to agree. He added, "And then we wait until Patrick turns sixteen before deciding what to do next."

He waited for an apparent consensus. The response was underwhelming, and he made the most of it. He smiled at them as if he had good news and explained, "This will be the third extension, and the favourable conditions from the previous contracts still apply." He nodded his head to encourage a positive response.

Beatriz seemed confused and asked, "The third extension. What happened to the second one?"

Peter thought she was joking as did a few of the others, but Maria laid her hand on Beatriz's arm gently, and when Beatriz turned to look at Maria she said, "Don't worry, it's surprising how time flies."

Beatriz just managed to tolerate Maria's kindness and forced her grimace into a smile. She calmed down enough to join in with the laughter that helped her hide her confusion and embarrassment.

Europa leaned forward and put one hand on the table, straightened her back and announced, "I want to return before Patrick's sixteenth birthday."

Peter gave her his full attention, she looked very serious. This wasn't part of his plan.

Steve sounded calm and thoughtful as he interrupted the silence, "It's three years until Patrick's sixteenth birthday that seems like a long wait to me. If there's a chance to go back earlier, I want to go, and I'm already on the returners list." Steve continued looking at Peter and watched for his reaction.

Peter kept his expression neutral. He could see that he meant it. It wasn't even a challenge, it was more of a polite request. He looked around at the team. They were getting tired of being stuck on the Moon. On the one hand they knew they were safe here and could easily stay, but on the other hand they were craving change and contact with different people.

Peter looked to Europa and asked politely, "Why do you want to return?"

Europa sounded both honest and resigned as she answered, "I have done a lot of research, and I'm slowly coming to the end of my work. I've had fifteen years with the most amazing equipment instead of the expected five. I want to go home to celebrate the two hundredth anniversary of Sputnik, and that means I have to fly before Patrick's sixteenth birthday."

Steve snorted and mocked her, "Do you really think people on Earth are in a position to celebrate?"

Liam looked at Steve disapprovingly and interrupted him, "I think it's more than possible. Decades of preparation have gone into making this anniversary special, and I can easily understand Europa's desire to want to be there."

With a touch of surprise raising the tone of Peter's voice, he asked, "Do you want to go as well, Liam?"

Liam froze and looked worried almost scared then he laughed briefly before he replied in a firm voice, "I don't have any urgent plan to return." Liam looked at Peter. He knew the reason why he'd never return. Had Peter expected him to just change his mind?

Apologetically Peter smiled at Liam and tried to appear nonchalant, but he worried about what could happen when the ship landed. They still had no idea what had happened and could die as soon as they landed, but then stopping them from returning, when they wanted to return, would also be dangerous. He observed the quick and questioning looks darting between the team and pretended to be waiting for a reaction, but he was weighing up the situation. They had to believe that they could decide freely, and if they didn't then they'd get the feeling that they were trapped. His eyes flicked through the faces before him, and he cautiously explained, "The escape pods travel with three people. We have to send three people together, or someone is left here without a possible return."

Their answer was a general silence.

Peter said, "Does anyone else want to return?"

Paul looked at the table in front of him as he said in a small voice, "I should return," he looked at Beatriz, "if I can."

Peter couldn't hide the disappointment in his face but managed to ask in a controlled tone, "You want to go back?"

Paul cleared his throat and half looked at Peter, he seemed sad as he said, "You all know about my DNA damage. I should have only stayed five years. The risk of problems increases with every year that I stay."

Peter eyes showed a deep sadness as he nodded stoically.

Beatriz looked at Paul sympathetically and said, "We have the situation under control. The medication and the regular check-ups keep everything under control. Don't worry about it. It shouldn't be a reason for you to return."

Paul relaxed in his seat and breathed out audibly. He smiled at Beatriz before saying, "I'd like to go with Patrick when he flies to Earth. I want to show him the things on Earth that we have talked about." As he smiled, the tears in his eyes caught the light.

Peter nodded, completely confirming Paul's feelings.

Dervla looked at Peter and said in a determined tone, "I'm not going anywhere without Patrick."

Charlie looked around and added, "I'm both happy to stay or to return." He looked pointedly at Maria.

Maria hesitated. She took her necklace in her hand, turned it over several times before saying, "I'd like to stay with my gardens, I don't want to return in a rush."

Steve looked at the people in amazement, "Do you want to die here? What are you waiting for?"

Peter remained calm and wanted to stop Steve from disturbing the others, "We are waiting until Patrick is strong enough to survive the journey."

Disparagingly Steve replied, "Have you looked at Patrick lately. He is already strong enough to survive the journey. We might have muscle wastage problems because we've gotten used to a lower gravity, but he doesn't."

Dervla turned to Steve, "He is too young. He's just a child."

Steve laughed, "Is that really what this is about, or is it one child too many. There are ten people and only nine options to return."

Dervla looked at him angrily, she remained quiet, but seemed about to explode. The rest of the group either looked at the table or were looking to each other for reassurance. Nobody wanted to say it, but they knew that Steve was right. They wanted to delay the decision because nobody knew what to do. They couldn't leave someone on the Moon without a plan of escape.

Peter took control, "Okay, does anyone else have anything to say? If not, I'll extend the contracts, and if anyone wants to meet with me, just drop by."

Peter looked around, there weren't any questions, and they seemed satisfied. At least nobody said anything. Peter's eyes searched for his captain's hat before he reminded himself that it was still in his office.

Shortly afterwards, Peter was sitting in his office. He had his captain's hat on his head, and was waiting patiently, or rather, he was trying not to think about who would come. He had a rough idea who would come, and he wasn't looking forward to it. The first to come was Charlie. Peter hadn't expected to see him, but he welcomed him anyway and offered him a lunchtime whisky. Charlie refused good naturedly. He explained that he was happy with the employment contract. He just wanted to talk about returning. He wanted to make it clear, that he wanted to stay with Maria. If she goes home, then he will go, and if she stays, he wants to stay.

Peter nodded and told Charlie that he understood. He'd never expected anything else of Charlie. He knew how much Maria meant to him.

Europa was waiting as Charlie left, and she wasn't happy, "I meant it. I want to go back. It doesn't have to be right away, and I know we need a third volunteer. I'm sure you can get someone to return with us." She looked at him challengingly. "We all want to go home sometime. It's only a matter of time." Then she avoided his gaze before admitting, "At first I was too scared to return. I pretended that I wanted to stay for work, and I think I even believed it myself. But it wasn't true. I was too much of a coward." She looked him straight in the eye, "I was scared, and I know I'm still scared, but I also know I'm not getting any younger. I don't want to wait so long that I can use my age as an excuse not to return."

Peter listened very carefully to Europa. When she was done, he glanced at his reflection in the mirror wall. He'd looked in the mirror before the meeting and not converted it back to a picture. Europa followed his gaze and looked in the mirror. They looked at each other's reflection and smiled broadly both showing their wrinkles. Europa laughed, "Neither of us is getting any younger."

She turned to him again, "I know that my family is probably dead. I'm also aware that if we land, Columbus won't be there to pick us up. I realise that it could be that I can't get to my sister or to the Sputnik celebration. It's risky to return to Earth, but if I don't try, I'll die here bit by bit, and I'll never be able to forgive myself."

Peter nodded that he understood but seemed a little lost in his sadness.

As Europa left the room, he watched her walk out. She was so sure. She knew exactly what she wanted, and she wasn't letting her fear stop her. He hadn't asked her if she had any other plans. She'd only mentioned the Sputnik celebration. He looked in the mirror again and thought about his wife. He still missed her even after fifteen years. It occurred to him that he didn't even know what she looked like. He'd already tried ageing her photo on the computer, but the resulting pictures never seemed real. He felt that they were more like a possible shadow of what she could become. He converted the mirror wall back into a picture and glanced at the clock. He was expecting someone else.

Steve was visibly upset when he walked in and started complaining immediately, "The offer for the contract extension isn't good enough."

Peter waited. He knew more was coming.

"And why isn't there any chance of advancement. I've been in the same job for fifteen years."

He stared intensively at Peter.

Peter thought quickly, "I need a deputy. I'll put it in the captain's logbook that you were promoted."

Steve took a little step back and was visibly calmer. He even smiled and nodded. He liked the idea of working as a deputy, "Do I get a captain's hat?"

Peter kept his expression serious and replied, "I think that's appropriate. Shall I arrange that, or would you like to do it yourself?"

Steve was flattered and self-satisfied, and said, "I'll do it."

Peter was relieved as he left, but then he realised that he had a new deputy. He needed to tell Liam and Beatriz. He was sure Beatriz didn't care, but he didn't want to hurt Liam's feelings.

Peter sat and waited a while, but no one else came for a private meeting. Peter stood up, laid his hands on the table and sighed. He checked that his uniform was in order, gathered his energy and went to Liam. He explained what he'd arranged with Steve. Steve wanted a promotion, and it would be officially published in the captain's log. There wasn't much else to offer him.

Liam looked at the screen while Peter spoke and shrugged his shoulders when he finished and said, "I know. Steve was already here to show off."

Peter looked apologetic, "I'm sorry."

Liam turned and looked at Peter. He saw in his face that he meant it, "I don't care. I understand why you did it, and also how little it changes my reality." Liam thought briefly, "Actually, I do care. I mean, it's a good thing, because it might make Steve act like a better person."

Peter smiled. He liked Liam's rational side.

Liam kept concentrating on his monitor and as Peter left, he said, "By the way, you've forgot your hat again."

Peter laughed and went back to his office, when he got there he sat down slowly. The captain's hat was on the table right in front of him. He stroked the hat gently and thought it means less and less to me. Then he called Beatriz and asked her if she wanted to take a break and talk to him. He sat back in his chair and wondered if he was happy, and was he doing with his life what he really wanted? He bit his lower lip and wondered if maybe a whisky would help.

Beatriz didn't take long before she arrived. She smiled beautifully at him and asked Peter if everything had gone well.

Peter ignored her question, "Do you think the experiment with the air quality worked well?"

Beatriz smiled, now she knew what he wanted, "No one but Maria noticed that we'd tried anything at all."

Peter was curious, "How did she know?"

Beatriz smiled and seemed relaxed, "She measures the air constantly to make sure her plants are doing well. She noticed on the first day."

Peter nodded. It was obvious to Beatriz that he wanted to say something, and that the current topic wasn't what he really wanted to talk about. She added as encouragement for him, "I think low levels of perfume to help people relax is a great idea."

Peter asked, "Do you think it had an effect on Steve?"

Beatriz decided to treat the question seriously, "I'm not sure about that. He was pretty worked up today, but it seems to work well for the others."

Peter seemed thoughtful.

Beatriz continued, "When the concentration of perfume gets too high, Patrick starts coughing. He seems particularly sensitive to perfume. I don't know if it has anything to do with him only having ever breathed the pure Moon Base air. Perhaps he needs an exercise in unhealthier air quality before he returns."

Peter laughed at Beatriz's joke, but then asked seriously, "Can we increase the concentration to help people feel better?"

She shook her head and looked at him questioningly.

He checked, "Isn't there another way that we can do something?"

Beatriz cleared her throat and told him, "We're taking fewer drugs than last year. It's not that bad. However, everyone except Liam and Patrick are taking something for depression."

Peter seemed to be listening, but he was somehow distracted when he asked, "Are you worried about getting old? I wonder what would happen if I broke a hip."

Beatriz laughed briefly, "You know. We have a body part 3D printer. To be honest, I don't know exactly how to use it, but it can't be that difficult, and if it is, we can always ask Liam. He can handle any machine."

Beatriz thought he looked worried and added, "Bone density is measured during the annual medicals, and everyone has very good values. Even you. Everyone has adhered to the regular training plan. I'm not worried about a broken hip."

Peter seemed a little distracted to Beatriz. She wondered what he really wanted to say as he explained, "I sometimes worry about the intelligent surveillance system. Maybe we should shut it down." Conspiratorially, he looked at her, "To protect our privacy."

Beatriz was a bit surprised and assured him, "No one is watching. There's no one here."

Peter felt like he was confessing as he explained, "Maybe someone hacked the surveillance system, and we are on a reality television show. They want to see how we react and they're experimenting on us."

Beatriz seemed concerned, "You're getting paranoid. I'm sure no one has hacked into the system. We can check with Liam, if you want."

With a deep voice he whispered, "He could be one of them."

Beatriz sharply said, "Have you heard yourself?"

Peter suddenly looked very sad, "I'm trying to make sense of what's happening."

Beatriz changed the subject, "Let's have a midday whisky."

Peter poured two glasses of whisky and handed one to Beatriz. He smiled and seemed to be his normal self again.

Beatriz took a closer look at him, "You know we have an Intellitoilet in the infirmary."

Peter nodded, sipping his drink.

Beatriz admitted, "It isn't the only one. All toilets are intelligent."

Peter dropped his head to one side and looked at her in surprise. Then he realised that his plan to hide how much alcohol he drank hadn't worked.

Beatriz continued, "I get a report on the health of our employees most days. The toilets have a so-called artificial nose, the same type that we use as safety locks and that checks breath for signs of disease, but in the toilet, they analyse farts."

Peter laughed, he was hoping it wasn't true.

Beatriz watched him very closely as she said, "We can even measure your rising intolerance to milk by the consistency of your farts."

He looked at her and shook his head. He didn't have any privacy.

Beatriz looked relaxed, relieved. She'd begun to confess her secrets and now wanted to tell him everything, "We do five medicals per year, but mostly we don't need them because we already know what's going on in each person's body. The medicals serve to distract everyone and makes them feel safe and not think about the data collection methods. Who wants to really know about intelligent toilets?"

Peter shook his head, it can't be true.

Beatriz continued, "The Smellaids can even predict mood pretty accurately, and whether someone is lying. They're not just there to open doors easily. They are a very useful addition to the general surveillance."

Peter pulled a face that showed his disbelief clearly, surely, he as Moon Major would have known about this.

Beatriz had more to confess, "That's why I knew about Dervla's budding bipolar disease last year. I could measure the lithium levels in her blood. Now she has a laboratory-on-a-chip on her Pulsera for easy and early identification of the necessary biomarkers. One single drop of blood is measured on a regular basis, and the correct dose of medication is automatically dispensed." Beatriz smiled reassuringly, "Of course, she also comes for a control examination from time to time."

Peter had heard enough. He wanted to think about it later when he had time, so he changed the subject, "Can you remember the Internet before it was separated? I miss the freedom of pointless surfing. The commercials for the things that I'm supposed to desperately need, even though I don't know what they are. The unverified content, the crazy theories, the old movies, I miss it. Sometimes I'd like to relive the freedom by surfing the Happynet."

Beatriz agreed, and hoped that he would soon get to the point, "It's a pity we don't have the Happynet here."

"Did you play with the virtual reality dementia program?"

Beatriz didn't look at him, "Yes, the result wasn't clear, but neither was it ideal. I'm starting to get worried."

Peter suggested, "Let's have some whisky and then try the dementia program." He laughed and poured two more glasses of whisky, and asked Beatriz, "Are you gaining weight? I'm putting on weight again."

Beatriz rebuked him, "You should do more sport and drink less whisky. Otherwise you won't fit in a spacesuit." She laughed and said, "Although, that would solve one problem."

He replied with a laugh and said, "You think I'm too fat to fly back, and I won't fit in my spacesuit."

With his fingers he felt how tight his belt was and thought he had to increase the maximum setting in his clothes again. Then he looked at her and finally admitted what he wanted to say when he blurted, "I promoted Steve."

Moonday Fourteen

Date: Thursday 2nd October 2155 – 09:45 CET
Location: Alpha 12 – Moon Base

Beatriz took a step back and looked up at Patrick. He was taller than she was, much taller. He'd shot up in the last year. She'd noticed but today at the start of his birthday medical it still came as a surprise. She smiled at him and said, "I'm very proud of you."

His smile spread wide across his face, and he twisted his upper body in a way that was so clumsy that it looked painful. Beatriz looked at him frowning and smiling at the same time, obviously it wasn't painful for him, otherwise he wouldn't be smiling so broadly. She let her medical eye look him up and down, he didn't look overweight, but with the weight measurement from the weighing chair she knew that he weighed above average for his height. His muscle and bone density had always been higher than normal and considering that he'd spent his whole life on the Moon, the values were impressive. The results supported Beatriz's suspicion that Dervla had made some adjustments to improve Patrick's DNA for a life in space. It annoyed her that without a genetic test, she couldn't prove it. She did wonder, if it was just for the science why she wanted to know the results of the test, but there was also extra information in the test. She knew that Dervla had repeatedly refused a DNA test and would probably never allow it while Patrick was healthy. Beatriz smiled at Patrick and thought, the problems with his rheumatism seemed to have disappeared as he'd got older. Beatriz didn't know exactly why and would like to. She knew she was curious about how far Dervla had gone with any DNA changes. She was sure Dervla had improved his muscle and bone strength and broadened his visual spectrum. She could only speculate about any other changes and who his father might be.

After Patrick had gone, Beatriz called Dervla, "I'd like to run a DNA test on Patrick."

Dervla replied harshly, "No."

Beatriz tried to keep the begging tone out of her voice, "I have some concerns about the results of his medical today."

Dervla sounded disbelieving as she replied, "He has a right to his privacy."

Beatriz felt annoyed with the refusal and tried to sound reasonable, "Nobody else here has DNA privacy. I have the DNA test results of everyone else on the Moon Base."

Dervla's thinning patience could be clearly heard in the tone of her reply, "We've discussed this topic several times, and you've already admitted that we don't have any medical reason to do a test."

Beatriz ended the call and slammed her fist on the table. She'd thought several times about doing the test secretly, but her conscience kept her from doing it. Then she realised that her conscience seemed to be bothering her less.

Patrick was sitting in the meeting room with Paul and Charlie. They were preparing for Patrick's first camping trip. His birthday present this year was a four-day Moon excursion accompanied by Charlie and Paul, and they needed to discuss and plan it. Patrick was looking excitedly between the two of them not really understanding what they were saying. He didn't know where to look and didn't want to miss anything. He wanted to know what the plan was.

Charlie stood up in front of the presentation stand and explained with authority, "We are here for the briefing for the camping expedition. First we are going to clarify the safety measures regarding our health and safety while we are on the road." He looked hard at Patrick until Patrick nodded in agreement.

"The first theme is which Moon vehicle." He grinned. "We'll travel in the Art Feldmann Antigrav Moon vehicle, which has a speed of up to 200km/h." He showed a picture of the large, cylindrical vehicle and smiled, "The so-called Arty." He pointed to the front of the picture of the vehicle, that hovered about half a metre above the ground, "The control area is at the front and in the rear part is the living area."

Charlie grinned almost impossibly wider, "We're going luxury camping, and in Arty we can spend the night asleep while Arty drives us with the autopilot." He brought up another picture of Arty and a tourist. He looked more serious as he continued speaking, "For the tourists, we called it a Moon-campervan to make it clear that it resembles a motor home, but for us she remains Arty." He smiled at Patrick, "Arty is much more than a motorhome and was built to travel very fast over the Moon's surface, and with enough space for sufficient supplies to last for several days. To be fair, not only to survive, but to be able to live in luxury."

He flipped to the next picture. It was the technical design of Arty with many controls marked on it. He explained, "The way Arty travels is more of a hover than a drive. Without floating above the surface, we are limited to a maximum speed of about 20 km/h. If we float above the uneven ground, we can achieve speeds of up to 200 km/h." His eyes lit up when he mentioned the speed.

Patrick looked impressed and a little scared as he asked Charlie, "Will I be able to drive? I have my Moon license."

Paul gently explained, "But your license only applies to the regular Moon vehicles, not to the antigrav vehicle."

Patrick begged, "But I want to have a go, and I can learn."

Paul tried insisting, "I'm sorry, but..."

Charlie interrupted Paul, "He can try, why not."

Paul glanced at Patrick, then looked at Charlie questioningly as he briefly considered his objections, Dervla wouldn't be there. He looked at Patrick, "Okay, if you don't drive too fast."

Charlie added, "The safety system takes over if you do anything too crazy." Then he laughed as he remembered an incident from his past.

Patrick watched as a new slide came into view showing the inside of Arty. Charlie explained, "Living conditions aren't the same as in the Moon Base. We'll be outside the Art Feldmann's field and gravity will only be one-sixth of Earth's."

Patrick was concentrating very hard. His eyes were wide open and his lips slightly apart, he looked spellbound.

Charlie continued, "The antigrav vehicle has a toilet, but it's important to follow the instructions when using it." He stared at Patrick to show he was serious, "Otherwise there could be bad consequences, and if the Sauberbots aren't there, then you have to clean it up yourself, or we have to end the trip early."

Patrick shook and nodded his head at the same time and promised to follow the instructions. He was so convincing that Charlie and Paul believed him and laughed at his seriousness.

The next picture was of the spacesuit, "Never take off your Moon Base outdoor uniform when you're outside."

Patrick nodded eagerly and squirmed excitedly.

Charlie showed a picture of the line between sunlight and shadow, "When you stand in the Sun, it will get very hot, but remember when you are in the shade, it will get very cold. This can mean that there is an extreme temperature difference between the two sides of your spacesuit. Try and avoid this."

Charlie showed a picture of Arty with him in his Moon Base outdoor uniform stood next to it. He pointed to the picture and explained, "Just in case you can't tell that's me. To summarise, there is a toilet but no normal washing facility, and that means we don't have to wash for four days."

Patrick looked from Charlie to Paul, his mouth fell open. Paul started to laugh, and the other two soon joined in. As they laughed Charlie flipped to the next slide and showed a Moon map with red markings on it. The red markings showed the landing sites of the Apollo missions from the 1960's and 1970's. Charlie explained, "The trip is going to take four to five days. And we're going to travel about 8,000 kilometres in total. We are going to follow the route marked with the red dots." Charlie checked to see if Patrick had understood, which was difficult to tell as he was just grinning madly. The next picture showed a radio. Charlie pointed at the picture and explained, "We need to talk about emergency procedures. Even though we don't expect any problems. Europa has done a thorough search for meteoroids and asteroids and found nothing. Nothing untoward should happen, but we still need to prepare."

Both Patrick and Paul were paying close attention.

Charlie explained seriously, "There is a radio in Arty which works by satellite when we're over the horizon."

Patrick pulled his body together and looked at Paul questioningly.

Charlie saw Patrick's reaction and said, "We don't have an ionosphere to reflect radio waves back to the base."

Patrick nodded. Charlie wasn't sure if he'd understood or not, but decided to continue, "Our location will be automatically sent back regularly to the Moon Base, and Liam is going to monitor our position." Charlie looked serious, "We have to remember that there is only one Moon satellite, which means we can't always get a message back to base. Arty has a special anti-gravity drone that we can send back if we have a problem." Charlie showed a picture of the drone, "We'll show you how to use it before we set off." He showed the next slide there were three names Oberon, Titan, Ganymede on it.

Charlie nodded towards the slide and said, "Columbus doesn't know we're leaving, and that means we're on a secret mission. So, we need to use our aliases." He looked at Patrick with a very mock stern expression, "From now on we only call each other Oberon, Titan and Ganymede."

Paul and Patrick both nodded in agreement, and Paul added seriously, "Thank you, Oberon."

Charlie replied, "You're welcome, Titan. Are there any questions? If not, we'll go to the party and eat birthday cake!"

Paul got up immediately, but Patrick remained seated. Charlie looked at him with a smile and said, "Aren't you coming, Ganymede?"

Patrick jumped up grinning.

When they arrived at the canteen, the others were all standing with a glass of champagne in their hands. As soon as they saw Patrick they spontaneously started singing, "Happy Birthday". He smiled and blushed embarrassed at the sudden attention.

Peter noticed, a little disappointed, that Patrick wasn't wearing his captain's hat. Peter stood well-groomed to attention. He was dressed in full uniform including his captain's hat. He was holding a certificate and a present in his hands.

When they'd finished singing, he walked right up to Patrick, shook his hand and handed him the annual good behaviour certificate as he spoke the usual words. Peter put on his best proud smile and explained to everyone that Patrick had had a wonderful year and had learned a lot and then he congratulated him on his birthday.

Patrick looked underwhelmed as he smiled and accepted the certificate. He turned and looked behind him and placed the certificate face down on the table.

Peter tried not to look offended as he watched Patrick discarding the certificate. Peter hid his disappointment before giving Patrick his second present.

Patrick took the present eagerly and tore off the wrapping paper and put it carefully on the table behind him. He looked at it in his hands and turned it over a couple of times. It was a book. He shook his head and looked at Peter questioningly.

Peter smiled and explained, "It's a captain's log."

Patrick shrugged his shoulders and holding the book in one hand and twisted his wrist to the side.

Peter explained patiently, "You need to keep a log of your own while you are on your expedition."

Patrick tilted his head to the side, turned the book over in his hands and looked closer at it before slowly smiling and said, "Cool. Thanks."

Steve made a show of presenting the birthday cake. Everyone was impressed. This year the cake looked just like Arty, and it tasted good as well. Patrick was talking enthusiastically about the expedition as he greedily ate his second piece of cake, they were going to leave as soon as the cake was finished.

When they'd finished eating, Paul explained that there was one last present. Patrick looked at the faces around him and then started shaking in excitement. He wanted to know what it was.

Paul went and picked up the long thin present from the corner, where he'd hidden it, brought it over, balanced one end on the floor and passed over it to Patrick.

Patrick held it carefully and looked at it curiously. He wasn't sure how to open such a large present.

Paul smiled and said mysteriously, "Guess what it is before you open it."

Still resting it on the floor, Patrick twisted the package around, then tried to bend it, and bent down and tried shaking it next to his ear. It didn't make a sound. He looked at Paul and shrugged his shoulders while shaking his head. He had no idea what it was.

Paul laughed briefly and then let him open the present.

Patrick smiled and ripped off the improvised wrapping paper dropping it on the floor. He recognised what it was immediately. It was a golf club.

Paul explained, "You're right-handed and can't use my left-handed club. You'll need your own right-handed golf club for our expedition."

Patrick immediately grabbed the golf club and holding it in both hands practiced his golf swing. Unfortunately, he was a little too quick for Peter, who almost lost his captain's hat.

Peter took a couple of steps backwards, straightened his hat and said smiling, "Everything's fine. Nothing happened."

Paul laughed and told everyone to take a step back before telling Patrick, "Try it with just one hand. The Moon Base outdoor uniforms are bulky, and you'll have to hit the golf ball with a onehanded swing."

Patrick nodded enthusiastically and tried his one-handed golf swing. As a precaution, Peter took an extra few steps to the side.

Steve was looking suspiciously at the golf club, "I hope you don't intend to enter the archaeological site and destroy it." He looked at Paul and Charlie threateningly. "They're important historical sites. You have to follow the official Apollo Tourist Plan, and don't touch anything." And just to be sure they'd understood, he added, "That means don't move or destroy anything."

Paul and Charlie looked at each other briefly before nodding.

Steve looked sceptical and emphasised, "The decision was taken against an Apollo archaeological excavation. The sites are to be preserved for the future."

Paul and Charlie nodded spontaneously and promised to act respectfully.

Steve looked at them closely. His facial muscles were like steel as he added, "And don't stand on Buzz Aldrin's footprint in the Moon regolith."

Paul looked at the floor as he answered, "We're just going to look and will look for two tiny golf balls."

Charlie added, "We'll take the tourist route and follow the rules."

Steve wasn't happy. He didn't trust them. He turned around in anger and left the room without saying anything.

Peter congratulated Patrick on his birthday once more before he said goodbye. After he'd gone, the three thought it was time to start the journey. Before they left, Dervla wished them a good time and made Patrick promise one more time to be careful and to behave. As they left the room everyone wished them good luck and lots of fun.

After they'd suited up and congratulated each other how good they looked in their Moon Base outdoor uniforms, they walked towards Arty. They were making stupid jokes and laughing through their intercoms. Patrick, who was trying not to be too excited, had only dropped his captain's log three times. The third time he dropped the book Charlie joked that it was lucky that he hadn't dropped Paul's bag. Patrick wanted to know why. Paul looked at Charlie before showing Patrick what he had hidden in the golf bag.

Patrick was confused, "But why so many golf balls?"

Paul pointed at the three golf clubs in the bag and smiled.

Ganymede's Captain's log –

Date: Thursday 2nd Oct 2155 – 13:57:22 CET (Central Eagle Time)

Location: Alpha 12 – Moon Base

My first entry in my Captain's log: ALMOST SETTING OFF.

Charlie said that the journey to Apollo 14 Landing site will take about 13 hours and we are going to travel most of the 1910 Kilometres overnight and when we get up, we will be there. Charlie, Oberon is driving first and then he is going to let me have a go.

The emergency Antigrav-Drone looks very similar to a normal drone.

Date: Thursday 2nd Oct 2155 – 22:05 CET (Central Eagle Time)

Location: On the way

Before I go to sleep, I'm writing my second entry in my Captain's log. Oberon told me that the autopilot is going to take over the trip for us. And that I'm learning quickly how to drive Arty. I drove well today, and tomorrow I'll get to drive again.

When we use autopilot, we travel slower, but we can't drive all the time because we need sleep, and if we kept stopping to sleep, the journey will take too long. Charlie is staying up first and is going to look at the landscape for a while, but I have to sleep. I think that I'm too excited to sleep. By the way, the toilet in the Arty is great.

I fell asleep straight away and slept great. We're at the landing site of the NASA Apollo 14 Moon mission from 1971 and are having breakfast. There's not much here. There's more junk than normal, but not much else.

~~Paul~~ Titan told me that Alan Shepard played golf here two hundred years ago. After breakfast we're going outside to find the two golf balls he lost, and to play some golf, too.

Golf is super. Unfortunately, we only found one of the golf balls. I'm taking it home with me. Oberon said it's okay as long as I don't tell Steve (Io) and also that I played golf on the Moon.

Titan says my right-handed golf club is a 6-iron and when I hit the ball it flew for miles and miles. None of us is sure how far a mile is, but it can't be that far, because we only made a few metres. It was fun trying but difficult hitting the ball with only one arm. Titan said I should try it with two arms when we are in the storeroom again.

We found a lunar vehicle that some NASA astronauts had left behind, and it seems to be in a good condition. Titan said that if we're here long enough, we could have repaired it and driven it around. Unfortunately, there wasn't enough time.

We did find the mirror reflecting to Earth quickly and cleaned it. It had a little lunar dust on it, but not much. Oberon told me it's called a retroreflector, not just a simple mirror. It looked like a mirror to me.

There should have been a flag, but we couldn't find it. We found the leftover equipment from the old ALSEP Systems experiments, but Oberon said only to look at them. We were very respectful to the archaeological site. Io would be happy with us. We also found the plaque inscription and showed respect and polished it up.

The Eagle descent stage was still in place, and we climbed on it. The Moon Base outer uniforms made it hard to climb but we managed, and it wouldn't have been possible without them. We didn't visit the ascent stage site. It's too far away.

Date: Friday 3rd Oct. 2155 – 14:30 to 17:00 CET (Central Eagle Time)

Location: Apollo 12 Landing site – Ocean of Storms

We only drove 181 kilometres to the Apollo 12 landing site, and I got to drive part of the way. And we found the white flag here, but it's pretty torn up. Oberon thinks it's a good thing they put up a white flag of peace.

The descent stage was still there, and we climbed it. We didn't see the ascent level. It had crashed somewhere nearby. Oberon said it wasn't interesting. But we did walk to Surveyor 3. There wasn't much to see, but the walk was fun. It's fun to run with little gravity and jump, especially when you're climbing.

We tried playing golf again and it was still difficult to hit the ball.

Day 3:

Date: Saturday 4th Oct. 2155 – 07:01 CET (Central Eagle Time)

Location: Apollo 15 Landing site – Hadley–Rille

Soon we are going to have breakfast and then we're going outside. I drove for two hours. For the rest of the 1188 kilometres we let the autopilot drive overnight. The landscape is rockier than the other sites.

We've seen the Lunar Rover vehicle, and we'll look for the retroreflector later.

Date: Saturday 4th Oct. 2155 – 11:03 CET (Central Eagle Time)
Location: Apollo 15 Landing site – Hadley–Rille

The Lunar Rover vehicle didn't start, and there wasn't enough time to fix it. We found the retroreflector and cleaned it. Although, it wasn't that dirty. We also found a small aluminium sculpture, Oberon says it represents a spaceman in a spacesuit, and that it was the first work of art on the Moon. We left it where it was.

We found the flag as well, but it was torn and lying on the ground. We put it back up. And we played golf and I'm getting better at hitting the ball.

The descent stage was still there, and I could climb on it. The ascent level was broken nearby, and Oberon said I shouldn't climb on it in case it broke, and I hurt myself.

Date: Saturday 4th Oct. 2155 – 17:03 CET (Central Eagle Time)
Location: Apollo 17 Landing site – Taurus–Littrow

Our almost 800-kilometre drive was great. I've drove for two hours twice and Titan says I'm an experience Moononaut. The white flag is still standing but is very torn.

We're going for a little walk, and to check the Lunar Rover vehicle out.

Date: Saturday 4th Oct. 2155 – 21:03 CET (Central Eagle Time)
Location: Apollo 17 Landing site – Taurus–Littrow

The Lunar Rover vehicle started after Titan repaired it, and I was able to replace the battery. It was fun, and we drove too fast, and there was often only one wheel touching the surface. This has to remain a secret and we can't tell Io. We parked as close as possible to the original landing place. Oberon said, when a meteorite hits, it will make our tracks disappear and no one will know. We all practiced golf again and we are all getting better at hitting the ball.

Day 4:
Date: Sunday 5th Oct. 2155 – 07:03 CET (Central Eagle Time)
Location: Apollo 11 Landing site – Sea of Tranquility

We are at the first Lunar landing site! We're going to look for Buzz Aldrin's footprint and the retroreflector. Oberon said the flag was blown away at the start of the ascent level, and we shouldn't look for it because we won't find it. After breakfast we're going outside.

Date: Sunday 5th Oct. 2155 – 10:58 CET (Central Eagle Time)
Location: Apollo 11 Landing site – Sea of Tranquility

We found Buzz Aldrin's footprint in the Moon regolith. Now there are four footprints right next to each other, Buzz Aldrin's is on the left. We took it in turns to jump and leave a footprint right there next to Buzz'. We took a photo of the four footprints, but we have to keep this secret as well.

The descent stage was still there, and we all climbed on it. I went down the ladder and made a pretend first footprint on the Moon. Titan said we shouldn't change things too much and to stop playing our game. We played golf, and the miles are getting bigger and bigger.

Date: Sunday 5th Oct. 2155 – 16:00 CET (Central Eagle Time)
Location: Apollo 16 Landing site – Descartes Highlands

We've arrived at the Descartes Highlands, and I drove Arty for all of the 400 kilometres. Except for a few minutes when I had to go to the toilet, but otherwise, it was a super four-hour drive. And I almost drove enough to get my license.

There's a very torn white flag, and Lunar Rover vehicles that we are going to look at.

Date: Sunday 5th Oct. 2155 – 20:00 CET (Central Eagle Time)
Location: Apollo 16 Landing site – Descartes Highlands

The trip is almost over. We're about to leave for 2700-kilometre journey home. We're feeling sad that the trip is over, and we're disappointed that there were only six Apollo missions. We've got to pack everything up and then make ourselves comfortable for the 18-hour journey home.

The descent step was there, and I climbed it. We didn't visit the ascent stage. It had crashed somewhere nearby. Titan managed to bring the Lunar Rover vehicle back to life, and we drove it around for a short time. One last event, we'll travel home via Surveyor 7 and will stop briefly to have a look at it, but we won't get out because there hasn't been too much to see since Surveyor 7 was hit by a meteorite.

We played golf again, and this time the balls really did fly miles and miles. We had to try a few times, and my ball flew the farthest. Paul says my one-handed golf swing is getting better and better. One of Paul's balls also flew far, but not as far as mine and Charlie's ball may have only flown a mile.

Day 5:
Date: Monday 6th Oct. 2155 – 15:17 CET (Central Eagle Time)
Location: Alpha 12 – Moon Base

We are home, and I drove enough hours to get my Antigrav driver license!!

Goodbye Captain's log.

Second Return

Date: Monday 19th September 2157 – 20:39 CET
Location: Alpha 12 – Moon Base

As the three figures, fully suited in their orange spacesuits and helmets, walked past him Peter straightened his back and saluted. He could feel the tense muscles in his back contract pulling his posture tauter. He held his position, his facial muscles rigid, but his eyes betrayed the emotion, and he was aware of the growing water droplets carefully balanced in the corners of his eyes. He glanced upwards and saw the light reflect off the black peak of his hat before deliberately blinking a few times trying to hold back the tears.

As he watched them go through the exit hatch, he lowered his hand and at the same time the muscles in his cheeks and also in his heart. He could still see the helmets turning to face him and saw the returners looking and nodding at him through the hatch. With a practised art, he stood to attention again, before nodding back both appreciatively and gratefully. His muscles remembered his training of standing emotionless to attention, but he couldn't banish the sadness from his face. He was going to miss the returners.

Peter took a few steps back to watch the action through the window wall. He could see them better as they walked to the escape pod. Even though they seemed to be moving slowly, it didn't take them long to reach the launch site.

Everything had been prepared. Liam had done a great job. He watched as one of the three turned and waved. Peter glanced at Maria, who was standing next to him and watched her as she, with sadness in her eyes and a half-hearted smile, waved back, even though she knew that he couldn't see her.

Peter said to no one in particular, "When they land, they'll have the advantage that it's full Moon on Earth. If they need light..." Peter didn't finish his sentence. He didn't really want to think about what could go wrong. He saluted again to stop himself from thinking. Patrick noticed Peter saluting and looked serious as he imitated Peter.

Maria watched them saluting and thought they both look good with their captain's hats. She smiled about Patrick's behaviour and at how they looked standing next to each other. Patrick was now taller, but lankier, than Peter, and he seemed to understand the gravity of the situation and was acting appropriately.

Peter looked at Paul and Beatriz, who were standing quietly next to Maria. He thought we're all here to say goodbye except Dervla, and of course, Liam was sitting at his workplace controlling the launch.

It only took a few minutes before Liam announced they were ready to launch, and he started the countdown. The ten second countdown seemed to last forever, and Peter froze his emotions and waited. He'd got an empty feeling in his stomach. He glanced around. They were waiting together, yet he had the feeling that he was alone. The escape pod launched and at first moved slowly upwards, but with an ever-increasing acceleration. Out of the corner of his eye Peter saw Paul waving to Patrick indicating that they should go. Peter was still watching the path of the escape pod and was aware of them respectfully going, and leaving Beatriz standing alone.

Peter noticed Beatriz turning her head and suddenly realising that she wasn't standing with the others anymore. She shook her head trying to shake off the confusion before she, almost faltering, stepped back, turned around and left.

Gently Peter took Maria's hand, she turned her head and looked at him directly, with wide open vulnerable eyes. Their eyes met, and fleetingly they shared their loneliness. He squeezed her hand, forced a smile and said half seriously, "Art Feldmann will be safe now."

Maria laughed briefly and spoke inappropriately loudly as she queried, "Because Steve is no longer here?"

Looking sad, Peter nodded a few times, then smiled and his expression relaxed, but only for a moment. Maria noticed his mood changing. His eyes became square and his expression serious. He was obviously worried, and she wasn't surprised when he said, "I have to go and check the statue." His voice became slower and calmer as he added, "Maybe he's left a surprise for us." Peter rushed to check on the statue.

Maria was still standing in front of the window wall, looking with her head bent a little forward and with her sad eyes at the empty landing site. Her closed right hand rested on her chest. She was holding her necklace and thinking about how much she was going to miss Charlie. The next launch was going to take place in less than a month, and she comforted herself with the thought that this wasn't so long to wait. A little smile grew on her face which despite its best attempt, failed to bring hope to her unhappy eyes.

Out of breath, Peter arrived at Art Feldmann's statue. He had the impression that he hadn't taken a single breath on the way there. He stood, bending forward at the waist with his hands on his hips, right under the statue and breathed in and out a few times deeply as he inspected it. He closed his eyes and was grateful that she was still intact.

Peter could feel the tension leaving his body. He'd been sure that Steve, before he'd left, had done something bad to the statue. Peter had intended to check before Steve's return, but with all the excitement he'd somehow forgotten. Peter couldn't fully believe that everything was okay and continued looking for something out of place. He didn't find anything, but still had a funny feeling that Steve had been up to something.

Peter admired Art Feldmann's statue, and he thought he'd really liked to have met her. He'd like to have had a beer with her. He shrugged his shoulders. She'd been dead a long time before he'd been born. If only he had a time machine, he would be able to travel back and talk to her. He smiled and shook his head slightly as he thought how crazy his thoughts were. A time machine, people tell such stories about time machines, and he wasn't even sure what time was.

He looked up at the statue and noticed her smile and wondered whether Art Feldmann could explain to him what time was. Maybe he should ask Meichun if she knows what time is. He took his communication device out of his pocket, felt a little guilty, and took a photo of Art Feldmann's statue.

He was breathing normally again, he put his communication device in his pocket and slowly walked back to his office. On the way he smiled and thought it was late enough in the day to have a whisky.

As soon as he stood in front of his desk, he carefully placed his captain's hat down and looked at it lovingly before stroking it once or twice gently. He turned his head and looked for the bottle, that he'd left on the desk. He took the whisky bottle firmly in his hand and poured himself a generous measure. He thought for a moment what his hat meant to him, and he wondered with an ironic smile as he slowly and lovingly stroked the soft fabric on the top of the hat with his fingertips, if he would have the opportunity to return to Earth whether he would take it with him, or not. He stood there lost in thought for a moment before his facial muscles hardened. He took the glass firmly but carefully in the other hand and sat down abruptly. He leaned back in the chair and let himself sink into his favourite memory of his wife while he sipped the drink slowly.

After just a few small sips, he felt how tight his clothes were around his waistline, and he wondered whether he should lose a little weight or even drink less whisky. Unconsciously he shook his head, he didn't want that. He'd rather do a little exercise. He needed to prepare for the possibility that he would one day return home, even though he knew he couldn't leave anyone behind. He thought of his wife and sighed. His eyes looked for something familiar, a comforting image to rest upon. He glanced in the mirror and looked at his reflection. He looked sad. He'd no idea if he would get the chance to return like Europa, Charlie and Steve had.

His last difficult conversation with Steve occurred to him. He sighed deeply and long and enjoyed the relaxing feeling that flowed through his body. The conversation had only taken place a few weeks ago, but Peter felt that with every kilometre that Steve flew away, the event was slipping further into the past.

Peter leaned his head back into the chair's head support, and his half-closed eyes relaxed as they stared aimlessly at the ceiling. He half smiled as he began to remember. Steve had never stopped trying to get closer to Europa. He'd even suggested that they do an additional bone density medical examination and could train together if necessary. Europa didn't have a problem with it. Both had passed their medical examination easily, and there was no reason for the extra training. Peter saw them both clearly in his mind's eye. He felt a passing closeness that drifted away with their growing distance. His neck muscles relaxed, and his head fell forward slightly. He straightened his head. He must remember to ask Beatriz if she would test his bone density.

He drank a sip of whisky and felt the warmth of the strong alcohol in his throat as he smiled and remembered that Steve had complained after the muscle and bone density test. He was angry and claimed that Beatriz was obviously confused. Europa, who was in the middle of her menopause, couldn't have a better result than he did.

Peter had tried to defend Beatriz and explained that bone density has a genetic component and the result could be valid. Peter shuddered as he remembered what Steve had said, "She's an old woman with dementia and no longer knows what she's doing." Steve tone had sounded accusing as he told Peter, "You have to do something. Things are getting critical. She's screwed up the test. You don't know what she could do next."

Peter had reacted cautiously and waited for Steve's next move. He had the feeling that it wasn't really about Beatriz. Steve had been emotional because he was torn about returning.

Steve's expression had been hard. He'd seemed to have the impression that Peter wasn't listening to him. Steve needed a reaction to help him calm his frustration. Annoyed, Steve had said, "We need a third volunteer to fly with us. Have you decided yet?"

Peter had looked at him in silence. He'd known Steve was angry and wanted a reaction. Peter had been surprised when it occurred to him that Steve was trying to lose his place in the escape pod.

Steve hadn't been able to stop himself, "The teenager has never lived on Earth. We don't know if he can even survive there. Maybe his muscles and bones won't be strong enough."

Peter had waited patiently until he thought Steve had said everything he wanted to. He'd started to get a sense of what Steve was afraid of and why his little outburst was happening. Peter became more compassionate as he thought, "It's almost as if he wants me to order him to stay here. He doesn't want to be left behind and is scared to go home."

Steve had been convinced that Peter wasn't listening to him, "Patrick has never been immunised."

Peter had nodded. He knew Steve was right.

Steve had laughed briefly, believing he'd won. He'd got a reaction from Peter.

But Peter hadn't been thinking about Steve. He'd decided to talk to Beatriz about Patrick and was thinking that he and Patrick could train together before they returned, then he'd be sure that his bones and muscles were strong enough.

Peter had looked pointedly at Steve, and as he spoke the determination was clear in his voice, "We're all going home even Patrick."

Steve looked angry and mocked, "How can that work. There isn't enough room for everyone."

Peter's voice had remained firm and clear, "Everyone will get the chance, even though it could mean that I have to stay here."

Steve's expression got grumpier.

Peter had sighed and asked gently, "You have your place in the escape pod, what's the real problem?"

Steve had ignored Peter's question, "Europa wants to be home for the Sputnik anniversary." He'd paused briefly, "But the shortest Moon-Earth distance is on the October 18th and the Sputnik Bicentenary will take place on October 4th." Steve had looked at Peter. He'd expected a reaction.

Peter had only shrugged.

Steve wasn't finished, "We'll return on September 19th and the next two groups will return on October 18th after Patrick turns sixteen."

Peter had remained mute. He'd waited for Steve to explain what he really wanted.

Steve had taken a deep breath before he spoke quickly, "I want to know who's coming with us."

Peter had been relieved and managed to suppress his smile before looking Steve directly in the eyes. When he spoke, his voice sounded conciliatory and understanding, "I don't know yet." Peter had shaken his head, "I'm sorry. I really don't know yet."

Steve had remained silent emitting a tense feeling, leaving Peter with the feeling that he was about to explode as he left.

Peter had relaxed after Steve had gone, but not completely. How could he answer Steve if he didn't know who else was returning? He went through the list of people on the Moon Base, and what he already knew about their wishes. Liam was determined to stay, but how could he leave Liam here without a possible rescue. Beatriz wanted to be in the last escape pod, so she could provide any necessary medical care. Maria wanted to stay and care for her gardens as long as possible, and Dervla won't return without her son, but then what did he want? He shuddered and forced himself to believe: He wanted to be the last to leave the Moon Base. The decision was between Paul and Charlie. Paul needed to return because of his DNA condition. He couldn't risk living much longer outside of the protection of the Earth's atmosphere.

Peter knew he had to talk to Paul, but he didn't really want to choose between the two of them. He hoped that they'd make his life easier and make the decision themselves.

Looking at the floor with his head bowed and a sick empty feeling in his stomach, which ended with the faint taste of vomit in his mouth, he walked along the corridor to Peter's office. His eyes followed the pattern on the floor with difficulty. He was reassuring himself, "Tread carefully, don't step on the small cracks on the floor." The walls floated past him unnoticed as his eyes concentrated on the floor pattern. This wasn't a decision he wanted to make, but it was time to be brave. Time to prove what he was really made of. Furtively he wiped his eyes and blew his nose. For a moment he stood nervously outside Peter's door, and he felt old-fashioned as he knocked.

The knocking at the door surprised Peter and brought him back to reality. He'd looked up curiously. Charlie had slipped in the room and spoke quietly as he announced, "Maria wants me to volunteer to return."

Peter looked at him with compassion.

Charlie added, "She's promised me she'll be on the next flight." He breathed deeply in and out and with a furrowed forehead and sad eyes he whispered, "But what will happen if there is no place for her in one of the pods."

Peter felt sorry for him and wanted to reassure him, "If necessary, I'll stay. I promise not to leave anyone behind."

Charlie nodded. His expression was sad, but he still tried to smile and look brave.

Peter wanted to comfort him. He understood why he'd volunteered and also that he didn't really want to go. Peter knew that he was torn because Maria had asked him. Peter's voice sounded kind, and he tried a brave smile, "We're sending additional communication equipment. Maybe you'll be able to send a message to let Maria know you've arrived safely."

Charlie nodded thankfully and said weakly, "She's already told me to send her a message to say we're fine as soon as we land." Charlie turned to go. He wanted to be alone. Peter thanked Charlie's back as he left.

The door closed silently behind Charlie. There wasn't anything to see, but Peter still stared at the door. He was grateful, but at the same time sad that it had come to this. He nodded and held his head in his hands, thinking of Charlie's pain and his own guilty relief that he didn't have to make the decision.

With renewed energy Peter said to Meichun, "We have a return plan." He almost sounded happy. "Europa, Steve and Charlie are returning on September 19th and six more will return on October 18th." The brief burst of energy was already spent as he added quietly, "And I'll stay on the Moon Base with you."

The gloomy mood didn't last for long, and he soon said, with a more positive note and a conscious portion of self-deception, "Of course, only if the others agree with my plan."

He thought of the three people who had accepted his plan and travelled today. Peter closed his eyes and remembered the faces as he had recently seen them. Europa had looked happy and determined. Steve had looked resolute and his behaviour had been rude. He didn't care what happened after he'd left the Moon Base, and he wanted to leave as soon as possible. Charlie's watery eyes sought solace in Maria's gaze. Peter could hear her reassure Charlie that she'd soon follow him. It was almost funny watching him trying to hug her while wearing that bulky spacesuit. He'd known it wouldn't really work, but he tried anyway. Maria smiled as he tried and waited until he gave up, then she embraced him and gently laid her cheek against his. She turned her head and kissed him lightly on the cheek before he turned his head and their lips touched each other fleetingly. Charlie closed his eyes, and Peter thought he's never going to forget the feeling her lips just made.

Steve was getting impatient and said gruffly, "Come on. Let's fly."

Maria let Charlie go and they looked at each other emotionally.

Maria whispered, "Have a good journey," and she smiled at him lovingly.

Europa and Steve had already got their helmets on. Charlie put on his helmet and turned on the radio.

Peter assured the returners, "We'll see each other again soon." Even though he knew this was a lie. He looked at Europa walking, she seemed happy and energetic. Steve's walk was rebellious and self-confident, while Charlie took only small reluctant steps, while repeatedly looking back.

Before they left the base Maria ran forward and stopped Charlie, she pushed a Moon flower in his hand. They could all hear over the radio as he said, "Don't forget me."

Maria wiped a tear from her eye as she said, "Never."

Peter rubbed his hands on his face and leaned back in his chair. The day had been exhausting, and he was happy that it was almost over. He poured himself a whisky, turned to Meichun and asked, "How long will we have to wait for a possible response?"

With her clear, sensible and friendly voice, Meichun replied, "It takes at least two days for the escape pod to return and then they'll be able to send a message."

Peter felt suddenly all alone.

Second Wait

Date: Monday 26th September 2157 – 11:40 CET
Location: Alpha 12 – Moon Base

Liam's fingers flew over the keyboard. He felt old-fashioned using it, but he liked the feel of the keys on his fingertips, and that he could work slower and think about what he was doing before committing to an action. He liked the privacy the keyboard offered and even though there was often no one there, he didn't like having to say the voice commands aloud. He knew he could have used the brain computer interface, but he didn't trust his thoughts. He enjoyed the feeling of the keys clicking as he slowly and exactly typed the commands he needed. He liked it to be quiet while he worked and today would have been fine if it wasn't for Peter's occasional sighing. His breathing came loud and short when he was agitated, but otherwise he'd not disturbed him and was waiting patiently.

"Did you get a signal?" Peter's voice sounded both hopeful and hopeless.

Slowly Liam shook his head. He saw no reason to try and explain the situation. The satellites had moved further away from their orbits, and he'd had to program his own devices precisely so that they could work with the signals from the new positions.

Peter sighed. He'd not expected anything else, but somehow this time he'd hoped that they'd get a message. He wanted to know what had happened on Earth, and after every failed contact it took him a while to come to terms with his disappointment.

Liam took a device out of a drawer near his seat. He showed it to Peter and said, "It's not finished yet, but you can take it with you next month." He looked at Peter for acknowledgement, who just looked at him, before he added, "It's not got any plastic parts, but it will work." He lowered his voice, "The signal is weak, but it should be enough for a simple short message."

Peter was a little taken aback, and he furrowed his forehead and smiled crookedly, he stared at the thing, "Is it made of wood?"

Liam didn't seem to notice Peter's reaction, and he replied casually, "Yes, partly."

Peter wanted to ask something sensible, something encouraging, "Is there a manual?"

Liam shook his head and said, "Paul knows how it works."

Peter nodded pleased, and he managed to keep a serious enough expression to conceal his inner relief that the machine was now Paul's responsibility, and he wouldn't have to worry about how it worked.

Peter had already started walking away when he realised, he hadn't said goodbye to Liam. Half-heartedly he turned his head in Liam's direction, then he felt his shoulders fall and the energy drain from him. He turned around and continued walking back to his office. He thought about his whisky and how he'd have a little one when he got there. It would help with the disappointment.

As he lifted the whisky bottle, he realised it was almost empty. He put the bottle on the desk and pulled open his whisky supply drawer, the bottom drawer in his desk. The quiet clinking of glass as he opened the drawer comforted him and he smiled automatically. Relaxing, he poured himself a whisky. He looked at his watch, it was still early in the day, but somewhere on Earth it was time to start drinking. He decided to add some water, because it was so early. He let a few drops fall slowly into the glass. He held it up to the light and looked at the light reflecting on the brown liquid, and he felt tired. He put the glass down and then sat down carefully before holding his face in his hands and rubbing his tired eyes. His palms touched his cheeks, and he remembered his two-day old beard. He took off his captain's hat and put it on the table next to his glass. He held his chin in one hand and felt the stubble. He still had his dress uniform on and was prepared, admittedly he was only half prepared with the two-day old beard, but at least he'd tried. He leaned back in his chair and put his feet up on the desk before he picked up the glass and started enjoying his whisky.

After the first satisfying sensation of whisky on the back of his throat and the quickly following heat that slowly seeped down his oesophagus, he smiled unhurriedly and was glad that he didn't have much to do today. Then he remembered that Patrick was coming to see him. It should have been the day after tomorrow, but Patrick and Dervla had had a fight. Paul had suggested that it would be better if Patrick took a break from working with Dervla. Peter smiled as he thought of Patrick coming, and he suddenly realised he was looking forward to Patrick's visit.

Peter reached into the drawer where he had hidden his wife's photo and took it out. He stared at it for a moment and thought about her. He tried whispering her name, "Jean." His favourite memory of his wife formed in his inner eye. It comforted him. She was standing on the porch and smelling the flowers in the bouquet she was rocking in her arms, but this time when she smelled the flowers, he saw the petals falling off and noticed the withered leaves. Had he waited too long?

The mirror was still there from his earlier preparations, he looked at his reflection and wondered what it would be like to see her again, and he realised that he was afraid, scared that too many years had passed by, and he no longer knew if she'd be pleased to see him again. He wondered if his decision that he could never leave Liam without an escape pod was just an excuse and the real reason was that he was too scared to return, scared of what he would find. He didn't like the unpleasant feeling that accompanied this thought. He turned to Meichun and asked angrily and almost tearful, "Are they all dead?"

Meichun reacted with lightning speed, she knew what he was talking about, "We don't know that they are all dead."

Patrick came into the room and unsuspectingly asked, "Who's dead?"

Peter hid his whisky glass under his hat, sat upright and smiled at Patrick. He was glad to see him. He jumped up, went over to Patrick, who was just standing in the doorway, and shook his hand energetically. Patrick was surprised and joined in smiling letting some of his positive energy flow into his hand. Peter enjoyed the feeling of Patrick's energy, and felt he was getting rid of his own negative feelings into the handshake. As they swapped hands and started shaking with the other hand, they both started laughing which spread to a twinkle in both of their eyes. It wasn't clear who'd started laughing first, and it wasn't important to know.

They heard Patrick's stomach growling and after laughing again, Peter suggested they get the meeting over and done with as soon as possible. Peter had a hard time stopping laughing, "I hear you have questions for Meichun and me."

Patrick nodded, took a deep breath to calm his breathing. When his voice was almost under control he said, "I even have a list."

Raising his eyebrows and smiling, Peter asked, "Where?"

Patrick held out his left palm and showed the questions he had written on it. Peter noticed how small and skilled Patrick's handwriting was. He was momentarily surprised that Patrick, who was usually so clumsy, could write so neat and tidily. Then he noticed that Patrick was wearing a Handpaper, a very thin conductive plastic that resembled half a glove because only the palm was covered. Patrick had made notes with a finger on it, and luckily for him while he wrote the Handpaper automatically improved the legibility and spelling of the writing. Peter smiled at Patrick and then turned to Meichun, "Are you awake?"

Meichun reacted immediately, "I don't sleep."

Peter ignored her answer and said kindly, "Patrick is here and wants to ask you a few questions." Peter turned to Patrick and encouraged him, "Ask the first question on your list."

Patrick cleared his throat, "I'd like to know something about the Earth." He glanced at Peter, his eyes searching for permission to continue.

Peter nodded encouragingly.

Patrick breathed in deeply and then said very quickly, "Will my Pulsera work on Earth?"

Meichun's voice was almost mechanical as she answered, "Yes, it will work."

Peter watched him relax and waited for him to ask his next question.

Patrick looked at Meichun and asked her, "How is the Earth's gravity going to feel on my body?"

Meichun remained with her mechanical professional voice, "Your body is going to feel heavier, and you will get tired faster than normal."

Patrick nodded then looked up to the ceiling before facing Meichun and asking his next question, "Is the horizon further away?"

Meichun responded immediately, "The Earth's radius is about twice the size of the Moon, but the Earth has an atmosphere with weather, that can block the view. Theoretically for someone approximately two metres tall the horizon on the Earth will seem twice as far away as on the Moon, but it isn't likely that you will get to see so far, and I've ignored the differences of standing at different locations on the oblique spheroid."

Patrick was impressed and made a mental note to check this out when he got to Earth. He looked at his list and made a little movement with his finger and then asked, "What does the air on Earth smell of?"

Meichun replied, "Humans can't smell oxygen, because they have never known a world without oxygen. Earth's atmosphere is made up of the same elements that we have here, but there are also unpredictable elements like pollen and dust. These elements can make a difference, but I think that it is going to smell sweeter for you."

Patrick looked at Peter and asked, "Does it really?"

Peter shrugged his shoulders, and pulled a general, I've-got-no-idea-face. He couldn't remember, and he didn't even know if he had noticed a difference. He could only think about barbequed meat.

Patrick nodded and turned his attention back to his list, "Does rain tickle when it falls on your face?"

Meichun remain quiet then admitted, "I don't know. I don't have any information about that."

266

Patrick accepted the answer and went straight on to his next question, "Is it safe in the sunshine on Earth?"

Meichun answered mechanically, "Sunshine is dangerous on Earth, but not as dangerous as here. The atmosphere acts as a filter, but you still need to protect your skin and your eyes. Don't forget your sunglasses."

Peter wondered if Meichun was trying to make a joke.

Patrick crossed off the last question on his hand and while Peter was watching him his stomach rumbled again.

Peter laughed, and he was relieved that Patrick hadn't asked about what had happened on Earth and what was waiting for them there.

Patrick raised his head and said, "I have one more question."

Peter felt fear growing up from the pit of his stomach, almost to the point that he could taste it. He managed to keep a calm exterior as he looked at Patrick and smiled weakly at him.

Patrick smiled and sounded curious as he asked, "How far will a golf ball fly, when you are playing golf?"

Peter laughed relieved.

Meichun took his question just as seriously as the others, "It depends on how hard you hit the ball."

Peter glanced over to the clock and calculated that the meeting was going to take place in about one hour. He suggested to Patrick that they go and get some lunch before the meeting started.

Patrick jumped up immediately and then stood there looking at Peter. His mouth was turned down and his arms were hanging loosely by his sides. He appeared sad. Patrick asked, "Why can't I come to the meeting? I'm almost old enough, and it's important to me as well." His voice had a high-pitched pleading tone.

Peter remained quiet, he didn't know how he could justify it. He smiled widely and said, "Let's go get something to eat."

As they ate, Patrick spoke about how he was going to discover everything on Earth. He wanted to see as much as possible. Peter let him speak, not hearing his words, just hearing his enthusiasm.

After a while Patrick said something that Peter heard, "Paul has told me that I could go for a walk with Astro during the meeting."

Peter said nothing, and thought, when Patrick was a toddler, it was clear that he couldn't come to the base meetings, but now, as he looked at Patrick, he realised how grown-up Patrick seemed, and he wondered if there was still a valid reason not to invite him to the meeting. Peter was still looking at Patrick and noticed that he didn't look happy, his lower lip was sticking out, but before Peter could say anything Patrick blurted, "I don't want to see Dervla, she's probably still angry at me because of the Re-Do machine."

Peter smiled and nodded, "Sounds like a sensible decision. We'll see each other later." Peter left Patrick sitting in the canteen eating his second dessert and went straight to the meeting room. His captain's hat was still in his office where he'd left it, covering his whisky glass.

As he entered the room, he was looking at the floor, but he still noticed that all five were already sitting on five of the six available chairs. Peter had made sure that the other six chairs had been hidden away. Three empty chairs hadn't been a distraction for him, but Peter couldn't cope with the sight of six empty chairs around the table, with the ghosts of their previous occupants sitting staring at him. He missed them. He caught himself thinking I missed the opportunity to spy on them before he'd come to the room. He could have observed them waiting. Peter looked up and smiled at them, trying to avoid looking into the eyes that were looking at him expectantly- It was an expectation that was briefly masking the habitual hopelessness of their everyday life. He shook his head slightly and said in an emotionless voice, "I'm sorry, but there hasn't been any contact from Earth."

He could almost feel the light breeze emanating from the deep sigh that slowly spread through the room. No one looked disappointed, they were resigned to the facts. Peter glanced over to Liam, smiled and raise his eyebrows questioningly.

Liam didn't smile and shook his head slowly. He'd not got anything new to say.

Peter's shoulders fell a little and while he was sitting down, he wondered if they were dead. He managed a small smile and explained calmly, "Let's reconsider the reasons why we think we lost contact. There is the improved Re-Do machines running out of control theory, society falling apart about the tensions around limited water sources, and not to forget, the possibility of a new form of avian flu." He'd forced his voice to remain steady and strong to the end of the sentence, but it didn't matter because no one was paying attention. Their thoughts were all somewhere else. Beatriz was seemingly looking at nothing on the wall opposite, and Maria, who had a distant look in her eyes, was twiddling with her necklace. Dervla, Liam and Paul were looking at the table in front of them.

Beatriz took her necklace, that was similar to Maria's in size, in her hand and still looking at the wall, she said quietly but firmly, "I don't want to go back." She looked both unhappy and relieved. Then she lifted her head up and looked directly at Peter and said, "I am already seventy-two. I'm too old to return."

Still looking at the table, Liam added in a quiet voice, "I want to stay as well."

Peter looked at them and thought there were always three, and there are three seats in the escape pod. He was waiting for someone else to say they wanted to stay. As he was waiting for a response, he started to smile. It'd occurred to him, there could be a place for him in one of the escape pods. He looked at Beatriz. She was qualified to take over as Moon Major. His relief didn't last long, and his expression showed his disappointment clearly as it occurred to him that Beatriz and Liam wouldn't have an emergency escape pod if he went home.

Maria was still playing with her necklace as she asked Liam in a quiet, inquisitive voice, "Why don't you want to return?"

Liam spoke slowly, and he looked to his left as he replied, "I don't have anything to return for and I like it here." His voice sounded determined.

Maria sounded apologetic as she said with a painful expression, "I didn't want to be nosey. I just thought that maybe you might know something that we didn't."

Liam nodded and smiled understanding.

Dervla interjected, "If we are planning on returning. I think it would be advisable for all of us to have a medical examination before we return."

Peter, who wasn't sure if Dervla wanted to return at all, smiled and nodded as he was forming a plan in his head. Liam and Beatriz were staying. Dervla, Patrick and Paul could fly in one of the escape pods and he looked kindly at Maria, who was clutching her necklace against her chest and looking at Beatriz, and he and Maria could fly in the second escape pod. He smiled pleased with himself ignoring Maria's unhappy expression. Then Peter's eyes followed Maria's gaze to Beatriz, who seemed confused and distracted as she asked, "Who's returned?"

Paul, who was sitting next to Beatriz, pointed discreetly at the medicine button on her arm.

Beatriz smiled and nodded, so Paul pressed the button gently.

Dervla insisted, "Patrick needs a medical examination before he can go home."

Peter watched the others nodding in response. He wondered if they were transferring their concerns to Patrick, so they didn't have to worry about themselves.

He knew there was nothing else to say, not at the moment, and there were only three weeks to the next return date.

Motherly Love

Date: Wednesday 28th September 2157 – 11:55 CET
Location: Alpha 12 – Moon Base

Peter was sitting in his office and was bored. He was ignoring his task list. It didn't interest him, and he couldn't believe the tasks were important. He felt and heard a low rumbling in his stomach, he glanced up and thought about eating something. He was craving something unhealthy, something full of sugar and preferably fried. Then he reminded himself that he'd decided to eat healthier. Nevertheless, his taste buds were longing for the taste of sugar, salt and especially for deep fried fat. He glanced down at his belly. He knew he wasn't really hungry, but his taste buds were longing for something to do. He glanced down at his supply drawer. Then forced himself to look away. He switched his attention to the surveillance system and tried to distract himself from thinking about the bottles of whisky in the drawer. He flicked through the surveillance cameras randomly looking at different views. Nobody seemed to be doing anything interesting, and the options were limited, so few people to observe. Patrick and Dervla were taking a walk through the small garden. It occurred to him that this was unusual especially at this time of day and he smiled at the thought that they were taking time for each other before returning to Earth. As he smiled, he thought of the salt on potato chips. He ran his tongue over his teeth, thinking maybe he was hungry after all. Maybe he should get something to eat. He put his hand on his stomach as it rumbled again, when he looked at the surveillance monitor, he noticed that they'd stopped walking and were turned to each other, both with a tense posture, as if they'd had a difference of opinion. He stared the picture and wondered if he should turn on the sound, but he didn't. He just looked at them standing under a tree near one of the small, fenced off displays that didn't properly contain the tree roots. There must be a microphone nearby, he could turn it on. His conscience started to bother him, their conversation was private, and he should keep it that way.

He looked at his watch, it was just before noon. He decided to wait until another hour before he'd pour himself a whisky and maybe get some lunch. He turned his attention back to Patrick and Dervla and smiled at how tall Patrick had grown. He was over 10 centimetres taller than his mother. Patrick had grown up. He seemed so much bigger and stronger than her.

Peter's eyes flicked to his captain's hat that was on the desk at the side of the monitor, he picked it up and started playing with it. He held it in both hands and turned it over slowly feeling the warmth of the felt material brushing against his skin, then he let it go and watched it fall lopsided onto his desk. He glanced back at the monitor with Patrick and Dervla. Patrick had grown very tall, and he wondered if the lower gravity had made a difference. He knew that Beatriz had told him that it probably hadn't made a difference, but how could they really be sure? He laughed briefly and quietly, he found the situation somehow funny, but didn't know why. Was he laughing at Patrick? He got an unpleasant feeling that he was prying and stopped watching them. He tried to appease his guilt by attempting to convince himself that he didn't want to witness a private moment.

He managed to look away from the monitor and felt pleased with himself. He slowly relaxed back into his chair and wondered about his morality. He smiled happily, but only for a moment. There was a little sick sinking feeling at the bottom of his stomach. He felt hypocritical because he knew he would watch them again, and his reasons for looking and what he was looking for didn't follow any rules or have any transparency. Moon Base surveillance was controlled only by his whims. Should he look again, just for a second? Who was going to know?

"Why won't you tell me who my father is?" Patrick's face turned red, and his voice sounded both excited and pleading.

Dervla looked at him concerned, "What's happened? You haven't known up until now, and it hasn't hurt you. Why do you want to know now?"

His body twitched, and he sounded stubborn and persistent when he said, "I want to know. I need to know."

She looked at him puzzled.

He breathed deeply and tried again, "It's not fair. I have a right to know who my father is." He looked directly at her. His eyes seemed full of pain, "I'm not just you. I want to know where I come from and who I'm going to become."

Her face was hard, and she shook her head decisively. He wasn't yet ready to know, "Wait until you are eighteen years old. Then I'll tell you."

Patrick didn't want to give up, and in a voice loaded with the unfairness of the situation, he said, "I'm almost sixteen years old. I'm grown up enough to know now."

Dervla replied without pausing, "When you are grown up and are eighteen, I'll tell you then." She sounded clear and unyielding. She knew that when he was eighteen, he'd be able to have his own DNA tested without her permission, and then he'd find out what she, for the moment, wanted to keep secret. She just wanted to delay him knowing, just for a little while, it won't matter when they were on Earth.

Patrick was angry and desperate, "But we'll be back in a few weeks. I want to know before then."

She turned to leave.

He automatically reached out for her to stop her from going. He wasn't finished. Patrick begged her, "Please tell me."

Dervla was visibly annoyed that he kept asking her. She frowned and told him, "You have to wait."

He took a little step closer to Dervla, frowned and said, "I don't want to wait."

With both arms she pushed him away from her and said rather angrily, "You're acting like a spoiled toddler."

That upset him. He raised his arms and pushed her back, "Tell me."

Dervla stumbled backwards, caught her foot against a protruding tree stump before she fell awkwardly backwards and hit her head against the fencing around the tree roots.

Patrick froze. He was shocked and couldn't understand what was happening. Then it was as if someone had turned on a switch in his head, and he bent over to see if she was okay. You could hear the rising panic in his voice, "Mother, mother." His voice broke, and he sounded frightened and alone as he said, "Mother, wake up. Please."

Dervla didn't move. As Patrick touched her to wake her, he noticed the blood leaking under the back of her head. He raised his head and cried for help. He slowed down his increasing panic and with a steadier voice he shouted as loudly as he could, "We need help. Dervla's hurt."

He knelt beside her and held her hand. He shook her gently to try and wake her, but she didn't wake up and she didn't move. Tearfully he looked at her and begged with a small, anxious voice, "Please, can someone help us?"

The distress call rang out in Peter's office. He sat straight up and looked at the monitor. He was puzzled for a moment. Dervla was lying on the floor while Patrick seemed to be shaking her. He called Beatriz and told her to meet him in the little garden as soon as possible. There's been an accident, and Dervla has been injured. Beatriz was already aware, the remote sensors had reported a problem with Dervla's life signs, and their representation on one of the monitors didn't present a healthy result.

Peter and Beatriz both ran separately to the scene. As they arrived, Patrick was crouching next to Dervla and crying softly. He looked up at them hopelessly, his face full of pain. His voice was soft and higher than normal, "I don't know what to do." He swallowed, "I think she's hurt."

Beatriz touched his shoulder gently and said with compassion, "Let me look."

Patrick kept quiet, and he didn't move. So, Peter put his hand on Patrick's shoulder and gently pulled him back so that Beatriz could get to Dervla.

Beatriz searched eagerly for signs of life. Peter saw the barely noticeable shaking of her head and understood how worried she was.

Beatriz said to Peter, "We need the robots."

Peter brought his eyebrows together and looked at her questioningly.

Beatriz replied, "We'll take her to the infirmary."

Peter nodded and then looked at Patrick, "Go and find Paul. He's in the warehouse."

Patrick hesitated. He didn't know what to do with himself. His head was hanging. He knew something bad had happened, and it had something to do with him.

"Go", ordered Peter.

Patrick nodded and left reluctantly.

After he left, Maria came by and asked if she could help, "I heard something. It took me a while to find where you were." She looked at Dervla, "We have to take her to the infirmary."

"The Sauberbots are bringing a hospital transport here. They'll do the work and we'll take Dervla to the infirmary." Peter explained.

Without looking at her, Beatriz gently and clearly ordered Maria, "Go back to work. We can take care of everything from here."

Paul was in the main store room trying to complete an inventory, he wanted to do it before they returned. He heard Patrick coming, and as soon as he saw him, he knew something was wrong. Paul looked at him for a moment before he suggested, "Let's go for a walk with Astro. We can go around and see if we can find something exciting in the warehouse." He tried to cheer Patrick up, but he didn't know what to do. Then he remembered it was almost lunchtime.

Paul smiled and cheerfully asked, "Are you hungry?"

Looking down at his feet, Patrick shook his head and said, "No."

Paul hadn't expected a refusal to food. Patrick's reaction was unusual. Paul knew that something was very wrong, that something must have happened. He asked compassionately if Patrick wanted to talk about it.

Patrick immediately began to say, "I pushed Dervla, and she tripped." With tearful eyes he looked at Paul, "She hit her head against a little garden wall."

Paul nodded in silence.

Patrick swallowed and continued, "Beatriz and Peter took her to the infirmary." He hung his head and whispered, "I didn't know I'd hit her so hard." His shoulders fell, he had bigger tears in his eyes as he said in a small voice, "I think I've hurt her badly."

Paul hugged him tight and let Patrick cry against his shoulder.

Peter was looking down at Dervla, who was lying on the bed in the infirmary. She looked very pale and wasn't moving. He looked at Beatriz, "Are you sure you can't do anything for her."

Beatriz didn't lift her head. She couldn't look at him, her voice sounded clinical and distant, "She's dead." She raised her head and looked him in the eyes, "There's nothing I can do."

Almost as if it were necessary, Peter protested. He didn't sound as if he was convinced of his own words, "But we have all this modern technology, and she just bumped her head."

Beatriz replied with resolve, "Peter, I'm sorry. It's over."

Peter shook his head in disbelief, "I can't believe it." Then he added, "What shall we tell Patrick?" He was shocked and didn't know what to do, how to feel, how to react. There had to be something they could do, "Let's look at the security camera footage and see what happened."

Peter used his privileged access codes to retrieve the security material from the garden and display it in the infirmary. Silent, they started watching the wide-angle view of the events in the small garden. Peter chewed on his lip as he noticed how the autumn colours were beginning to appear in the leaves. Peter zoomed in on the them standing under the tree. They watched for a few minutes without speaking, until Peter asked, "Should I turn on the sound? Or is that enough with just the picture."

Beatriz replied, "No sound. We can turn it on if we need to."

Peter looked at her still unconvinced.

Beatriz closed her eyes, swallowed before she said quietly, "Let's just watch."

They watched the scene and looked at each other as they recognised the apparent quarrel. The significant angry look on Dervla's face as she pushed Patrick away couldn't be overlooked. The position of the camera had automatically adjusted during the conversation, and they could see Patrick's face as he reacted. They saw how angry he was as he pushed her back, how she tripped and fell. They watched as he bent down to see if he could do anything, and they saw him full of panic looking around for help. They watched him scream silently, saw him helplessly asking for assistance. Then they noticed the blood seeping from under her head, and they could see his body shaking as he started crying. They stopped watching when they saw themselves appear.

Paul kept his voice steady when he asked, "What were you arguing about?"

Patrick sniffed, "I wanted to know who my father was."

Paul nodded, but was puzzled, and he wanted to know, "But why, I thought you didn't care."

Patrick wiped his nose with the back of his hand, his voice was firm, "Yes, I didn't." His tone got higher as he continued, "But I got a message from Steve this morning saying that I really should know before we return to Earth."

Paul's face froze, and he shook his head as realised that Steve had sent a time-delayed message to stir things up.

Patrick didn't understand why Paul looked so angry.

Beatriz looked at Peter's downcast face and wondered how he felt. She felt tired, and he looked it and also visibly shocked. She said to break the tense silence, "He doesn't know how strong he is." She stressed, "He hasn't got used to his body." She shrugged her shoulders and shook her head, saying in an attempt to convince them both, "He's grown so fast."

Peter's head moved erratically from side to side. His voice was weak and sounded uncertain, "I'm sure, he didn't want to kill her." He cleared his throat. The strength returned to his voice as he said, "I don't even believe he wanted to hurt her."

Beatriz nodded in agreement, adding in a small voice, "I wonder how he feels now."

Peter looked sad as he shook his head, "I can't imagine." Peter was annoyed with himself. He was the Moon Major. He should know what to do, but he was just standing there undecided. He was trying to get control of himself. His mind focused on the practicalities, what needed to be done. He heard his father's advice repeating in his head, "Take care of the necessities and let the emotions come later."

Peter ordered the Sauberbots to clean up the blood. Then he turned to Beatriz and asked, "What do we do with the body?"

Beatriz answered without emotion, "We've got a disposal station in the infirmary. It's a kind of organic material Re-Do machine." She looked at Peter and sounded a little concerned as she added, "It'll make fertiliser out of her." She shrugged her shoulders and continued, "I think that's all right, isn't it?"

Peter looked at Beatriz and grasped that she was looking for permission. He thought everyone does that nowadays, and that she was very old-fashioned. Then he smiled as he realised that there could still be a chance of finding life on Enceladus. He suppressed it and said, "Maria will be pleased for the plants."

Beatriz nodded in agreement.

He looked down at the body briefly before he looked up at Beatriz, and his face was full of sadness as he said, "We have to tell the others."

Beatriz reacted quietly, "There's only Liam who doesn't know."

Peter nodded, and said, "Yes, of course. There are fewer of us here, and now there's one less."

Beatriz took a blanket and respectfully covered the body as she stated, "We can take care of her later." She sighed and sounded reluctant as she said, "I am going to talk to Maria."

Peter nodded. He wanted to be alone and was glad he could return to his office. On the way he passed Liam. He knew he had to stop and explain that there'd been a terrible accident and that Dervla was dead.

Liam was obviously shocked.

Peter, who felt numb inside, perceived Liam's feelings but had nothing left to be able to offer him comfort.

Liam saw Peter stressed expression and offered, "Can I do anything?"

Peter shook his head slightly and kept his voice as normal as possible, "No, at the moment it's okay." He smiled and added, "We'll meet later." He turned to go, then he remembered, "Actually, yes. Could you prepare to say a few words? We'll have a little funeral ceremony later, maybe even tomorrow. So, we can say goodbye to Dervla."

Liam nodded and explained that he'd prepare something.

Peter's eyes expressed both his gratitude and his need to be alone.

Not long later Peter was sitting quietly in his office when Beatriz came to see him. She sat down in the visitor's chair and explained in a soft voice, "Maria wasn't surprised at all. She didn't think Dervla looked very well." She relaxed in the chair and leaned back and imitated Peter's position before saying something positive, "She suggested planting a tree for her."

Peter raised his head slightly and turned it slowly until they were looking at each other, both of them looked sad, and they both knew that they had a lot to process. They sat there in silence for a while before Peter said in a dampened tone, "I only spoke to her this morning. Everything seemed fine." He looked at his captain's hat on the table and added, "We have to ask Patrick what they were talking about."

Beatriz nodded, and she looked away from Peter.

Peter's voice sounded normal again as he asked, "Meichun, is there a protocol when someone dies in the Moon Base?"

Meichun reacted immediately, "The protocol states that a complete autopsy must be performed, and the body should be disposed of as soon as possible to stop the spread of disease on the base. After a few days there should be a small ceremony to say goodbye to the deceased colleague."

Beatriz and Peter looked at each other and nodded. The plan sounded good.

Meichun waited about thirty seconds before explaining, "If the person was murdered, then the murderer should be locked up in the base prison."

Peter and Beatriz stared at Meichun before searching each other's face for the doubt they felt themselves.

Beatriz spoke first, "Most of the time I think it makes sense if we consider the protocol as a guideline and not as a fixed rule."

Peter sounded determined as he said, "I'm not going to lock him up. He's spent his whole life here at the Moon Base. If we take away the little freedom that he has, it would be unfair."

Beatriz clarified, "He's not a murderer. It was an accident."

Peter agreed readily.

They both fell silent, both absorbed in their concerns.

Peter picked up his captain's hat and held it in his hand, his voice sounded almost dismissive as he said, "I'm looking at the practical side. At least we have enough escape pods now. It makes it easier to decide who has to stay behind."

Beatriz laughed briefly and leaned her head to the side, but she didn't say anything.

Peter sounded honest and almost relieved as he admitted, "We'll have room for everyone in the escape pods. I didn't think I would ever get the chance to go home." He poured himself a whisky. Beatriz refused.

Peter looked over at Beatriz holding his glass in his hand and asked, "Could we really lock him up more than he already is?"

Beatriz replied, "No, we're all already locked up."

Peter knew exactly what she meant but didn't want to have that kind of conversation. He pulled himself together and changed the subject, "Life must go on."

Beatriz sighed and reminded Peter, "We haven't told Paul and Patrick. We have to tell them."

Peter put on his captain's hat and ordered, "Meichun can you locate the clothing chips for Patrick and Paul."

Meichun obeyed and said, "They are in the big warehouse."

Peter nodded contentedly and thanked Meichun before downing his whisky in one.

Beatriz asked, "Shall we meet at the infirmary?"

He sent Paul a message, "Is Patrick still with you?"

Paul reacted immediately to Peter's question with a simple, "Yes."

Peter answered, "Please come to the infirmary."

Peter was breathing hard through his nostrils as he left the infirmary. Patrick stayed with Beatriz and Paul. They were trying to comfort him. Peter wasn't in a position to do that.

He was angry, and there was something he wanted to know. He went to Liam and asked him if had Steve left a message for anyone else.

Moonday Sixteen

Date: Sunday 2nd October 2157 – 08:30 CET
Location: Alpha 12 – Moon Base

Patrick was on his bed laying on his back and could feel the pleasant heat and light from wake-up lamps on his face. He opened his sticky eyes briefly and started the slow process of waking up. He heard the soft, gentle birthday music and grinned. He stretched excitedly. Today was his birthday. Finally, he was turning sixteen years old and would be allowed to join in with everything. His mother couldn't tell him what to do anymore. He sat up and smiled, but it was a fleeting smile that melted away as he remembered that his mother was no longer there. He thought about the farewell ceremony and the words that Liam had spoken. He'd heard the soft comforting tone and seen that Liam had teary eyes, just like the others, but he hadn't heard what Liam had said.

Patrick felt an empty feeling in his chest, and heard his mother's voice in his head say, "Get up and brush your teeth now." He got up and obeyed. He wanted to make his mother happy.

After brushing his teeth, he carefully opened the door to his mother's room still expecting her to be sitting on the bed. The air conditioning was running, but the room felt cold and deserted. He sat down on the edge of her still-made bed and hung his head. He looked at the floor. Everything was very orderly. The Sauberbots had tidied and cleaned up. It seemed to him as if no one had ever lived here, but he knew her belongings were still in the cupboards.

Next to her bed was the bedside table with the top drawer, where she'd always hidden a little present for him. He looked at the closed drawer for a few seconds, and then holding his breath he leaned forward, and carefully pulled open the drawer. Had she left a present for him?

He looked into the open drawer full of expectation and fear. Had she forgotten him? He gulped and smiled as he noticed a carefully wrapped package. Was it for him? Had she remembered. He saw his name printed on it and smiled as his chest filled with joy, and his eyes filled with tears. He took it out of the drawer and opened it carefully, putting the wrapping paper on the bedside table. He held it in his hand, it was a small torch, and it had a note stuck to it. There were instructions on the note. He ignored it and pressed the switch on the torch. Wherever he aimed the light, the colours changed. He laughed. It was strange and funny. He played with the flashlight for a while and then he picked up the note and read it. It was a UV torch. He wasn't sure what it was and thought he'd have to ask Paul.

He walked out of his mother's room holding the torch and put the instructions in his pocket. He shone the torch on the height markings on the door frame, they looked different from normal. He smiled, because he could see them more clearly.

He turned and looked at the now closed door of his mother's room. He remembered that Peter had asked him if he wanted to move downstairs and join the others. Patrick had said, no. He didn't want to leave the security, the comforting familiarity of his room, despite this, it felt strange without her, lonely. It was in the morning when he missed her most. She'd used to spend a lot of time in the lab, and he hadn't seen her much in their suite during the day.

He thought it was only going to be for a few days more. He leaned against her door and hugged himself to try and make himself feel better and managed to drop the torch. He leaned over to pick it up, smiled faintly, and was relieved to see that it wasn't broken and put it in his pocket with the instructions.

The communication device on his belt beeped. He looked at it, he should visit Beatriz. The results of the DNA test were ready. As he took the stairs, taking two at a time to walk down, he felt sad, even the view of the Sun from the stairs didn't brighten his mood.

Beatriz was waiting for Patrick to arrive. She recognised the sadness clearly in his face. Normally she would have asked him if everything was okay, but today she smiled at him. She knew how he was feeling.

She given him the DNA test two days ago and had had the results since yesterday. She'd already discussed it with Peter, as she hadn't known how best to explain the results. She thought Peter's suggestion was good and was going to use it. In as cheerful a voice as she could muster, she said, "I have good news and bad news for your birthday."

Patrick, who'd been expecting to hear his father's name, looked confused. He looked at her and frowned, then shook his head and shrugged his shoulders.

Beatriz suggested that they both sit down before they continue.

As Patrick made himself comfortable in his chair, Beatriz watched him and thought it didn't look comfortable at all, but then he was sixteen and at that age you could sit comfortably in any cramped position. She smiled and checked if he was okay. She noticed Patrick looking at her expectantly.

"First, the bad news, your father didn't live on the Moon Base. We have a large stockpile of genetic material on the

Base. We're holding the genetic store that was destined for the Mars Base. Your father was one of the sperm donors. We have his personal information on file." She showed Patrick a photo of a tall, handsome, red-haired man on the screen. Beatriz smiled and said, "He's good looking and clever. I can understand why your mother chose him."

Patrick briefly looked at the picture. Then raised his hand and tried to touch it with his fingertips. His gaze was distant, and he seemed lost at first.

Beatriz watched him and waited as he got used to it.

Patrick looked her in the eye and asked, "And the good news, what's the good news?"

Beatriz bent her head to the left and breathed in and out deeply, "Your mother was a geneticist, and she specialised in working with DNA, and she was very good at her job." Beatriz looked at him closely, "She applied her skills to you and has made some small improvements in your DNA." She smiled wistfully and looked at him intensely to see if he'd understood.

Patrick was curious and confused, "But what has she improved?"

Beatriz glanced down at her list, "You have an improved immune system, which means you don't get sick as often as other people."

He nodded not really understanding what that meant.

She continued as objectively as she could, "Your bone and muscle density are higher than normal. That means you are stronger and faster than other people."

He nodded and smiled.

"And there's something unusual about your vision. I haven't found any research to explain exactly what it is, but you have a wider visual spectrum than normal. It explains why you can see UV light."

He smiled, got out his torch and showed her, then he looked a little worried, "Isn't that normal?"

Beatriz was touched by his naivety, "It's not normal, but I'm sure you'll be fine on Earth if you wear your sunglasses in daytime."

Patrick seemed happy. He looked at the picture and without moving his eyes away from it asked Beatriz, "Why did Steve send me the message?"

Beatriz looked sad and thoughtful, "I don't know. I'm sorry." She would have liked to have known, but she had the feeling that it had just been one of his stupid jokes. She continued, "We'll do your normal examination. If that's okay." She smiled friendly, "It's Moonday. You always have an examination on your birthday."

He laughed, and they played the normal examination routine. But this time, Beatriz knew what she was looking for, and she was more careful and thorough than usual. It was, after all, going to be his last examination with her.

This time she gave him an injection to keep him from growing too much, for the time being and she made a note of his bone and muscle density. She smiled when she wrote in his medical notes that it was safe for him to return to Earth.

After they were finished, Beatriz checked the time. It was a little too early for the party, so she sent Patrick to Paul.

Patrick found Paul sat behind his monitor in the warehouse experimenting with the robots. When he arrived, Patrick took the flashlight out of his pocket and asked Paul, "Do you know how it works?"

Paul looked at the device, smiled and nodded before he explained, "This is a UV or a black light torch. UV light is just outside the visible light spectrum, that's why, the human eye can't see it." Paul pointed to the torch, "Inside your flashlight is a light bulb with a black light filter glass bulb." Paul was watching Patrick to see if he understood.

Patrick was impressed that Paul knew so much.

Paul went on to say, "There's more." He smiled, "Fluorescent dyes absorb a little energy from the short-wave invisible UV light and convert it into less energetic visible light."

Patrick got the feeling that Paul was reading the explanation from the screen and went over to check. An explanation of UV light was displayed on the screen.

Paul laughed briefly, slightly embarrassed and then warned Patrick, "You have to be careful, the light bulb generates energy that can harm your eye, even if you can't see it, the energy is still there, and it can damage your eye by looking at it."

Patrick thanked him for the explanation but wanted to know, "How did you know I would ask?"

Paul raised his eyebrows and laughed before lying, "Your mother told me before she died and that I should prepare to explain it to you."

Patrick believed him easily, and he nodded as he looked at the flashlight. It didn't occur to him that it might have been Paul, who'd hid it in the drawer.

Paul had a plan and suggested that they turn off the lights and go on a flashlight discovery tour. Patrick liked the idea and ran off laughing to turn off the main lights. Paul looked at him with a smile as he ran off and thought it wasn't necessary to go to the light switch, but he knew that running there was fun for Patrick. As soon as it was darker, the discovery tour began. They chased each other through the warehouse, looking for things on the shelves that fluoresced.

Paul ordered Astro to follow them, and from time to time Paul checked where Astro was, and made sure he was still following. Every time Patrick found something fluorescent, he laughed and called Paul to come over and look. There were so many different colours of plastic that changed their colour under black light and the white boxes glowed a light blue. The light of the UV torch caused the weak colours that Patrick saw under normal light to shine out brightly. Patrick smiled at Paul and explained to him how funny it was to see the colours brightly, then he ran off again to investigate the small electrical appliances in the vicinity of Paul's workplace. Paul followed slowly. He liked seeing Patrick enjoying himself.

Patrick shouted to him and told him to hurry. He'd found something. When Paul finally arrived a little out of breath, Patrick said in admiration, "Someone's written Happy Birthday on a parcel."

Paul looked at the bright green text on the package before smiling broadly and tauntingly saying, "Really?"

Patrick, who was still in awe, asked, "Do you think it's for me?"

Paul kept his voice serious, "Lots of people have birthdays."

Then Patrick remembered something, "You did it, didn't you?"

Paul started laughing and Patrick joined in and forgot his sadness for a moment. The discovery tour was over, and Paul suggested that Patrick should look at Astro with the flashlight. Patrick called Astro to him, then bent down and shone the flashlight at his side. He looked up at Paul and grinned before saying, "Astro is wishing me happy birthday. It's written on his side."

Paul's armband gadget beeped and without looking at it, he said, "Let's go to the canteen." He smiled, "There might be something there for you."

It wasn't long before Patrick and Paul arrived in the canteen. They hadn't run, but then they hadn't exactly walked. Everyone was already there to celebrate Patrick's birthday. They were trying their best to follow Patrick's normal birthday routine. They were standing around the table talking about the birthday cake. Patrick was surprised, and his eyes lit up and shone as he saw the cake. Steve wasn't there anymore, and Patrick hadn't been expecting a birthday cake. He didn't think anyone else could bake.

Maria noticed his confusion and joy and explained, "Steve baked the cake just before he returned. He wanted to leave a present for you."

Peter, who was wearing his captain's hat, shook Patrick's hand and congratulated him on his birthday. He hadn't brought a certificate and Patrick didn't seem to notice. A few days ago, they'd talked about the certificate, and Patrick didn't believe that he deserved one. The accident had changed everything. Peter had tried to convince Patrick that it wasn't his fault and had told he shouldn't feel guilty about it. He'd emphasised that accidents happen sometimes, but Patrick didn't want to know. The lack of a certificate was Peter respecting his wishes.

Before they cut the cake, Liam lowered the projection screen and the lights, then as he played the video mail, he said, "Just before they returned, Steve, Europa and Charlie filmed a birthday video mail for you." He smiled at Patrick. Liam could feel Peter watching him intensely. He ignored Peter's gaze. He pointed at the screen and continued happily and said smiling, "Let's watch the video."

The video mail showed the three waving and looking happy on the screen. Maria was there briefly in the background as she tried to get out of the way of the camera. They sang Happy Birthday for Patrick and then congratulated him on his birthday. They explained how sorry they were they couldn't be there for his party. When it was over Liam put everything away, and Beatriz gave Patrick a well-wrapped gift.

Patrick was pleasantly surprised and eagerly tore off the wrapping paper, which he let fall on the floor. It was a piece of fabric, and he wasn't sure what it was. He looked at Beatriz questioningly.

She laughed briefly and explained to him, "It is a sunhat. You have to take it with you on the journey to Earth. You'll need protection from the Sun."

The hat was light beige with a large brim going down to his shoulders at the back and a brim at the front to keep his eyes in the shade. Patrick put the sunhat on his head and smiled broadly showing off his present to the others. Patrick liked the attention and felt proud when he showed off the torch from his mother. He found it comforting to see their interest in his mother's last gift.

Beatriz laughed and said, "Maybe now you can imagine how other people see the world."

Paul started cutting the cake and joked, "It'll be the last Moonday. In the future there'll be an Earthday for Patrick's birthday." Everyone laughed loudly and mostly to hide their confused emotions about the end of an era and the start of a new one.

After they'd finished eating the cake, they all went to the meeting room where the last meeting was going to take place. Patrick, who was there for the first time, was nervous and didn't know which chair to sit in. With a hand gesture, Beatriz suggested the place where Dervla normally sat. Patrick looked at Peter for permission.

Peter smiled, closed his eyes briefly and nodded to Patrick before putting his captain's hat on the table in front of him. Patrick sat down, and Peter smiled to welcome them especially focusing on Patrick. Peter began to speak with a serious tone, "Today will be our last meeting together." He watched people nod slowly and sadly. He felt sad and knew that today was kind of a goodbye.

"There's room for all of us to return, but I know that not everyone wants to go home."

Patrick was fidgeting in his seat, looking at the others excitedly and curiously.

Liam said quietly and shaking his head, "I want to stay. I'm not coming with you."

That wasn't a surprise for Peter. He'd expected Liam's statement.

Beatriz spoke next and announced, "I'm staying too. I'm too old to go back, and I don't think I can survive the trip," She looked at Peter, "and without my medication, I'd become a shell of myself."

Peter nodded. He knew exactly what she meant. As they were still thinking about Beatriz's words, Maria took her necklace in her hand and said quietly but clearly, "I'm staying as well."

Liam and Paul were both surprised and looked at Maria incredulous. Beatriz looked at the table. Maria's statement was nothing new to her, and Peter just looked sad.

Patrick blurted out, "But why?"

Maria smiled apologetically at Patrick, "I've a little problem with my heart, and it's constantly monitored by my necklace. I don't want to risk going back," she looked at the table and continued slowly and quietly, "and I need a supply of medication."

Peter looked closely at Maria. He'd always thought that he'd have to stay, but everything was settled. She was serious. He wondered if she was afraid of returning home, just like he was.

Paul interrupted the silence and said in a sad and calm voice, "I definitely want to go home."

Patrick agreed energetically, and his whole-body trembling with enthusiasm as he said, "I'm coming too."

Peter looked at his team and smiled. He had tears in his eyes as he said, "We were a great team, and we have a plan." He smiled at each person in turn before adding, "Paul, Patrick and I will return in a rescue pod on October 18th, and Liam, Maria and Beatriz will remain here with the last rescue pod. You can return if you need to."

Peter looked sad as he got up and put his captain's hat back on, and he said, "This is our last meeting, it's the end of an era." Then he watched the small group standing up and shaking hands with each other. As Beatriz walked over and shook his hand he said quietly, "And it's our last Moonday."

Third Return

Date: Tuesday 18th October 2157 – 07:27 CET
Location: Alpha 12 – Moon Base

Standing in their orange spacesuits, holding their helmets in their hands, the three returners stood just outside the communication room near Art Feldmann's statue. Beatriz and Maria were standing in their full white Moon Base uniforms. They all looked good. Although it was early in the morning they were all wide awake. There was something final about the day, and they sensed both the end and a new beginning.

Liam came to join them. He'd been supervising the final preparations and he told them that a message had come from Steve. He wished them good luck and a safe journey.

Peter looked visibly annoyed. He wondered if that was all Steve had done. He wanted to check but knew that it was too late for him. He'd handed the responsibility over to Beatriz. He suppressed the thought and turned to Beatriz asking with sad eyes and a strained smile, "Are you sure you want to stay?"

Beatriz nodded tenderly. She looked both sad and determined as she replied in a steady voice, "Yes, very sure. I'm too old to go back." Then she smiled at him.

Peter looked with regret as he said, "I'm going to miss you."

Beatriz smiled a little embarrassed and replied, "I know, but I might not miss you. It depends on whether I'm on my meds or not." She laughed quietly.

Peter snorted, and one of the inconvenient liquids of human emotion squirted down his nose. He hadn't expected that and tried holding his gloved hand up to wipe his nose, which didn't work very well. Laughing Beatriz took a tissue out of her pocket, and she smiled at him before wiping his nose and she joked, "I thought I'd be doing this for Patrick and not for you."

He looked guilty, embarrassed and tried explaining, "I'm sorry. I can't believe I'm going home. I'm going to get to see my wife."

Beatriz grinned broadly, as she threw the dirty tissue to one of the Sauberbots, "It's understandable, don't worry. I'll remember you like this."

He pulled a painful smile in response and offered her his hand to shake. She inspected it carefully before she took it and shook his hand with a deep feeling of respect and love.

When they let go, Peter looked over to Patrick, who was looking good in his spacesuit and seemed very excited. He could barely keep still. Peter hoped the sleep medication would work on Patrick, and he would sleep most of the journey home. Then he looked around at the familiar fixings in the Moon Base and then back at Patrick and Paul standing next to each other, and he smiled wistfully. Patrick was almost as tall as Paul, although when Paul smiled, he showed his wrinkles and looked old, so much older than the last time Peter had seen Paul in an orange spacesuit.

Peter heard Patrick telling Liam, "We have our orange spacesuits on, so that we can be easily found by the search and rescue teams." He saw Liam nodding in response, and he smiled at Patrick's inexperience, and his optimism.

Paul, who was still standing next to Patrick, explained gently and compassionately, "It could be that no one comes looking for us when we land."

Patrick, who had the advantage of youth on his side to keep him positive, replied, "We'll be okay." Then he looked at Liam, "Did you get an answer to the message you sent to Columbus?"

Liam shook his head, "Not yet."

Paul kept quiet, he didn't want to take Patrick's hope away. This positivity was going to help him on his way home. He looked over to Peter before glancing at the others' faces and realising that no one believed what Patrick had said, but then neither was anyone willing to disappoint him.

Patrick didn't notice the looks, and asked Paul, "Are you taking your golf club back? We could play golf on Earth."

Paul smiled, "We have to keep the weight as low as possible."

Patrick nodded. That made sense.

Paul told him with a smile, "You never know, maybe I'll come back sometime. There'll be golf clubs on Earth, and we can track some down and play there."

Patrick laughed and thought it was a great idea and tried swinging his arms in a golf swing. Peter took a cautious step back.

Liam's communications device beeped, and he held up his hand with the checklist written on it. The robots were done. Liam looked at Peter and said, "The preparations are finished."

Patrick suddenly looked sad and glanced at the floor before whispering, "It's a pity Mother can't come with us."

Liam looked at Patrick and smiled compassionately, "She'll always be there for you. She's staying on the Moon. When you're on Earth looking up, you'll see the Moon and you'll see her smiling back at you."

Patrick listened to Liam's words with tearful eyes and smiling weakly. He liked the idea of seeing his mother when he looked at the Moon.

Liam turned to Paul and gave him a small bag with the small communication device. Paul nodded, he knew what to do. Peter remembered that it was some kind of signal amplifier of Liam's own design. He watched Liam smile as he said modestly, "I hope it works. The connectors are easy to identify and replace."

Peter looked at Paul. Paul knew how it worked and how to assemble it, when the time came to try and send a message back to the Moon.

Peter turned to Beatriz and pointing at the device he said, "It has no plastic parts, we might be able to get a message back." He looked thoughtful and worried before saying quietly and slowly, "I guess we'll soon find out what happened on Earth."

Beatriz joked, "Send me a postcard explaining what happened, when you find out."

Peter smiled weakly. He thought about whether he'd forgotten anything. He'd already said goodbye to his office and Meichun. She hadn't changed much over the years, she knew a lot of facts, but she didn't make any mistakes and because she didn't experience the physical world, she had no external prompts forcing her to develop her character. She was often boring, but even so Peter thought he would miss her. He'd deleted his private logbook, and he'd told Beatriz that she could continue the official logbook if she wanted.

Maria looked at the group and thought how good they looked and suggested, "Let's take a farewell photo." Everyone thought it was a great idea, and they moved closer together, nobody caring about the order. They stood as friends and equal colleagues. Peter automatically breathed in, even though you couldn't see his stomach under the spacesuit, until the photo was taken. Liam put the picture on the window wall, and they admired it together as Liam went to fetch a hard copy.

Peter laughed when he saw himself in the picture and said, "We could all do with a haircut. I hope when we land that we find Steve."

Everyone laughed. They looked good in that picture, everyone was smiling it was a moment of happiness during the sadness of the departure.

Peter added, "I wonder if Steve took his hairdressing scissors with him." He hoped so because Peter was still mad at Steve and still wanted to stab him.

Peter overheard Maria talking to Paul. Her voice sounded taut and full of regret, and her words came slowly and consciously as she said, "If you see Charlie, tell him. Tell him I'm sorry I lied to him." She swallowed, "It was for his own good. He can start a new life on Earth. He still has time." She gazed into the distance and sounded resigned as she continued, "I can't leave the gardens." She looked directly at Paul, "I have to take care of them."

Paul nodded and patted her shoulder with as much feeling as he could in his bulky suited hand.

Peter looked at her with tears in his eyes. It'd been a hard decision for her. He hadn't expected it. He asked her, "Are you sure?"

Maria nodded. She seemed relaxed almost at peace, "Yes, very sure." She was holding her necklace as she spoke. Then she added, "I wouldn't be able to survive long without my medication." She looked down, "I'm sorry. Please tell him for me."

Peter assured Maria, "We'll find Charlie and tell him."

Maria nodded but then she looked Peter directly in the eyes and said, "We don't know what the future holds, but I feel safer here than somewhere where there may not be any medication."

Peter smiled friendly. He guessed she was trying to justify her decision to herself.

Liam said, "It's time."

Paul hugged Beatriz as best he could in that bulky spacesuit and said, "I'll miss you."

Beatriz smiled and gently touched his cheek, "I'll miss you too. Take care of yourself."

He raised his hand and covered hers still resting on his cheek, "Thank you for all the medical help."

Beatriz smiled with faint melancholy and said, "Safe journey, and take care of the other two."

Paul nodded and promised he would.

Liam returned and handed Peter the photo. Peter indicated for Liam to put it in the gadget bag that Paul was holding. Then he shook Liam's hand, "Thank you for the work. You did a great job."

Liam nodded appreciatively and replied, "Have a good trip, and don't forget, you're not abandoning us. It's our choice to stay."

Patrick was playing with his helmet and passing it gently between his hands. He said to Paul excitedly, "I want to see the Earth."

Paul raised his hand to stop him from playing, "Watch out. Don't drop it. What are you looking forward to the most?"

Patrick held the helmet still and smiled broadly, "That's an easy question. I want to see the Moon."

Paul laughed and replied, "Of course, there are many things that you've never seen including moonlight, rainbows or shooting stars. You are going to have so much fun when we get there."

Patrick giggled. He was happy and excited.

Maria added, "There's real wind and rain, and you'll see the beautiful plants and trees everywhere." As she smiled, she looked beautiful as she did whenever she spoke about plants, she looked carefree and for a moment much younger than she was.

Peter looked around one last time before leaving checking that he hadn't forgotten anything. He'd already said goodbye to Art Feldmann's statue, but he looked at it one last time and pretended to toast it. He invited Paul and Patrick to join him. Patrick pulled a face, he thought it was stupid. Paul looked at Patrick and raised his eyebrows threateningly. Patrick reluctantly raised his arm and joined in with the pretend toast.

Peter, who was still wearing his captain's hat, took it off and handed it to Beatriz and said, "Look after it." They were both holding the captain's hat, he seemed reluctant to let it go. Thoughtfully he added, "I've always found it funny that we have a Moon Major wearing a captain's hat." He and Beatriz smiled at the same time, "But I guess you need alliteration for Moon Major. Moon Captain doesn't sound so good."

Beatriz smiled briefly, and then she became serious, "Don't let Patrick forget that even when there is an atmosphere the Sun can do damage. He could get sunburn. And take care of yourself." She patted him lightly on the shoulder.

Peter looked around and thought, what have I forgotten. He knew it was too late now. They put on their helmets and walked through the first door of the airlock. Peter didn't look back as they headed for the escape pod. He walked on automatic pilot. He felt stunned. It was really happening. They climbed into the escape pod and took their places, Patrick in the middle, Paul on the right and Peter on the left.

As Peter leaned back and tried to relax, he remembered that he had never found out if Steve had left a final prank, but then he reprimanded himself, he hadn't really looked during the last month, everything had seemed calmer than normal. Then he remembered that he was no longer in charge. Beatriz was going to take good care of his Moon Base. He could trust her. As he thought of the three who were remaining, he was surprised at how quickly he had gotten used to the fact that the others weren't there, and he wondered if Beatriz, Liam, and Maria would get used to them not being there as quickly.

Peter heard the count down and realised he wasn't worried. He was just happy and relieved that a decision had been made, and he was going home.

He braced himself as he felt the power of lift off, and as the escape unit flew higher and higher, he realised he wasn't looking forward to the next thirty-six hours of the return flight.

Landing

Date: Wednesday 19th October 2157 – 19:20 CET
Location: Earth

The air was pure and full of oxygen. Peter took a deep breath and tried to replace the musty air in his lungs with the fresh air around him. At first smiling with relief and then pulling a pained face. The cold air hurt his teeth. Why hadn't he accepted Beatriz's advice and made a last visit to the automatic dentist.

He looked at the other two. He was relieved and happy. They'd survived re-entry. The escape pod hadn't been shaken so badly that it had fallen apart, and the braking parachutes had worked as planned. He'd been a little sceptical about them, but he had to admit that Steve and Damian had done a really good job. Although, there'd been a few moments during the re-entry when he'd thought they wouldn't make it, but even the reinforced heat shields had survived the extreme heat of atmospheric braking and done their job protecting them.

Patrick had wanted to get out immediately, and Peter had stopped him. They'd landed somewhere in the countryside, they didn't know exactly where, and it was dark. Peter had needed a few minutes to pull himself together. He was concerned, you never know what could be waiting for you. Peter had wriggled his toes slowly and laboriously. He'd checked his whole body to see if it was still intact but had been mostly relieved that he could still move his toes. He'd nodded to himself. That was a good sign.

When he was ready, he'd given the signal, and Paul had got out first. After that Patrick had followed nimbly. He'd jumped down the last step, so he could leave a clear footprint in the mud. Paul warned him to stay alert and look around. Slowly and awkwardly, Peter had climbed out of the escape pod. After thirty-six hours, without the opportunity to move around, Peter felt each one of his fifty-nine years clearly. His reluctant muscles were stiff and could only be moved slowly.

As he stepped on the ground, he wondered if they'd find the others. The calculations were good and only had a fault tolerance of less than half a percent, but this could mean that they'd landed kilometres apart.

The three of them stood before what was left of the escape unit looking at each other. Peter was thinking that anyone nearby had undoubtedly heard and definitely seen the re-entry into the Earth's atmosphere. Now they were standing in their bright orange spacesuits. They'd already opened the helmets in the escape pod to breathe the fresh air. Now he gave the sign that they should take off their helmets.

Patrick wanted to take his off right away, but Peter insisted that he go first. It was a precaution, probably a meaningless one, but he wanted to protect Patrick. He released the holding mechanism and slowly lifted off his helmet before bending down and putting it on the floor. He stood up straight feeling lighter and took deep breaths of the cool, sweet evening air. It was glorious. His smile showed him relaxing, and then he looked around. There was no obvious danger. Paul and Patrick took off their helmets together. Paul got his helmet off first while Patrick still struggled with his, when he finally got it off Paul laughed. Both Peter and Paul watched Patrick as he breathed the Earth's air for the first time.

When Patrick sneezed, Paul looked at Peter anxiously. Was this an allergic reaction? They held their breath until Patrick was breathing normally. They sighed and laughed briefly with relief before they noticed that it was starting to rain. Patrick looked up and felt the small cooling droplets hitting his face for the first time and smiled.

Peter had ordered that they only speak in an emergency while in the escape pod, and Patrick had had to wait with his questions. Now he was eager to ask and looked at Paul, "Why was it so hot in the escape pod?"

Paul smiled and explained, "The heat was caused by air compression, and from the friction of the Earth's atmosphere against the heat shields, as the escape pods slows down the energy is converted into heat." Steve had explained it to Paul years ago, but he didn't tell Patrick how he knew.

Paul took off his gloves and got the bag with the communication device. The escape pod had automatically sent a message to Columbus on re-entry and on landing. Liam had adjusted the communication sender, so a signal had also been sent to the Moon Base. He unpacked Liam's communication device and handed Peter the photo before he setup the device and tried sending a message. He looked at Peter, "We can try it again tomorrow."

Peter looked at the photo and then up at the sky and searched for the full Moon. A thin layer of clouds obscured the night sky. He waited briefly until the clouds had moved on and the surrounding area lit up in the moonlight, and then he looked up and searched again. As he saw the full Moon it made Peter smile, and he felt far away from home. Peter thought he'd miss his life there, his whisky and his captain's hat. A growing pressure from his bladder reminded him that he needed to go to the toilet. He'd miss the Moon Base toilets as well. Peter nudged Patrick and pointed upwards. He looked up and smiled as he saw the white-blue full Moon.

Back on the Moon

Date: Monday 24th October 2157 – 08:50 CET
Location: Alpha 12 – Moon Base

The air was pure and full of oxygen, perhaps too much oxygen Maria thought as she inhaled deeply. She took one of the small gravel paths in the main garden and walked slowly along the shadowy path. She smiled and smelled the fresh clean odours of the plants. The leaves were green and autumnal brown but healthy. A branch growing out of control stroked her face and arms gently as she walked by. She enjoyed the cool touch of the leaves. It had been almost six days since they were just the three of them. Just three people to exhale carbon dioxide. Her plants probably needed more.

Soon she came to the closed moonflowers, they'd planted Dervla's tree nearby. She stood before the flowers and looked over to Charlie's drones, still there, where he'd last parked them. She missed Charlie. She missed his permanent presence. She missed that she couldn't call him, and that he'd show up minutes later worried that he'd not got there quick enough. Where was her Oberon? Was he safe? She hoped he was all right. She took her necklace in her hands and looked down at her feet. Was he waiting for her? Peter would have found him and told him that she wasn't coming, that it wasn't her fault that her heart wasn't strong enough to travel.

She heard one of the birds calling, and it distracted her from her depressing thoughts, and she wondered if it was cold enough in the garden. It didn't feel cold enough, even though the autumn weather program had started at the beginning of October. She was thinking of Beatriz. It was a perfect Spanish autumn. It wasn't too cold for people, but it was cold enough for the plants to start changing for the next season. Yet she shuddered.

She went to find Beatriz, who was sitting in Peter's office. It remained and would always remain Peter's office. Beatriz was trying to have a conversation with Meichun. Maria couldn't understand what they were talking about. Beatriz reacted slowly to acknowledging Maria's presence. The elapsed time felt just a little too long for it to be a comfortable pause before Beatriz put her glasses on her nose and looked at Maria.

Beatriz said dreamily, "I'm waiting for shooting stars."

Maria sounded patient and caring, "We don't have them on the Moon. There's no atmosphere." Maria knew what to do, "Have you taken your medication?"

Beatriz seemed confused. She smiled broadly and carefree, "Have you seen my glasses?"

Maria went to the infirmary and fetched Beatriz's medication. She put the medicine button on Beatriz's arm. Beatriz didn't stop her. She trusted Maria and just let it happen.

Maria gently pressed the button. After a few seconds, the drug began to take effect in Beatriz's brain. Her gaze intensified, and her eyes focused on Maria, and she smiled slightly embarrassed. She thanked Maria and explained, "It hurts less if I don't take the medication regularly."

Maria sat down, and they sat there silent for a while until Beatriz looking sad said, "I miss the others."

Maria nodded, and her expression betrayed the extent that she agreed.

Beatriz sighed, "We'll have to get used to it. It's our choice to stay in our luxurious prison."

Maria suggested, "Let's go see Liam."

They went together to see Liam, who was looking at his monitors in the communication area. Astro was sitting next to him, waiting for someone to play with him. Beatriz and Maria walked up and stood behind Liam. The atmosphere seemed too calm, so calm that it was oppressive, and Maria didn't like it.

Liam noticed them behind him and said, "It's five days and they haven't been in touch." He looked at her, "To be honest, I didn't expect them to, but I'm disappointed anyway. I'd like to know what it is that prevents communication." He was thoughtful. "I guess we'll never know, will we?"

Beatriz smiled compassionately, "Let's continue as normal. Peter would want that." She didn't have a good feeling because she realised, she was talking about him as if he were already dead. With a lighter, forced tone Beatriz said, "The Annual Closure is coming up in three weeks. We need to prepare for it."

***

www.ingramcontent.com/pod-product-compliance
Lightning Source LLC
Chambersburg PA
CBHW070223260626
47160CB00002B/665